D0953474

this I side of
jealousy

this I side of jealousy

LILI PELOQUIN

razOr
bill

An Imprint of Penguin Group (USA) Inc.

Published by the Penguin Group
Penguin Group (USA) Inc., 375 Hudson Street, New York, New York 10014, USA
Penguin Group (Canada), 90 Eglinton Avenue East, Suite 700, Toronto, Ontario M4P
2Y3, Canada (a division of Pearson Penguin Canada Inc.)
Penguin Books Ltd, 80 Strand, London WC2R 0RL, England
Penguin Ireland, 25 St Stephen's Green, Dublin 2, Ireland (a division of Penguin Books Ltd)
Penguin Group (Australia), 707 Collins St., Melbourne, Victoria 3008, Australia
(a division of Pearson Australia Group Pty Ltd)
Penguin Books India Pvt Ltd, 11 Community Centre, Panchsheel Park,
New Delhi–110 017, India
Penguin Group (NZ), 67 Apollo Drive, Rosedale, Auckland 0632, New Zealand
(a division of Pearson New Zealand Ltd)
Penguin Books, Rosebank Office Park, 181 Jan Smuts Avenue, Parktown North 2193,
South Africa
Penguin China, B7 Jaiming Center, 27 East Third Ring Road North, Chaoyang District,
Beijing 100020, China

Penguin Books Ltd, Registered Offices: 80 Strand, London WC2R 0RL, England

Published simultaneously in Canada

Library of Congress Cataloging-in-Publication Data is available

Printed in the United States of America

10 9 8 7 6 5 4 3 2 1

This is a work of fiction. Names, characters, places, and incidents either are the product of
the author's imagination or are used fictitiously, and any resemblance to actual persons,
living or dead, businesses, companies, events, or locales is entirely coincidental.

To Robbie

July Seventh

PROLOGUE

*A*lice could smell the blood even from more than a hundred yards away. It hung on the air, sweet and sticky and faintly rotten. And she could hear, above the din of the crowd, the roar of the ocean, the sharp crack of a fist on a face, bone colliding with bone, the dull thump of a knee in a midsection or groin, of a body crumpling in on itself. In the distance, a police siren wailed, soft but growing louder. Sickening sounds.

She scrambled to get to the other side of the dune, panic shooting through her, driving her forward. She didn't want anyone to know where she'd been or who she'd been with. Yet it seemed the faster she tried to move, the slower her progress, her heels sinking deep into the sand, her legs leaden, like weights were strapped to the ankles. Only in nightmares was her run so heavy and lurching, so thick-limbed and strange.

"Stop!" she tried to yell, but the word didn't come out of her mouth, was stifled by her closing throat.

At last she reached the edges of what up close she could see was more mob than crowd: beer-fueled and wild-eyed, primed for action, rumbling and growling, erupting in shouts any time a blow landed or blood was spilled. The guys and girls who made it up looked rich but also somehow loutish, their smooth cheeks slick with sweat, their soft lips flecked with saliva, their braces-perfect teeth bared in snarls. At the center of it were Tommy and Patrick.

They were still grappling, but their punches were losing sting, their movements growing sloppier, more sluggish and ragtag by the second. Even if the boys wanted to keep on trying to kill each other, it didn't look as though their bodies were going to let them. Their knuckles were cracked and streaming, their legs trembling, their knees buckling. Both their shirts were ripped, Patrick's missing a button, the right sleeve hanging on by a thread. And their faces, dear God, their faces—they were beginning to resemble hamburger meat.

It horrified Alice to see the damage they were inflicting on each other, but at the same time, it relieved her as well. It meant that while she was the reason for the bloodshed, she was also, weirdly, irrelevant to it—beside the point. Superior masculinity was the point. Or, as her sister Charlie might have put it, the fight was a my-dick-is-bigger-than-yours thing. What's more, the boys had probably been too busy trash-talking and chest-bumping before it started to register her absence. And they'd probably be too busy testing for broken bones, trying not to wince when hydrogen peroxide was applied to open wounds after it finished to ask any questions. She was off the hook.

Alice turned to look for Charlie. As she did, there was a sudden shift in the air, a rushing onslaught. The crowd exploded, began chanting with renewed vigor. She turned back. Jude and Stan had joined Tommy and Patrick in the fray, the two rolling around in the sand. *What has gotten into everyone?* she wondered. Was the beer spiked with testosterone? And then Stan's fist connected with Jude's jaw in a particularly vicious uppercut, causing her to wince-cringe in sympathy, duck her head.

Which was when she spotted Charlie, standing a dozen or so yards away, on the opposite side of the crowd, a book in hand, eyes wide with shock.

"Charlie—" Alice started to say, but once again, her voice failed her, dying in her throat.

She began pushing her way into the mass of thrashing bodies that separated her from her sister. When she'd broken through, made it to the other side, she was almost distracted enough not to notice that Charlie's lipstick was kiss-smeared, faded at the center of her mouth but not at the corners.

Almost.

And it wasn't Jude or Stan who'd done the smearing, Alice was nearly positive. She'd been watching both boys all night, tracking their movements. And the sole time Charlie had been out of her sight, Jude and Stan had been in it.

Hmm, Alice said to herself as the cops descended, swarming the beach, pulling apart the brawlers. *Looks like I'm not the only one sneaking off with a guy who isn't my boyfriend.* Charlie had gotten good at keeping secrets since moving to Serenity Point. Very good.

Well, that was okay. Alice had gotten even better at uncovering them.

*Six Days
Earlier*

CHAPTER ONE

*A*lice stood outside Charlie's bedroom. The *I'm sorry* was already in her mouth, formed and waiting, all set to drop from her lips. Not that she expected an apology to fix what she'd done. The damage was too great. How could she have fought with her sister like that, so cruelly, so viciously, showing no mercy whatsoever? Though, she had to admit, if anyone was entitled to a bad-behavior hall pass it was her.

Just before she'd said what she'd said to Charlie, her mother Maggie had said what she'd said to her: that Phil, the man who'd raised her since she was a baby, was not her father; that Richard, the man Maggie had recently married, the one Alice didn't like or understand or trust, was her father; and that Camilla, the dead step-sister she'd never met, was, in fact, the dead half sister she'd never met. Three blows in rapid succession, any one of which was powerful enough to knock her sidewise, have her seeing stars.

Still. It was no excuse.

The recollection of the words she'd spoken to Charlie sent

sickening waves of shame through her entire body. She couldn't face Charlie, she realized, in a burst of panic. Not now, not yet. She needed to wait. For a bit of time to pass. For the memory to fade a little.

Alice was just about to release the knob, slink off to a more private part of the house where she could hide out, when she heard stirring sounds from across the hall in her mom and Richard's bedroom. They must be waking up. Swiftly she turned the knob and stepped through the door.

Charlie was in her bed, sprawled out on top of the sheets in a small T-shirt and smaller underwear, limbs splayed starfish style, blankets kicked to the bottom. Her eye makeup was smudged. One arm dangled over the side of the mattress. Her bikini and cutoffs were in a tangle on the floor.

Alice walked over to the bed, sat on the edge. Charlie moaned in her sleep and shifted, rolling Alice's way, from her stomach onto her side. As she did, her T-shirt rode up, exposing the angel's-wing tattoo on the small of her back. Actually, exposing the Band-Aid covering the angel's-wing tattoo on the small of her back.

The last time Alice had seen that Band-Aid-covered tattoo it was moving away from her, not toward her.

Yesterday. Late morning. Alice had just left her mother in the garden. She was walking fast around the side of the house and up the staircase to the deck. Her brain was churning and hot and all over the place. How could her mother have lied to her—lied to all of them—for so long, and about things that were so important? Alice's mind latched onto the phrase *How could she?* and began repeating it frantically until the words slurred together—*Howcouldshehowcould-*

shehowcouldshe—became empty sounds, utterly meaningless, bouncing off the walls of her skull.

At the top of the steps, Alice had run into Charlie. She didn't think there'd ever been a time in her life when she was so happy to see someone. Charlie, with her open, clear-eyed face and blunt, head-on nature that was too impatient to engage in deception. Too honest, too.

The happy feeling hadn't lasted, though. It had vanished as soon as she realized that Charlie was behaving uncharacteristically twitchy, fidgeting with her eyes and hands. And for good reason, as it turned out. Charlie was hiding something. Or, rather, some*one*.

Jude. A boy as troubled and self-destructive as he was rich and good-looking.

When Alice put it together that Charlie had been lying about her relationship with him, had been sneaking off to meet him, was about to sneak off to meet him at that very minute, all the rage she'd kept a lid on with her mother had suddenly blazed up in her. "You're pathetic," she'd said.

As soon as the words hit the air, Alice learned the meaning of another word: *regret*. So long as she drew breath, she'd never forget the look on Charlie's face—stunned, just slack-jawed with surprise and pain. Nor would she forget the things Charlie had said to her in response, the crimes she'd accused her of—of living in the past, of being a loner and a weirdo, and, most painfully of all, of jealousy. And Alice couldn't defend herself because she couldn't explain herself. If she told Charlie the truth, Charlie would be wrecked. Charlie so wanted to be a part of this new family, her stepfather's family, the Flood family, it would devastate her to learn she was the only true Flaherty among them.

Charlie had run away from Alice straight to Jude and Cybill—Jude's cousin, distant but sometimes not, sometimes as close as close can be—soaking up sun and gin on the private beach below. The sight of the three of them walking off together, Charlie, in the middle, first Jude's arm, then Cybill's, snaking around Charlie's slim back, the intertwined arms blocking the Band-Aid-covered tattoo from view, had made Alice's stomach grab.

Next to her, Charlie shifted again—restless dreams, obviously—this time rolling from her side to her back, her arm flopping across Alice's lap.

Looking down at the pale underside of the tanned arm, the delicate blue veins running through it, Alice's stomach grabbed again. She realized for the second time that morning that she wasn't up for this scene. Her life had become nearly unrecognizable to her: the setting, the context, the players had changed, almost everything she thought was true turned out to be false, even her own face seemed to have altered, the features becoming less her own, more Flood-like. Charlie was the one constant. And suddenly Alice understood that the only thing scarier to her than the prospect of hurting Charlie was the prospect of being rejected by Charlie.

For the last three weeks, ever since they'd move out of the rented ramshackle duplex in Cambridge they'd lived in their whole lives and into the swankiest house in the swankiest town in swanky Connecticut, their relationship had been strained. The ties that bound them were, Alice feared, frayed down to a few fragile threads. What if learning about this missing chapter in the family backstory caused them to break entirely? If Charlie were to decide she'd had it, was done, Alice would have no one.

Gently, Alice raised Charlie's arm, placed it on a pillow, then began creeping toward the door on tiptoe.

She'd just reached for the knob when Charlie's voice, thick with sleep, said, "Allie?"

Alice stopped and turned around. At first her heart gave a hopeful lift because Charlie looked happy to see her. But then Alice saw the memory of the fight coming into Charlie's pearl gray eyes, saw Charlie's pretty, sleepy-creased face clouding. Forcing her mouth into a smile, Alice said, "Good morning."

Charlie gave her a sour look. "You better have come to serve me breakfast on a gold platter because that's the only reason I'd allow you in here."

"What about an apology on a gold platter?"

By way of reply, Charlie rolled onto her side.

"Come on," Alice said, "don't you want it?"

"Not particularly."

Alice sighed. "Well, you're getting it anyway. I'm sorry. For yesterday. For what I said."

"Yeah, right."

"I am. Very."

Rolling back, Charlie said, "Really?" her tone doubtful.

"Really." Alice leaned forward and hugged her sister. At first Charlie was stiff in her arms, but gradually her body went soft and she began to hug back.

"I'm sorry, too," Charlie said, pulling away so she could look Alice full in the face, her eyes shining. "Oh, Allie, if you give Jude a chance, you're going to love him. He's different than you think. He's different than everybody thinks."

Alice dropped her eyes, shook her head. "No, not sorry for what I said about Jude. Sorry for what I said about you."

Charlie, her voice flat, disappointed, said, "And here I thought you were actually being nice."

"I am being nice. For me, anyway." Alice tried out a smile on Charlie, but Charlie just stared back at her, stone-faced. "I don't think Jude's a good person is all," she said quietly.

"Oh really? That's all? And do you have any reason for thinking this?"

Alice did have a reason, in fact. Tommy, Camilla's former boyfriend and Alice's current (if secret) boyfriend, had told her that when he and Camilla were still together, before she killed herself by driving her car off Greeves Bridge nearly a year ago, she was cheating on him with Jude. After she and Tommy split, Camilla had continued to see Jude. Already depressed over her mother's death from breast cancer a month before, she'd slipped further into drugs and debauched behavior. Tommy blamed Jude for aiding and abetting this slide. Not that Alice could share any of this information with Charlie. Not when Tommy had made a point of asking her not to. So, instead, she shrugged lamely. "Call it intuition."

"How about I call it bullshit? You're really starting to get predictable, Allie."

"What do you mean?"

"First, Richard was the boogeyman. Now it's Jude."

Alice cringed at the justice of the charge. There had been a period in which she'd blamed her stepfather for everything wrong in her life, wrong in her world. And Charlie didn't even know how far Alice's suspicions of Richard had gone. For a brief time, Alice had suspected him of foul play where his first wife Martha was concerned, believed that he might have helped the cancer along in some fashion. (How exactly did she imagine Richard had helped the cancer along? By tampering with Martha's drugs? By pulling out her IV line? By putting a pillow over her face? It all sounded so ridiculous now, so elaborate and far-fetched. Like something out of one of those British mystery series she and her mom sometimes watched on PBS. A case to be cracked by the chubby guy with the waxed mustache and the Pepé Le Pew accent.) Alice had even brought her suspicions to Maggie and nearly gotten laughed out of the room for her trouble. "Oh, honey," Maggie had said, between fits of disbelieving giggles, "Richard can't even flush a spider down the toilet."

"Charlie," Alice started, "I didn't mean to—"

But Charlie didn't want to hear it. Holding up her hand like a stop sign, she said, "Look, I think we need a little space from each other. I don't mean I'm going to ignore you, give you the silent treatment or anything childish like that. Let's just steer clear of each other for a bit, okay? You do your thing, I'll do mine."

Alice could tell from Charlie's tone, the set expression on her face, that her mind was made up and arguing would be pointless. And after giving her sister's limp hand a squeeze, Alice rose from the bed.

As she exited the room of one sister, her mind jumped to another sister. She had the same thought she'd had yesterday when she'd watched Charlie disappearing down the beach with Jude and Cybill: that Camilla—a suicide, a dead person, a ghost!—had duped her. Camilla had *wanted* Alice to quarrel with Charlie, had *wanted* Alice to alienate Charlie, had *wanted* Alice to have no one but Camilla. And Alice had played right into her hands.

• • •

When Alice stepped into the hall, she came face-to-face with her mother, still in a nightgown. It was one Alice hadn't seen in a while, an old one, from the Cambridge days, a thin and worn white cotton covered in little yellow and pink flowers, nothing like the sexy, filmy, shortie movie-babe negligees she'd been wearing since she and Richard started sharing a bed. Maggie's gaze was fixed on Charlie's now shut door. Not for the first time, Alice noticed how closely her mother and sister resembled each other: gray eyes, hair so dark and slinky-glossy you could practically see your reflection in it, small, athletic bodies with plenty of curves in them, the kinds of bodies men liked.

Maggie's eyes appeared tired and worried. Looking at them, Alice could feel the sympathy welling up inside her. Quickly, she looked away so she wouldn't have to feel it anymore.

Her mom, she reminded herself, didn't deserve her sympathy.

Her mom, she reminded herself, deserved the opposite.

When she'd fortified herself sufficiently, made her mind steely-cold, Alice turned her eyes back to Maggie's. "Rough night?" she said, gathering her lips together in a sneer.

Maggie appeared confused. "What?"

"Those are some serious bags under your eyes, Mom. You should tell Richard to take it easy on you. After all, you're no kid. Can't go all night anymore. Not without showing the effects the next day."

Alice was shocked that she was speaking to Maggie in this way, would never have dared to in the past, and was almost hoping that Maggie would stop her—yell at her, slap her, do *something*—but Maggie did nothing, other than look pained. She'd forfeited all moral authority when she'd told Alice the truth about her relation-ship with Richard, an affair that began eighteen years ago, resumed two years ago, and involved the betrayal of not just Alice and Charlie's dad—Charlie's dad, anyway—but Camilla's mother, dying at the time, as well. Ethically speaking, Maggie didn't have a leg to stand on. She knew it, Alice knew it.

A door opened and closed downstairs. Luz, their cook, no doubt, or maybe Fernanda, their maid. Maggie pulled Alice into a small cove behind the staircase and out of earshot. "Did you tell her?" she asked anxiously.

Her meaning Charlie. After their little scene yesterday, Maggie had asked Alice to let her be the one to tell Charlie about Rich-ard. Alice had denied the request, said that she'd do it. Looked like Maggie was going to get her wish now, though, because Alice, it turned out, was too much of a coward for dirty work. Not that Alice was about to admit this.

"Did you tell *him*?" Alice demanded right back. "Does Richard know I know he's my . . ." She trailed off, unable to say the word *father* as it related to Richard out loud.

Maggie shook her head.

Alice felt a tension she wasn't even aware she'd been carrying slacken and dissolve. "Are you going to tell him?" she said.

"Not until I speak to Charlie."

"Speak to Charlie whenever you want. I didn't say anything yet either."

Maggie let out the breath she'd been holding. "Thank you," she said.

Annoyed that she'd pleased Maggie. Annoyed, too, that Maggie thought that was her intention, Alice said, "I didn't mean to do you a favor, believe me. The timing just wasn't right on my end."

"Still, thanks."

"Hey, I've made your secret mine. You've turned me from a victim of your lies into a collaborator in them. So I should be the one thanking you."

"Alice, honey, I wish you'd be less . . ."

"Less what?"

"Angry."

"Can't see that happening anytime soon," Alice said, but it wasn't true. It was already happening. Just observing how fatigued Maggie seemed, how on edge, the dark puffed-up circles around her eyes, the deep lines on either side of her mouth, affected Alice. Made Alice want to put her arms around her mom's shoulders, rest her cheek against the fabric of her mom's nightgown, soft from a million washings, smelling of detergent. Be nice, basically. (So much for steely-cold.) She couldn't, though. The betrayal Maggie had perpetrated was big time. Alice needed to punish her. Kindness, she told herself, was just another word for weakness. But the truth was, in punishing Maggie she was punishing herself every bit as hard.

Alice, seeing Maggie's gaze flitting again to Charlie's door, the hesitant look on her face, said, "So, what are you waiting for? Aren't you going to tell her? You wanted the chance so bad, now you have it."

"I think I'm going to wait a bit, give myself a little more time to work out what I want to say. Do you mind?"

Alice shrugged. "You've lied us our whole lives. What's a few more days?" She pushed past Maggie. "I'm going to change before breakfast. I'll see you downstairs. And don't worry, I'm sure I've inherited your ability to dissemble and deceive. Nobody'll know anything's wrong. Promise."

Alice crossed the hall to her bedroom slowly, deliberately, stagily, knowing Maggie was watching her. Once inside, though, she closed the door as fast as she could so she wouldn't have to look at Maggie's face. The expression on it, she knew, would be one of hurt and bewilderment. And, honestly, she didn't want to see it. She wanted to spare herself.

She saw it anyway, though—just a flashing, fleeting glimpse— and the sight twisted her heart so that she almost couldn't breathe.

CHAPTER TWO

*C*harlie grabbed her racket bag and headed straight for the club after breakfast. Unusually for her, she hoped Jude and Cybill wouldn't be there yet. She was still mad at Alice. Furious was more like it. Where did Alice get off telling her what to do, who to be with? Alice was barely even older, had Charlie beat by a measly year and a day. What made her think that she knew more?

For Charlie, the quickest, most efficient way to get rid of anger was to discharge it on someone—or, ideally, some*thing*—else. She didn't want to banter or flirt, to sneak sips out of Jude's flask or tiptoe around Cybill, be sensitive to Cybill's feelings now that she and Cybill were no longer competing for Jude, now that Jude had definitively chosen Charlie. She just wanted to roll out the ball machine, hit the cover off a couple hundred Wilson Titanium All Courts. An hour or so of that and she'd be as good as new, ready to face whatever was coming.

The Serenity Point Country Club, known locally as "the club," as if there were one and only one in the entire universe, was half a mile of private beach away from Richard's house. Charlie crossed the strip of pristine sand, soft under her feet. The horizon was a hard straight line in front of her. The water to the left of her was as smooth and clear as polished glass. She marveled at how different the beaches here were from the beaches in Boston. On summer weekends back home, she and Alice would get up at seven, pack a bag—towels, sunscreen, a few dollars to buy treats from the snack shack, a snow cone for Alice, a Choco Taco for Charlie—then head to Rindge Avenue. At Rindge, they'd pick up the bus that would take them to Porter Square. And at Porter Square, they'd switch to the Red Line, getting off at the JFK/UMass station, skipping the stairs to walk over the bridge to Carson Beach. Carson was crowded, it seemed, no matter how early you got there, the noise levels positively assaultive: competing stereos and screaming kids and teen mating calls, the tootings of car and truck horns on nearby Day Boulevard, and the squawk of black-and-white sirens (the beach was a stone's throw from the South Boston Police barracks).

There were no traffic noises on the beaches in Serenity Point, no people noises either. Just the sounds of the birds in the sky and the breeze in the dunes, the cracking of the surf and the flowing of the water. Sounds that made you notice the absence of other sounds.

At last Charlie reached the club. The sheer physical beauty of the place, which she now took for granted to the point that she no longer even registered it, struck her anew today: the tall wrought-iron gates that served as an entranceway, the long lines of green grass—most of it golf course—rolling gracefully out to the blue sea, the road winding through it made of crushed white seashell. Dotting the landscape were tennis courts and croquet lawns. And at the center was an enormous clapboard structure with a wraparound porch: the clubhouse.

Charlie needed to make sure that all the courts weren't booked before heading out to them, so the clubhouse was her first stop. She took the long way around, avoided passing any of the grounds that the café windows looked out on, to lower the chances of Stan spotting her. Stan worked at the club as a waiter. He and Charlie had a relationship that was too flirtatious to be called a friendship but wasn't quite a romance either. Well, whatever you called it, it was no more. The last time she'd seen him had been bad. Really bad. She'd just gotten into a fight with Jude, was all churned up inside when she ran into him. The things she'd said were so unabashedly vicious, so through-and-through rotten she cringed remembering them. Honestly, thinking about her behavior that night made her sick to her stomach, so she stopped. She'd be lucky if he didn't actively hate her now.

At last, Charlie reached the clubhouse. She opened the door, stepped inside, the air-conditioning immediately cooling the sweat on her skin. The pro behind the desk that morning was Lucy Entwhistle. Lucy was a pretty brunette entering her sophomore year at Amherst College. She had a telephone receiver pressed to her ear, was listening to the person on the other end of the line. She held up a *one-second* finger to Charlie.

While she waited, Charlie let her gaze do a lap around the room. It stumbled on a photograph hanging on the far wall. This photograph was such an object of obsession of her sister's that Charlie couldn't help but become a little obsessed with it, too. It had been taken two years ago—a year before Camilla killed herself. She and

Tommy had just won the club's mixed-doubles championship, were accepting a trophy. They looked so beautiful. Like a golden couple, literally, the rays of the sun hitting them in such a way that they seemed illuminated, surrounded by a halo of light.

As great-looking as Tommy was, though, it was Camilla who really drew the eye. She was a knockout, no question: tall and slender and blond, more poised than anyone her age had the right to be. A prom queen and an ice queen in one. But there was something about her mouth, the lower lip in particular, which had a sexy droop to it, a pout, that let you know that the debutante ingenue act wasn't the whole story with her, not by a long shot. In terms of facial features and body type, Camilla and Alice bore a resemblance to each other, a strong one, in fact. Their attitudes, though, were so different, the energies they gave off—Alice so studious, so virginal, so buttoned-up—that Charlie only ever registered the likeness long enough to dismiss it, which was exactly what she was doing at that moment.

At the sound of a receiver being replaced in its cradle, Charlie turned around. "Hey, cute top," she said, going out of her way to be nice because she'd always been a little cool to Lucy in the past, back when she thought Lucy was a rival for Jude's affections.

Lucy glanced down at her striped Polo shirt. "Thanks. I stole it from my mom's closet. She never throws anything away."

"So it's vintage? Nice. Hey, I don't suppose there are any courts available, are there?"

"Like whenish?"

"Like nowish?"

"You're in luck. That was Mrs. Perkins calling to cancel. Must've just remembered that the doctor said no strenuous exercise twenty-four hours after an injection."

Charlie laughed. Mrs. Perkins was one of the many seemingly ageless women who prowled around the clubhouse in formfitting workout gear, waiting for the next calorie-burning class to begin—kickboxing, Zumba dance, *vinyasa* yoga, didn't matter what—sipping lemon water and avoiding carbohydrates, eyes edgy and angry from excessive self-discipline. She could have been anywhere from thirty-five to sixty-five, her face shot so full of Botox and filler it resembled a Kabuki mask, her body lean and tight enough to be called girlish, though too stringy to be truly youthful.

"Court three's all yours until noon," Lucy said.

"Is anyone scheduled to use the ball machine?"

"That's all yours, too. Think you can wheel it out yourself?"

Charlie said she'd manage and thanked Lucy for her help. She was about to walk out to the equipment shed behind the courts when a familiar voice said, "No need to resort to a machine to meet your needs. Not when I'm around."

Charlie turned to face Jude, a sideways grin on his face. She'd missed him when she entered the room because he was lying on a couch, out of sight. He was standing now, picking up the racket and glass of orange juice resting on the table in front of him. He began walking toward her. As always, he looked ludicrously handsome. He had the kind of face that, without being effeminate or girly, would be as striking on a female as it was on a male: cornflower blue eyes, full mouth, narrow nose, long-boned and aristocratic. Not quite, actually. Cybill had his face and though she was, by any standards, extremely good-looking, she missed true beauty by the slenderest of margins, her chin a shade too long for a girl. Jude's body in his tennis whites was on the small side, but compact and well formed. On top of his head sat a baseball cap from St. Augustine's Academy, one of several schools from which he'd been kicked out, navy blue, sun-faded, and tilted at a rakish angle.

Charlie snuck a quick peek over his shoulder, checking to see if Cybill was stretched out on another couch. She wasn't. Charlie breathed a sigh of relief. Ever since Jude and Charlie had become an established pair, things had been weird between the three of them. No, that wasn't accurate. Things hadn't become weird, which was weird in and of itself. They soon would, though. After all, the dynamics had changed. The trio was no longer, strictly speaking, a trio. They were a couple plus one. And Charlie felt like she was holding her breath, just waiting for Cybill to lose it.

True, only yesterday, Jude, Cybill, and Charlie had spent the day together and there had been no problems to speak of. In fact, Cybill had gone out of her way to be sweet to Charlie, show her that she bore her no resentment or ill will. Even when Jude had done boyfriend-y things with Charlie, like take her hand or save her the last bite of his ice cream sandwich, Cybill hadn't reacted. But Charlie was wary of the peace-and-harmony act, didn't trust it. Jude was Cybill's, and now he was Charlie's. It didn't matter that Jude and Cybill were never together together, not officially. How could they be? They were related. And their sexual involvement—fleeting, Jude assured her, and not ever very enthusiastic on Cybill's part—was no more. Still, Charlie could feel in her bones that a freak-out was imminent, and she'd just as soon it come later rather than sooner.

"I've been hanging around all morning looking for a pickup match," Jude said, moving in close to her.

"I'll be your pickup."

"Will you now?"

"Anything for you," she said, letting her voice drop a couple registers, get sexy-husky so he'd move in closer. When he did, she reached for his hand. "But we have to get moving. We've only got the court for an hour."

He laughed. "Hang on. Let me finish my orange juice first." He gulped down the glass's contents, then kissed her hard on the mouth.

"Eighty-proof orange juice," she said, wrinkling her nose, though she liked the kiss, screwdriver-flavored or not.

"Well, I might have added a splash of vodka." Off the look she gave him: "What? How else am I supposed to get it down? You don't want me to die of thirst, do you?"

Charlie rolled her eyes. "Just don't puke on the court, okay?"

"No promises."

Jude and Charlie stood at the baseline, trading ground strokes for ten minutes or so.

Catching Charlie's last shot with his hand, trotting to the net, Jude said, "Let's play a match. I hate just practicing. If there's nothing at stake, my attention starts to wander."

Charlie remembered the last time they'd played tennis. Strip tennis. After midnight. The feel of Jude's fingertips on her naked skin. She could tell from the smirk spreading across Jude's face that he was remembering, too.

Charlie, feeling the color flooding her cheeks, quickly spun her racket to decide who served first.

Charlie and Jude were in the second point of their fifth game when Charlie rushed the net on an approach shot that clipped the tape, had less on it than she'd hoped, was a sitter, in fact. Options winnowing, she darted to her right to cover the deuce court because she had to pick a side, leaving the ad court wide open. Jude replied with a heavy topspin lob, rising way above her head and dipping down fast, a beautifully executed shot that landed just past the baseline. Charlie raised her index finger in an *out* call.

The sound of laughter. Charlie turned. She was surprised to see that she and Jude had a spectator, a guy she'd never seen before. He was tall, young, though quite a bit older than they, and dressed in a suit. Something about him struck her as off, sinister even. Maybe it was the suit, the neatness and formality of it, the shirt buttoned almost to the Adam's apple, the tie cinched tight. It was so at odds with the environment—the sunshiny heat and pastel beach colors and atmosphere of leisure. Or maybe it was the shades he'd paired the suit with, the lenses reflective and concealing the upper part of his face. His hair was dark and slicked back. And his skin was pale, as if he spent most of his time indoors.

The guy said, addressing Jude, "Now, the percentage play would have been to hit a crosscourt forehand, an easy winner. But you had to go the showboat route. Opted for the stylish shot rather than the smart one. Story of your life, huh, buddy?"

"Fuck you, Nick," Jude said, his voice oddly unemphatic and toneless.

"Hey, if I could do that, I'd never leave the house."

"What do you want?"

"Want?" Nick repeated slowly, like he was giving the question serious thought. He took off his sunglasses, tucked them in his breast pocket.

His face, Charlie decided, wasn't handsome, not conventionally anyway, but it was striking. An intelligent face. An alert face. The face of somebody you wouldn't want to tangle with.

"Yeah," Jude said. "From me."

"I don't want anything from you. I just wanted to say hi. Let you know I was back in town."

"So now I know."

"So now you do know. Well, I'll be seeing you around." Nick flashed Charlie a smile. His teeth were small and white and sharp. Putting a hand to the side of his mouth, he said, in a stage whisper, "Old Jude here's easy to beat. All you've got to do is let him beat himself. But I expect you've already figured that out." Advice dispensed, he began moving away from the courts. Sauntering more than walking, his pace relaxed, taking the time to look around, check out the scenery, hands in his pockets.

Charlie watched Jude watch Nick disappear into the clubhouse. When the door closed, Charlie said, "Who was that?"

Jude, his eyes still on the clubhouse door, "Nick."

Charlie grinned. "Yeah, that part I got."

"I don't like him."

"That part I got, too. I mean, who is he to you?"

"Just a guy." Then, realizing that she wasn't likely to be satisfied with this response, Jude pried his gaze off the door, turned to her, said, "He worked for Dr. van Stratten last summer, interning or something. Hung around the club a bit."

"So he's a medical student?"

"No, he's still in college. But he wants to be a doctor."

"You're kidding. I thought he was way older than college age."

"I think he's only, like, a sophomore."

"I wonder what he's doing in Serenity Point this summer. Not like Dr. van Stratten's in a position to be mentoring bright-eyed young hopefuls in the art of healing these days."

Jude shook his head sullenly. "Not unless it's mentoring them in how to almost kill your patients, miss getting sent to prison by a pubic hair, then being stripped of your medical license."

"Right," Charlie agreed, "not unless he's mentoring them in those things."

Jude, suddenly seeming to come outside his mood, looked at Charlie. They smiled at each other at the same time. He took off his baseball cap to wipe the sweat from his brow. A strand of dark brown fell forward, across his eye. He brushed it back with a tawny forearm. God, he was gorgeous.

Charlie used her racket and the side of her sneaker to pick up a ball. "So, it's two-all, fifteen-all. A dead heat. Should we keep playing?"

"I think I'd rather get drunk. Or drunker."

"Somehow I knew you were going to say that."

"You mind?"

Charlie sighed. It worried her that he drank so much. He'd been sent to rehab before by his father, lieutenant governor of Massachusetts Billy Devlin, and would be sent again if he wasn't careful. But she knew the encounter with Nick had shaken him up. And she was still on edge from her fight with Alice. A drink or two might be just the thing. "I'll even keep you company," she said.

He leaned over, bit her softly on the neck. "I knew you were the right girl for me."

She laughed, and they strolled off the court hand in hand.

CHAPTER THREE

*T*ommy called Alice just before noon. She was in a bit of a panic because lunchtime was fast approaching and she didn't want to get stuck eating it with Maggie and Richard. She'd holed herself up in her room after breakfast to avoid them, Maggie in the garden checking roses for black spots, and Richard in the office bent over his drafting board.

Trapped herself in her room was more like it.

If evasion of Maggie and Richard was the goal, the simplest means of achieving it would have been to go somewhere they weren't. Only she had no car (Richard, after the fate that befell Camilla, was understandably wary of mixing adolescent girls and motor vehicles), and the club was off-limits since Charlie was there and she'd promised to respect Charlie's need for space. Consequently, when she picked up her cell after seeing Tommy's name lighting up the screen, all he had to do was get out the words, *Would you like to*, and she'd already said yes. He laughed, told her he'd be right over.

Alice stood with her ear pressed to her door. When the loudest sound she could hear was her own heartbeat, she opened it, started down the wide, turning staircase that led to the first floor. She used to be afraid of the men and women in the portraits lining the walls of the front hall and entranceway. Floods, every last one of them, their dark eyes—watching eyes, Mona Lisa eyes, eyes that seemed to move from right to left—following her from inside the heavy gilt frames, tracking her activities, storing up information on her comings and goings to report back to Richard. His informers. His *spies*. She was one of them now, though. Blood. They wouldn't dare tattle.

Keeping what Jane Austen would call her countenance, what Charlie would call her shit together, Alice walked toward the front door, calmly returning any gaze she happened to meet on the way. She maintained an even, unhurried pace, showing her hard-eyed ancestors that she wasn't frightened, that she wouldn't be cowed. At last she was blinking in the sunshine.

She knew Tommy wouldn't want to run into anyone from her family. Nor would she for that matter. So she decided to intercept him at the top of the driveway. As she walked, she threw a quick glance over her shoulder. From this vantage point—from any vantage point—Richard's house appeared jaw-droppingly, eye-poppingly, heart-stoppingly grand. When she'd first seen it, she'd thought it looked like a castle in a fairy tale, beautiful but forbidding at the same time, the people inside it leading charmed lives that had been cursed. She was one of the people inside it now, and a cursed charmed life sounded about as accurate an assessment of her situation as she could imagine: it turned out she was really of noble birth, a princess disguised as a peasant girl, but with a father who might or might not be an evil king, and though her mother was still her mother, it was possible she was also a wicked witch, too, and as for the handsome prince who'd come to rescue her, well, he was still handsome and still princely, only he seemed in need of rescuing himself.

Speaking of which, here he was, on his white horse. Or, rather, in his cream-colored Volvo.

As he was pulling up, it occurred to Alice to wonder: should she tell him that she and Camilla were half sisters? Until that moment, she'd just assumed she would. After all, she'd been honest with him about everything else. Even the ugly, shameful stuff like Maggie and Richard's affair, conducted on the deathbed—okay, not quite but practically, might as well have been—of Martha Flood.

Alice had put her trust totally in Tommy. And it wasn't a lack of trust that made her hesitate now. It was a fear of rejection. His feelings toward Camilla, his ex-girlfriend—his *dead* ex-girlfriend, his *dead, unfaithful* ex-girlfriend—were both powerful and complicated. (So were hers toward Camilla come to think of it.) What if the thought of being with someone who was so intimately connected to Camilla, shared blood with her, turned him off? Like, what if he found himself repelled by Alice in ways that were instinctive and involuntary and thus un-get-over-able? That would be it for their romance. And Alice loved Tommy. She hadn't told him yet, had figured it out herself just the day before, but she did. The thought of losing him was painful to her to a degree that was almost unbearable, almost as unbearable as the thought of losing Charlie.

So, for the second time that day, Alice decided to keep someone she was close to in the dark because she was afraid honesty would exact too high a price. It was a despicable move, she knew, craven and cowardly. But the truth of the matter was she didn't think she could handle any more change or loss in her life. At the moment she was at her limit.

It occurred to her that from another perspective she was only evening the score between them. After all, Tommy was keeping a secret from her, too. A big one. And one that also concerned Camilla. "It didn't happen like everybody thinks it did," he'd said to her at Redbone's Café the day before about Camilla's death. This statement matched up with her intuition, which told her that a girl like Camilla, a tough and tough-minded girl, a girl who wasn't a victim, who victimized, a girl who'd rather wear blood than lipstick, wouldn't be driven to the edge by the loss, however painful, of a parent from a natural cause, that there had to be more to the suicide than the official story allowed. Yet when Alice had asked Tommy to explain himself, he'd basically shut down. Had said that Serenity Point was more dangerous than she knew. It was a variation on the old if-I-told-you-I'd-have-to-kill-you joke. Only he wasn't joking. To prove her trust in him, she'd backed off. Had that been the right move, though? Should she have pushed harder? Insisted?

Alice dismissed these thoughts from her mind, resolving to sort them out later as Tommy applied the brakes and rolled down the window, turned his face to hers. She loved looking at him. He was handsome in the cleanest, most straightforward way imaginable: light brown hair and even features; long body, lanky but muscular; strong, white teeth, the front two slightly overlapping, this minor imperfection only serving to make him seem *more* perfect by drawing attention to how flawless the rest of him was. His beauty was of a totally different order than, say, Jude's. There was nothing decadent or androgynous about his appearance. He was what you envisioned when you were a little girl dreaming of your first boyfriend.

"Hop in," he said, and when she did, kissed her twice. The first kiss was soft, the second hungrier, more lingering.

As good as his mouth felt, she pulled away from him, worried that Richard would get a sudden hankering to play a round of golf, jump into the Mercedes, happen upon them idling in the driveway. She reached for her seatbelt. "We going anywhere in particular?" she said.

"I told my mom I was taking the car to get a jump start on picking up college supplies. That's the only way she'd let me borrow it."

"This is your mom's car? I just assumed you had your own."

"I did. But we're down to two now. My dad had to trade in the Lexus."

Tommy's dad, Dr. van Stratten, had recently been sued for malpractice after a patient had almost died from a medication he'd prescribed. While Dr. van Stratten had managed to evade a prison sentence, his medical license had been revoked. And when the wife of this patient had announced that she'd also be seeking damages, and thus potentially bankrupting him, Mrs. van Stratten had filed for divorce as a way of protecting the family's assets. Light, however, seemed to be shining at the end of the tunnel for Dr. van Stratten. He'd just been offered a position at a hedge fund in Stamford. Had, in fact, used Tommy—much to Alice's annoyance and dismay— to grease the skids for him a little, convincing his son to woo the daughter of the man who ran it.

"Sorry," Alice said.

Tommy shrugged. "It wasn't only about the money. We needed to get rid of one of the cars anyway since I'll be heading off to college in the fall. Late summer, actually. Pre-season starts at the end of August."

Tommy was Harvard-bound. Had been heavily recruited by the crew coach.

"Yeah," she said, "it's not like you're going to be doing much driving in the city."

"Nope. What is it you have down there? The T?"

"That's right. Which I can totally help you master. I'll teach you how to buy a T card, tell you which stops and stations to avoid, which lines break down the most often—all that."

"My own private tour guide," Tommy said with a tender smile.

They had a prolonged moment of eye contact, which Alice, suddenly shy, broke off. Looking down at her lap, she said, "So, shopping for school supplies. Okay, I'm up for it even though it's barely July. What should we buy first? Dry-erase boards? Laundry bags? Ethernet cords? I guess I'm going to be needing that stuff, too, for Wolcott."

Alice and Charlie would not be graduating from Rindge and Latin, nicknamed *Sy*rindge and Latin because of its druggy rep, the public high school located in the heart of Cambridge, where they'd begun their academic careers. (The main building was a tall, mean slab of concrete that looked like it was designed to house criminals, not students.) Instead, this fall they'd be transferring to Wolcott Academy, a boarding school situated on thirty wooded acres just outside of Montpelier, Vermont, where every girl seemed to wear a wool sweater and every boy seemed to carry a lacrosse stick. Alice would be a senior, Charlie a junior.

"No, no," Tommy said, "that was just a line to get my mom to hand over the keys to the Volvo. I'll do that boring stuff with her, not you."

"All right. But I really don't mind."

"Hey, maybe I'm not the smoothest guy around, haven't read enough *GQ* or whatever, but I can manage to put together a better date than the local Staples, okay?"

She laughed. "Okay."

"How about I show you around Serenity Point?"

"You do realize I've been living here for almost a month now."

"Yeah, but how much of Serenity Point have you really seen? The club? The downtown area? A private beach or two?"

"I thought that was all there is."

"Oh, no. That's only *mostly* all there is."

Alice laughed again. "Then by all means, show me the rest."

"The rest" turned out to be the Serenity Point lighthouse, which was just across the bay on the western bluff. Tommy had in fact taken Alice once before. Had tried to, anyway. They'd driven to the lighthouse, had parked in front of the lighthouse—actually, in back of the lighthouse, more privacy—but never quite made it out of the car and *inside* the lighthouse.

This time they were more purposeful. They exited the car and followed a sandy path that wound around the lighthouse's surprisingly wide base. At last they came to a small door. Alice thought it would be locked, but when Tommy tried the primitive latch it gave easily under his thumb, and they stepped inside. There was no window, only the light from the door. No furniture either. Just a spiral staircase at the center. The air was dank, moldy, dense. But Alice was suddenly less aware of the details of her surroundings than she was of the darkness and seclusion they provided.

Assuming Tommy must be thinking the same thing, she turned to him. Instead of looking back at her, though, he was looking upward, at the staircase twisting to the roof, to the sky. "This is the oldest lighthouse in the country," he told her, eyes still raised. "Built out of wood in 1777, rebuilt out of stone in 1812 after a fire destroyed the original. It was a suspected, though never proven, case of arson."

Taking her hand, he led her over to the staircase. Climbing it frightened her a little, reminded her of the staircase in the Hitchcock movie *Vertigo*. It was that wooden and rickety and swirling, seemed that prone to collapse.

Once they reached the upper floor, though, her anxiety disappeared. It was much less spooky than the lower, containing as it did a single large window. Alice moved toward it, standing directly in front of it, mesmerized by the view it offered: pure blue, the sea stretching out like an azure carpet, the sky above it a deeper shade of azure, intense and mute and luminous. The air blowing in felt light on Alice's skin, warm but not hot, caressing. She could smell the honeysuckle plants growing below, the scent sultry and summery, mixing deliciously with the tangy balm of the ocean water, sweet and salty.

And then she heard Tommy coming up behind her. "This isn't the top," he said, "there's one more level—the lantern room—but it's not open to the public. What we're in now is called the service room. It's where the keeper used to prepare lanterns for the night, stand watch."

Alice sensed Tommy wanted her to keep her back to him so she didn't turn, even when he was finished speaking. Other than his breath—damp, soft, heated—hitting her neck in little puffs, stirring her hair, though, no part of him touched any part of her. She could feel her pulse beating all over her skin, making her whole body throb. And a tickling sensation started in the pit of her stomach, grew stronger with each second that passed with no contact between them. Then, just when she thought she couldn't take it anymore, was about to thrust herself at him, unable to wait, self-control gone, he pushed her gently up against the window. Began kissing her neck, at the base right above the vertebrae of her spine, his lips moving over to her shoulders, her collarbone, the side of her throat. He reached up to the straps of her tank top, had just slid the left one down when a sound made them both freeze: the door below opening and shutting, a pair of garrulous voices, male and female.

Alice twisted her head around to look at Tommy. They clung to each other tightly for a moment. And then, once again, he took her hand, leading her down the staircase this time. At the bottom step, they passed an older couple, retirees probably, clad entirely in khaki. Alice and the woman exchanged a smile.

Once they were out in the open air, Tommy slammed the door shut. He seemed mad, pacing back and forth, shoulders high and tense. But when he turned to her, said, "So you like the spot?" his expression was nervous, sweet.

Alice slipped her tank-top strap back up her shoulder. "I love it."

He looked hard at her face, like he was trying to gauge the truthfulness of her statement. "Really?"

"Really. It's the best thing I've seen in Serenity Point. It's so lovely and unspoiled here, I bet it looks the same way it looked a hundred years ago." She could tell he wasn't quite convinced, though, so she kept going: "Looking at it makes me feel lonesome but in a way I like, the same way I get when I'm standing in front of an Edward Hopper painting."

His voice happy, "You should paint it."

"Somebody should."

"Why not you? I thought you loved to paint."

"Well, I brought my sketch pad and pencils from home. They're sitting on my desk in my room at Richard's. And I know I brought my acrylics, too. But I can't find the box I packed them in. They must've gotten lost in the move. I'll just have to get another set, I suppose. It's just, I hate to spend money on something that still might turn up. Richard didn't want Charlie or me to get a job this summer, which means I'd have to ask him for the cash. Oh well"— shaking her head at herself, smiling—"it'll teach me not to be so casual about labeling."

"Just the paints?"

"Unfortunately, no. Brushes, canvases, easel, palette. All of it, pretty much. Everything was packed in the same box, you know?"

He nodded. "Sure. Well, that explains why I've never seen you paint."

It did and it didn't. While a lack of supplies was part of the reason Alice hadn't been painting, it wasn't the whole reason. She also connected the activity with her father, or rather the man she used to think was her father, Phil. Phil was a trumpeter, jazz by training and inclination, but often taking jobs with rock bands to pay the bills. He was in Japan right now, doing sideman work for a pianoless quartet, and had been out of contact with the family since he and Maggie split at Christmas. He and Alice had always been close, their shared artistic interests a strong bond between them. Picking up a paintbrush or a sketching pencil now only reminded her of him, of all she'd lost in learning the secret of her paternity.

"I've got something for you," Tommy said. "Well, for us. Wait here."

He walked off in the direction of the road and a minute later she heard the slam of a trunk. When he returned, he had a blanket draped over his shoulder, a couple of plastic bags dangling from his wrist.

"You brought lunch?" Alice said, delighted.

"I wasn't sure what kind of sandwiches you liked so I got a few— tuna salad, ham and Swiss, roast beef. There's a vegetarian option in there, too. Avocado and cheddar, I think. Take whichever you want. I like them all equally. And there's fruit salad and soda and chocolate chip cookies for dessert. You haven't eaten yet, have you?"

"Not since breakfast. I'm starved."

There were scattered tables and benches around the base of the lighthouse. Alice and Tommy, though, chose to have their picnic on a shady spot a couple hundred yards away from the area designated for the public, just on the other side of a swell in the land and, therefore, out of sight. They spread the blanket on a bit of ground that was half grass, half sand, laid out the food and drinks.

After they'd finished eating, Alice curled up next to Tommy, settling her head in the crook of his arm. A soft breeze passed over her, working its way into her clothes. As she stared at the sky above, watching a fat white cloud blow across the sun, momentarily eclipsing it, she realized that she hadn't thought about her mom or Richard or her fight with Charlie in almost an hour, and it was because of Tommy and the perfect afternoon he'd arranged. She stretched her neck up, pressing her lips to the underside of his jaw. He laughed and told her she was tickling him, then leaned over and kissed her for real.

They kissed and talked, talked and kissed. And in such a pleasant manner, the day began to pass. After a while, though, the kissing and the talking tapered off, and they fell into a drowsy half sleep.

"Well, well, well. What do we have here?" a voice said.

Alice surfaced from unconsciousness and looked up. The sudden glare of sunlight after the dimness of her closed eyelids made it difficult for her to see the figure standing above her as anything but a tall, sharply angled shadow. After a moment, though, her vision adjusted and details emerged: the figure belonged to a man, young, in a suit and tie, sunglasses. He was grinning. The grin, in fact, was the first thing she was able to make out, the teeth inside it so white they almost glowed.

Frightened, confused, too. Was the grinning young man real or was he a figment from her dream—or more likely nightmare— leaked out into daylight? She sat up in a panic, breath trapped in her throat, heart thumping wildly. What kind of person snuck up on a sleeping teenage couple in an out-of-the-way spot? An insensitive one, possibly a dangerous one. She glanced over at Tommy. He was rubbing his eyes, grinding his fingers deep into the sockets, digging out the sleep. He seemed as confused as she was. Not frightened, though, which calmed her down.

"Did I travel from Hanover in a time machine or a car?" the young man said.

He reached into his jacket pocket, pulled out a bottle of iced tea, took a long drink. He looked at the label, frowning as he read— black tea leaves, organic, lemon-infused—before delicately screwing the top back on. He was weird, she decided, but not dangerous weird.

"You tell us," she said, smoothing down her skirt, tugging the hem to her knee.

The young man returned the bottle to his pocket, made a disappointed face. "A car, apparently. You're not who I thought you were."

"Sorry."

Not registering the sarcasm of her tone, or pretending not to, the young man said, "Oh, don't be. It's just, you look like someone I used to know."

Alice tried to see the eyes behind the dark, reflective lenses. She couldn't, though. All she could see was herself. Herselves, rather. Two of them, shrunk down and slightly warped. "Let me guess," she said, "a girl who you used to know but don't know anymore because she's dead."

"You must get that a lot around here."

"You have no idea."

The young man laughed, clapped Tommy on the shoulder. There was something off about his manner, Alice thought. It was odd, a little too intimate, friendly when friendliness wasn't warranted.

"So, did you grow up around here?" she asked.

"Yes, but not in the way you mean," the young man said to

Alice. And then to Tommy, "Well, I think it's safe to say you have a definite type, kiddo."

Alice looked over at Tommy in surprise. Tommy was sitting up, perfectly still, staring at the young man. Obviously, Tommy knew him. Equally obviously, Tommy didn't like him.

The young man held Tommy's eye. "You going to introduce me to your little friend here?"

"Hey, you stole my line," Alice said, confused, a bit angry as well. She didn't appreciate being referred to as a *little* anything, not in this context, not by this guy.

"Alice Flaherty, Nick Chillingworth," Tommy said.

"Nice to know you, Alice."

"Nick used to work for my dad."

Nick shoved his hands in his pockets, rocked back on his heels. "How is the old man, anyway? I was sorry to hear about his troubles. The bad news traveled all the way up to New Hampshire."

Nick's words were the proper ones, Alice observed, polite and sympathetic, yet somehow his tone negated that politeness and sympathy. Changed the words' meaning, made them nasty and jeering.

"My dad's fine," Tommy said, a defensive note entering his voice. "Better than fine, actually. He's about to start working as a consultant on the pharmaceutical industry for a hedge fund."

"Glad to hear it. Not that it's a surprise. Your dad's a survivor. I always tell people, bet on Dr. van Stratten. He'll come through. No matter how dire the circumstances, he'll figure out a way to save himself."

Again Nick had said the right words, the words any courteous person would say in such a situation, but in a way that subverted their meaning, somehow turning a generic compliment into the most pointed of insults.

Tommy nodded once, tightly, clearly wishing to close the subject.

Nick, though, kept going. "Even if everybody around him is drowning, he'll find the one life preserver. Tear it out of the hands of an infant if he has to." This last line got a laugh from the speaker, if no one else. "So, Tommy, I was thinking about swinging by your parents' house later today, saying hello. Think I should?"

"I think you should do whatever you want."

"I was planning on talking to your dad. Telling him I'll be interning this summer at Dr. Rose's office. Do you know Dr. Rose?"

Another tight nod from Tommy.

"Of course you do," Nick said smoothly. "Serenity Point is a small town. Not too many concierge doctors in it."

"No there aren't," Tommy agreed grimly.

"I just interviewed with Dr. Rose at the club over lunch."

"You must've really wowed him if he offered you the position right then and there."

"Oh, he didn't offer it to me. Not yet. But he will. I understand he's the primary beneficiary of your father's misfortune. A lot of new clients—excuse me, patients—have been coming his way in the last few months. Can't imagine him turning down an extra pair of hands. Especially an experienced pair like mine."

When Tommy said nothing in response, and the silence started to grow into an awkward one, Alice stepped in. "So, where are you staying, Nick? Do you have family in town?"

Nick turned to her, taking off his sunglasses. For the first time, she got a real look at his face. It was sharp-featured and keen-eyed.

Foxy. Also, younger than she'd initially thought. Much younger. He was probably only a year or two older than Tommy, two or three years older than she.

"Serenity Point's a little rich for my family's blood," Nick said. "I'm renting a room in a house one town over."

Alice was racking her brain for another neutral topic when he abruptly straightened. "Enjoy the rest of this beautiful afternoon, you two. A pleasure meeting you, Alice. Tommy, I'll be seeing you around."

As he sauntered off, his movements loose-limbed and springy, Alice thought to herself, *my first impression of him was right. He is dangerous, the danger in him coiled up and controlled.*

And all the more deadly for it.

The spell of the day had been broken. There was no mending it. In silence, Alice and Tommy stood, began gathering together their trash, repacking the uneaten food, shaking out and folding up the blanket. Tommy carried the bags back to the car as if they were full of something heavy, though they were much lighter than when he carried them from the car. Alice, meanwhile, tried to restrain her curiosity until they were strapped in their seats, the engine humming, definitively out of earshot of Nick and anyone else, but wanting answers so badly she thought she'd burst with all the questions she had.

Relief, however, was not forthcoming.

"So, who's Nick besides your dad's former assistant?" Alice asked, attempting to start a conversation.

In response, Tommy made a sound that was somewhere between a mumble and a grunt.

"Where did he come from if not Serenity Point?"

Again, Tommy's response was part mumble, part grunt.

"How did your dad happen to hire him? Like, what were the circumstances?"

When Tommy mumble-grunted a third time, Alice started to get angry. It was as she turned to him to express this anger, though, that she noticed the pained, almost pleading look in his eye. His reluctance to speak obviously had something to do with Camilla—didn't *every*thing have something to do with Camilla where Tommy was concerned?—and thus something to do with his desire to protect Alice. (Nick knew Camilla, had to have if he mistook Alice for her. The question was, how well did he know her? What was the nature of their relationship?) Clearly Tommy wouldn't be providing Alice with any of these answers even though he had them. Alice was starting to get this itchy sensation, like when she got a scratch at the back of her throat and no amount of coughing or rasping would relieve her of it. Only now the itchy sensation was in her brain. She wanted to cry out in frustration.

To distract herself, Alice turned her attention to her window, letting the scenery slide past her eyes and into her mind. And it was as they crossed Greeves Bridge, the site of Camilla's grand exit, the repairs in the section of the barrier that Camilla had rammed her car through still visible, that it occurred to Alice to wonder: was her relationship with Tommy damned, doomed from the start, the secrets between them too many and adding by the day, piling up, higher and higher, creating a wall so tall and so thick that soon they wouldn't be able to see each other over it, feel each other through it?

Tommy dropped Alice off at the top of Richard's driveway. She leaned in to kiss him, but he just brushed his lips against her mouth, so lightly she barely felt them. And when she got out of the car, turned to say goodbye to him through the open window, he was already driving away. Fast. In the growing darkness, she watched his taillights receding. Going, going, gone. Then she began the long trek to the house, her movements as heavy as his had been back at the lighthouse.

At last she reached the front door. Just as she was opening it, her cell phone, an old model and not a nice one when it was new—unlike Charlie, Alice had refused to let Richard buy her an iPhone—buzzed. A text message. She looked down eagerly, hoping it was Tommy, as unhappy with how they left things as she was, wanting to say goodbye properly, make up even though they hadn't officially fought. But it wasn't. It was Patrick.

Thinking of you.

For the first time since she'd arrived in Serenity Point, certainly for the first time since she'd met Tommy, Alice was tempted to return one of Patrick's text messages, maybe even give him a call. It was funny. She wanted to talk to the boyfriend who was still not officially her ex so she could take her mind off the boyfriend who was not officially her boyfriend. Funny in a way that made her want to cry rather than laugh.

No, Alice decided, calling Patrick was not an option. She did her best to quell the surge of affection rising up in her. It wasn't easy, though. (Patrick, so uncomplicated! So easygoing! So what-you-see-is-what-you-get! And with a backstory she knew by heart!)

But if she did call him, she'd just be giving him false hope, especially since she couldn't mention Tommy. He'd just hear the sadness in her voice, and, not knowing the cause, think she needed him. And she couldn't mess with his emotions that way. He was too nice a guy.

CHAPTER FOUR

"*B*e careful of the plate, miss, it's hot," the waiter, an unfamiliar one, said to Alice as he slid the lobster gnocchi in front of her.

It was family dinner at the club that night. Alice had been pleased to discover that their reservations were for the café rather than the formal dining room. Formal dining room meals took, on average, one and a half times as long. And what Alice wanted to do more than anything was go home and up to her room, stare at her phone and wait for Tommy to call.

She'd elected not to order an appetizer in the hopes that she could speed things along. It was a useless sacrifice, as it turned out, as Richard, Maggie, and Charlie had all ordered salads. The only thing Alice could do was sit in her seat, will the forks to move from their plates to their lips faster.

At least they were onto the main course now.

And then Richard cut into his steak, frowned. "Excuse me," he said, summoning the waiter back to the table with an impatient hand wave. "I asked for medium rare. This is medium."

"I'm sorry, sir. I'll have the chef prepare you a fresh cut of meat straightaway."

Alice ground her teeth in frustration. Great, tack on another fifteen minutes to the already never-ending meal.

As the waiter whisked up Richard's plate, Charlie blew out her breath in a sigh. Alice looked curiously across the table at her sister. Clearly Charlie didn't want to be at the café any more than she did. Would have preferred, no doubt, to be off somewhere with Jude and Cybill, drinking dinner out of a flask. Though Alice was guessing that's how she'd consumed her lunch. She seemed ever so slightly wasted to Alice, her eyes glassy, her movements not slurred or wobbly, instead overly deliberate in that drunk-but-trying-to-hide-it way. She was distracted, too. Kept turning her gaze to the set of doors that led to the kitchen, the waitstaff swinging in and out.

"Go ahead, everyone," Richard said. "Don't let your food get cold on my account."

Alice and Charlie exchanged an eye roll, exciting for Alice because otherwise Charlie had ignored her all night. Exchanged a second one when Maggie picked up Richard's wineglass, drank from it even though she had a glass of her own. And then a third when Richard and Maggie continued to hold hands while Maggie twirled the pasta from her duck confit and foie gras bolognaise around her fork.

Not that Richard or Maggie noticed Alice and Charlie's shared irritation. They were as caught up in each other as they usually were, no eyes for anybody else. When Richard's entrée arrived—cooked, or rather undercooked, to perfection—he began talking about what he'd been talking about since they'd all sat down: the big-time job he'd recently been tapped for, designing the new wing of the Art

Institute of Boston, the city's premiere museum of the visual arts. How would he achieve the ideal balance of modern and classical? Could he create a glass-and-steel facade without being accused of ripping off Mies van Somebody's Something Gallery in Berlin, that apparently towering landmark of twentieth-century architecture? Where should he and Maggie rent a condo, Back Bay or Beacon Hill? Would they be able to get up to Richard's co-op on Park Avenue regularly or should they close it up for the fall? It was as if, Alice thought, the volume on his internal monologue had been turned up full blast. There was no conversation, no shared dialogue or exchange of ideas, just him holding forth. At least he didn't require much in the way of response. Throw in the occasional nod or "Uhhuh, yeah" and she was free to let her mind wander.

Wander back to Tommy, of course. How could she have left things with him the way she did? She shouldn't have tried to pressure him to talk. She'd said to him at Redbone's that she trusted him, and she *did* trust him, so why couldn't she simply let her questions go? Assume that if she needed to know something, he'd tell her? Why had she allowed herself to doubt him? The doubt was just Camilla poison, and she'd let it infect her, seep into her bloodstream, taint her mind. Whenever a rift came up between her and Tommy—between her and Charlie, too—it was a victory for Camilla. She was going to have to wise up, toughen up as well if she wanted to be more than a cardboard cutout opponent for Camilla, for this to be any kind of fight at all.

The dishes had just been cleared and Richard had begun speculating, with lip-smacking glee, on the reactions of his various professional rivals upon hearing of his coup, the dreams dashed, the hopes crushed—"Mario thought he had this one in the bag, the arrogant Heidegger-quoting prick. He'll probably be crying into his copy of *Being and Time* after Pollard's people call him with the news"—when Cybill's mother, Muffie Buckley, approached the table.

To Alice, Muffie almost wasn't a person, she was a caricature, a parody of a moneyed New England WASP: painfully thin, painfully tan, painfully blond. Painfully oblivious, too. She and Cybill's father were divorced, and she gave off this weird vibe—on the prowl but stiff about it. Like, man-hungry and sexless at the same time. The single men in the club, the few that there were, headed the other way when they saw her coming.

"Rich*aaard*," Mrs. Buckley said, drawing out the second syllable of his name at least three extra beats in that way of hers.

Alice noticed that she came as close to ignoring Maggie—a brief nod, no eye contact—as civility would allow. She was one of those women, Alice suspected, who only paid attention to her own sex when no member of the opposite was present.

Richard, in a magnanimous frame of mind after a good dinner and a chance to pontificate on himself and his future achievements virtually uninterrupted for a solid half hour, stood. Leaning forward, he pressed his lips to the emaciated, leathery cheek turned his way. "Muffie, how are you? We were just about to have coffee. Join us. I'll get a waiter to pull up a chair."

"Oh, no, we"—she turned to gesture to a woman Alice had seen around the club, another older, too-thin, too-tan, too-blond divorcee, hovering in the background, waving shyly—"were just leaving. I'm Pricilla's ride and she promised the sitter she'd be home before ten."

"What a shame," Richard said, though his face looked none too cast down. "You'll just have to come by the house for a cocktail sometime."

It was obvious to Alice, would have been obvious to anyone, that the invitation was a pro forma thing, a polite conversation-ender. (It sometimes seemed to Alice that the good manners that were on such prominent display in Serenity Point were just another way for people to be two-faced.) But Mrs. Buckley's eyes lit up.

"I'd love to," she said eagerly. "When? Tomorrow? This weekend?"

Richard swapped a panicked look with Maggie. A quick cup of coffee was one thing. A cocktail that could turn into a dinner that could turn into an entire evening was quite another.

He opened his mouth to speak. Before he could get the words out, though, Maggie placed a silencing hand on his forearm. It was a casual gesture, but a telling one: *He's mine*, it said. *He does what I say*. And its meaning was not lost on Alice.

Or, Alice noticed, Mrs. Buckley.

"Actually, Muffie," Maggie said, "the next few days are no good for us."

Mrs. Buckley looked back and forth, from Maggie to Richard. "They aren't?" she said in a small voice.

Maggie shook her head.

"That's too bad."

"We'll all get together after the Fourth, though."

Mrs. Buckley perked up. "I'd like that."

"Yes, we would, too."

"Shall I call you at the house to arrange something?"

"Why don't you call Richard's office?" Maggie said. "His

assistant handles his schedule. It's easiest to make appointments with us through her."

Mrs. Buckley nodded her head in meek acquiescence.

Alice was still angry with her mother but couldn't help admiring her, too: Maggie wasn't going to let this stuck-up bitch push her around.

"Enjoy the rest of your evening," Maggie said, and lifted Richard's wineglass, clearly dismissing Mrs. Buckley.

But Mrs. Buckley wasn't to be dismissed so easily. Instead of leaving, she turned away from Maggie, back to Richard. "I'm pleased to have run into you, actually," she said.

He raised a polite eyebrow. "Oh?"

"I've been meaning to tell you how delighted I was to hear that you were going to be holding a memorial for Camilla."

Alice stole a quick look at Richard's face. She could see the good cheer draining right out of it along with the blood. His expression darkened and clouded, then hardened until it became almost rigid— a mask. Maggie spotted the transformation too, Alice noticed, watched it taking place with worried eyes.

Mrs. Buckley kept on talking, oblivious to the effect her words were having: "I've been longing for a chance to properly honor her poor, dear memory. There really wasn't one at the time. The whole thing was handled in such a disjointed fashion. No sense of closure was given. Not that I blamed you for that. Not when it took so long for them to—" She broke off here, doubtless realizing that there was no good way to finish this sentence.

Fish Camilla out of the Atlantic would have been the most efficient way, if not the most tactful. It had been weeks after Camilla disappeared that she reappeared. She washed up on the shore of a beach in Old Lyme, a town nearly twenty miles south of Serenity Point. Richard had to drive down to identify her. Alice could only imagine the state that Camilla's face and body were in after all that time under water, strong currents and hungry sea creatures having had their way. It must've been a gruesome sight because Richard decided that the funeral would be a closed-casket one.

It was agonizing waiting for Mrs. Buckley to continue speaking, fill in the space that she'd left blank, watching her mouth open and close soundlessly. Finally, in a whisper, she said, "Bring her home."

In a voice that was a little bit tight but otherwise normal, Richard said, "Yes, well, honoring her memory's the idea."

"When will it be held? Do you know the date yet?"

"We're thinking July 9 since that was the day she died."

Alice couldn't tell if he was being sarcastic or just giving information in a matter-of-fact way.

Evidently Mrs. Buckley couldn't either. Stuttering, she said, "I-I-I loved Camilla. The girl was like a daughter to me."

"How lucky for her," Richard said. Again, it was impossible to know if he was being sarcastic or not.

After casting an apologetic look at Maggie, Mrs. Buckley said her goodbyes, hurried over to her friend.

For a long time, nobody spoke. The silence was unbearable. Alice didn't know what to do with hands or her gaze, so she ended up putting both in her lap.

At last the waiter came by with the coffee. Richard was particular about how he took it, and Maggie immediately set about determining which pot contained decaf, which regular, if the milk was skim rather than whole, if substitute sugar was available or only real. "And do you have Splenda tonight or just Equal?" she asked the waiter, looking up at him as if her life depended on the answer.

Maggie was, Alice knew, obsessing over the dinky and inconsequential problem she'd been presented with because she wasn't sure yet how to deal with the massive and momentous problem she'd been presented with. Like tending to the paper-cut wound sustained by a man who'd just had his throat slit.

Charlie, registering Maggie's momentary state of distraction and not about to let an opportunity pass, said, "Hey, Mom, Alice and I were thinking of meeting up with some people. I mean, if that's okay with you."

Alice glanced at her sister, puzzled, but not about to question.

Maggie stared at Charlie blankly for several seconds before saying, "You want to . . ." She trailed off. Then she shook her head, and, in a stronger voice, said, "That would be fine." She turned to the waiter. "Is the coffee fresh-brewed or has it been sitting in a pot all night?"

"So you wouldn't mind if we cut out a little early?" Charlie was looking at both Richard and Maggie as she asked this question, but Richard wasn't looking back. He was staring straight in front of him as if he'd fallen into some sort of trance.

Maggie reached for the Mercedes key in his jacket pocket, held it out to Alice. "Go ahead, you two. Take the car. Richard and I will finish up our coffee and find our own way home." She turned to him, smiling brightly. "It's a beautiful night for a walk on the beach, isn't it, darling?"

Alice and Charlie didn't wait to see if Richard shared his wife's enthusiasm for moonlit strolls. They stood and headed to the door, throwing thanks for dinner over their shoulders, walking fast. Neither girl wanted to give Richard a chance to emerge from his stupor.

Or Maggie a chance to change her mind.

Alice was making a beeline for the back door, the one that led to the gravel lot where Richard's car was parked, when Charlie tugged violently on her arm, hissed, "This way," and shoved her toward the front door.

As Alice stumbled outside, she said, "God, you almost yanked my arm out of its socket. I didn't know you were so particular about your means of egress."

Charlie glanced over her shoulder, then started walking fast. "Sorry for the manhandling. I was just afraid of running into Stan. He sometimes reads on the back porch during his breaks. And what's an egress? That's some kind of bird, right?"

Curious, hurrying to catch up with Charlie, looking over her bobbing shoulder into her face, Alice said, "Stan? The cute waiter?"

Charlie appeared irritated by Alice's description. "He's not just a cute waiter. He's also our cute future classmate."

"Really?"

"Yeah, he's going to be a senior at Wolcott. Wants to go to Yale. And I'm sure he will. Probably on a scholarship, too, just like at Wolcott."

Talking about Stan, Charlie's voice had taken on a protective tone, which Alice immediately noticed. Noticing Alice noticing, Charlie rolled her eyes. "All I meant was that he has his nose buried in a book even more often than you."

"I didn't even see him working tonight, did you?"

"No. But he usually does on Thursday nights." Then, after a beat, "Don't give me that."

"Give you what?" Alice said, surprised.

"The raised eyebrow."

"I didn't realize I'd raised one."

"Well, you did." Charlie was quiet for a bit. "It's not like I've memorized his shift schedule. Actually, I have. But not because I'm obsessed with him, because I'm ashamed of myself. I was a total bitch to him the other night. Really, Allie, I was so bad I think I've blocked out the worst bits. Like, for self-defense purposes. So the memory doesn't make me shoot myself."

"Why were you such a bitch?"

Covering her face with her hands, Charlie said, "It was a Jude thing. It was before he and I came to our, you know, understanding. Stan said something about him that was true but that I didn't want to be true. I was jealous, upset. And I behaved badly. Really badly."

Alice thought for a bit. "You could always apologize."

"I could. Or I could just spend the whole summer trying to avoid him."

"That's another way to go, sure."

They'd just reached the Mercedes. Charlie tossed Alice the keys.

"You want me to drop you off at Jude's?" Alice asked, catching them.

"No. I'll let Cybill have him for the night. Let's you and me hang out. We could go into town, get ice cream. That is, if you're up for it."

Shocked that an olive branch was being extended so quickly and after so little groveling on her part, Alice said that she definitely was. (Take that, Camilla!) The obsessing over Tommy could wait till later. She hit the button to unlock the doors, and the two girls climbed into the car, headed into town.

Alice and Charlie strolled out of Dips Ahoy Creamery on Serenity Point's main drag. Alice was holding Charlie's chocolate-dipped waffle cone containing one scoop of amaretto crunch ice cream, one scoop of cake batter fudge ice cream, and one scoop of caramel chaos ice cream, so Charlie had both hands free to sample from Alice's single-scoop cup of vanilla frozen yogurt.

When Charlie'd had her fill, she passed the cup back to Alice with the words, "I made the better choice."

"What a dinner, huh?" Alice said, wiping her sticky hands on the napkin in her pocket.

"Eek, yeah. So, there's going to be a memorial for Camilla, looks like."

"And soon. I wonder why Richard decided to have one. He sure didn't seem to want one."

"No kidding. I thought he was going to have a stroke or something when Cybill's mom was talking to him about it." Charlie grew quiet for a moment, thoughtful. "He must be doing it for the town."

"That's the only explanation I can come up with too. It sounds like Camilla didn't get a proper funeral the first time around, so there was no real chance to publicly grieve."

"No . . . what was that stupid talk show word that Mrs. Buckley used?"

"Closure," Alice said.

"Right. There was no closure." Charlie became quiet and thoughtful again. "It's funny, though. A memorial seems redundant. I mean, if ever there was a girl who people were in no danger whatsoever of forgetting, it's our stepsister."

Alice laughed. "So true. All a memorial will do is remind people that they're not forgetting."

Charlie began laughing too, then ran her tongue over a melty spot on her cone.

"Charlie!" a voice called out. "Hey, Charlie!"

Charlie and Alice turned, saw Cybill waving to them from the other side of the street. As they stood there, watching while Cybill waited impatiently for a slow-moving SUV to pass, Alice said to Charlie, "I've got to say, Cybill's taking the news of you and Jude better than I would've expected. Like, way better."

"Tell me about it. I thought she was going to boil my pet bunny."

"You don't have a pet bunny," Alice pointed out, confused.

Charlie rolled her eyes. "Obviously I don't have a pet bunny. I was, like, making a cultural reference."

"To what?"

"*Fatal Attraction*."

"An oldie. Huh. I didn't know you'd seen that one."

"I haven't. They showed a clip of it on VH1's *I Love the 80s*."

"Oh."

"It looked kind of good, though."

At last Cybill reached them. Cybill was the alpha, the top girl in Serenity Point. There was something about her, though, that, to Alice, suggested a sleek and expensive animal, a racehorse maybe, a

Thoroughbred. She moved gracefully and had beautiful tawny skin and hair, and her features, so similar to Jude's, were even and well proportioned. Her only flaw was her chin, which looked perfect on her male cousin but was a touch large, in Alice's opinion, for a girl's face. There was certainly nothing wrong with her legs, that was for sure. They were fantastically long and lean and perfectly shaped, and the black high heels she wore to set them off reminded Alice of polished hooves.

"Did you get my text?" Cybill asked Charlie.

Charlie glanced down at her phone. "I'm getting it now. One from Jude, too. What's Red Sky?"

"A dive bar in Scumthrope." Scumthrope, nickname for Scunthrope, was the next town over from Serenity Point, also on the water. It was a poorer town, rougher. A fishing town, as opposed to a vacation town.

"What's so great about this bar that you're willing to leave town to go to it?" Alice asked.

"Lax ID policy. You two should come. Jude'll be there, a bunch of people from the club, and I think—" Cybill stopped talking abruptly, the chirp of her cell cutting her off. She pulled the phone from her bag, spilling a bottle of Korres Walnut & Coconut Suntan Oil onto the pavement. Alice bent down to pick it up, hand it to her. She accepted it without thanks. Frowning at the name flashing across her screen, she said, "I've got to take this."

As she stepped aside to do so, Charlie turned to Alice. "Let's do it. It'll be fun. We haven't gone out together in ages. And it'll give you the perfect opportunity to spend time with Jude, get to know him better. Plus, you never drink, so you can designated-drive me."

Alice snorted. "What an honor."

Charlie looked at Alice, then she cocked her head to the side, brought her lips together and stuck out the lower one: sad clown face. Sad clown face was part of Alice and Charlie's private language. It was the face you made when you were expressing your unhappiness but also, at the same time, making fun of that unhappiness.

"Come on," Charlie said. "You sort of owe me."

Alice looked at her sister. She sort of did. With a sigh, she nodded, said, "Okay, but you're the only underage drunk I'm hauling around. The other underage drunks can call a taxi."

"Sure, great, of course."

"And we're only staying for one hour."

"Two hours."

"Fine, two hours. But that's it."

Charlie clapped and jumped up and down. "We're in," she crowed to Cybill. "You need a ride? Should we pick anyone up?"

CHAPTER FIVE

*J*esus, Charlie thought, Cybill wasn't being too rough on Red Sky when she called it a dive. The bar was housed in a squalid building on an abandoned-looking strip of dock strewn with empty wine bottles and fast-food wrappers. It didn't even have a sign other than the red neon one in the window that blinked "BUD." As she breathed in the urine-y stench, she realized she could take off the Band-Aid that was almost part of her skin now, flaunt her angel's-wing tattoo. It set her apart in Serenity Point, but here it might actually help her fit in. Charlie couldn't believe someone like Cybill even knew about a rough-trade place like Red Sky, never mind frequented it. She was careful, though, not to let Alice see her shock. If she did, Alice, she knew, would turn the car around, head back home. So she kept her face deadpan and blank-eyed.

Alice found a parking space in front. The girls piled out of the Mercedes. Charlie was patient with Alice as she checked, then re-checked the doors to make sure they were locked. When she moved to check a third time, Charlie grabbed her arm, dragged her across the sidewalk.

The door to Red Sky was heavy. Charlie needed to use both her arms to pull it back. The bartender, a bald guy in a sleeveless shirt, tattoos up and down his massive arms, turned as the girls entered. Even though it was night, and dark outside, Charlie's eyes still needed a second to adjust to the extreme dimness of the interior.

A few customers, old-timers mostly, all men, were hunched over their drinks at the bar. Everyone else in the place, though—and it was packed—was young. *Young* young. Too young to legally buy cigarettes, never mind alcohol young. Half were local kids, meaning tough-looking. The other half were Serenity Point kids, meaning tough-looking in a different way: arrogant in their khaki shorts and shirts with the little crocodiles on them, aggressive in their sense of privilege, confident nobody would mess with them even off their own turf. The two groups were on opposite sides of the room and seemed to be coexisting peacefully enough, though Charlie sensed that could change in an instant.

Jude and a couple of other guys, a few of whom Charlie recognized, a few of whom she didn't, were clustered around the pool table at the back, playing a game. Looking on were Cybill's worshippers, Sasha and Bianca. (Charlie had known these two girls for several weeks now, and though they didn't look alike feature by feature, their imitation Cybillness made them weirdly hard to tell apart.) It wasn't Jude's turn to shoot, and he was just leaning against the wall, watching the action on the table, his stick propped against his hip, a bottle of beer dangling by its neck from between his fingers.

When he saw Charlie, he gave her a small smile, a cool little two-fingered wave around his beer bottle. She dropped her head, unsure if the wave was a signal for her to approach him or to stay away. They were still so new as a couple she didn't know how to act in public. What was proper protocol? Proper etiquette? Should she even expect acknowledgment of their change in status? How much? And how much should she give in return?

Evidently, though, Jude shared none of her self-consciousness or doubts. While she'd stood there, dithering, he'd shouldered his way through the drunken masses. Reaching her, he pulled her into a kiss, a deep one that went on for some time. There were a few hoots and catcalls, all good-natured. Charlie laughed with embarrassment and pleasure when they finally broke apart. She checked for her sister's reaction, but Alice was no longer by her side, must've gotten lost in the crowd. Cybill winked at her, made a kissy face.

"I didn't hear from you," Jude said. "I wasn't sure if you got my texts."

"I wanted to surprise you."

"Nice surprise." He held up his beer. "Should I get you one?"

"Sure. I'm going to have to make room for it first, though." Craning her neck, "Do they even have a bathroom here?"

"Jude," one of the guys called out, annoyed. "It's your shot."

He shrugged. "Look around. You'll find it. Or pee in a corner. Can't make this dump smell any worse than it already does."

He leaned over, kissed her cheek. And as he returned to the pool table, she went off in search of that bathroom or corner.

Charlie was just wiping her wet hands on the tops of her thighs—no paper towels in Red Sky's bathroom, naturally; she counted herself lucky there was toilet paper—when she walked smack into some-body. A guy her age in a white T-shirt, apron, carrying a gray food-service bin filled with empty glasses. Stan.

"What are you doing here?" Charlie said, too surprised to re-member that she was supposed to be shamed by her recent behavior, had been ducking him for nearly a week.

"I could ask you the same question," he said back.

Charlie just looked at him, at the wide green eyes, at the dark tousled hair framing a face that was cute rather than handsome. It was a nice face, a likeable face.

At last he sighed either in irritation or anger, and said, "I work here."

"As what?"

"An exotic dancer," he said. Then, rattling the bin with the glasses in it, "As a busboy. My friend's brother, Izzy"—tilting his head to indicate the Mr. Clean–looking guy behind the bar—"owns the place. He gave me the job."

"But you already have a job."

"Had. I quit last week."

"Last week," Charlie repeated, mystified. Then, recognition suddenly dawning, "You mean after our . . ."

"Yeah, after our dot, dot, dot. The money here isn't as good as it was at the club, but, hey, at least I don't feel lower than dirt at the end of the day, so it all balances out."

Stan started to push past her, but Charlie stopped him. "Look, I know an *I'm sorry* isn't going to even begin to cover it but—"

"Exactly. Wouldn't even begin. So save your breath."

"Stan, I—"

Throwing a quick glance at the bar, he said, "Izzy's watching us. I can't afford to lose another job."

Charlie stared at him, blinking, trying to think of something to say, something that would make it better between them, fix things.

He sighed again. "Just forget it. We're cool, whatever, I forgive you. Okay? Can I go now? Do I have your permission?"

Charlie, realizing she had no other choice, nodded. Stan walked off. She watched him as he moved from table to table, dropping empties in the bin, running a rag over damp patches.

And then a voice said, "I thought you were Jude's girl."

Charlie turned. It took her a second to identify the person standing behind her, grinning. It was that Nick guy, the one who'd watched her and Jude playing tennis that morning. She didn't recognize him at first because the sunglasses were gone. Also, he was dressed differently. Or at least he was wearing his clothes differently. The jacket was off, the tie loosened, the top couple buttons of his shirt undone and the sleeves rolled. The air of being out-of-place, though, was certainly the same. (Casual Fridaying his outfit helped, but not much.) So was the face: the sharp, white teeth, the eyes that didn't miss a trick, the heavy, dark hair brushed back from the forehead.

He must've realized that she recognized him because the grin suddenly screwed itself into a new shape, got even bigger.

"So?" she said.

"So why aren't you giving *him* the hard time?"

Charlie reached for the beer in his hand and took a swig, not to quench her thirst, to show she wasn't afraid of him, even though she was. Of course she was. He'd rattled Jude, and Jude didn't rattle easily. "I like it better when Jude gives me the hard time. Rock hard. Know what I mean?"

Nick threw his head back and laughed.

At that moment Jude came up to her, and, in a gesture that was either protective or possessive—she wasn't sure which—put his arm around her shoulders. "What's going on here?" he said to Nick, his tone aggressive.

Casually, Nick took back his beer from Charlie. "Oh, hey, Jude. I was just asking your girlfriend here why she was fighting with some other guy when it's your life she's supposed to be making miserable."

"What other guy?"

"Why don't you ask her?"

Turning his body toward Charlie, turning his aggression toward Charlie, too, Jude said, "What's he talking about?"

"Nothing. It's that waiter from the club. Stan. He's a busboy here now."

"What do you care if he's a busboy?"

"That's what I was wondering," Nick said.

Shooting Nick a look but otherwise ignoring him, Charlie said, "I don't. It's just, I think he quit his job for me."

"What do you mean, *for* you?"

Finding herself on the defensive without quite knowing how she got there, Charlie said, "Not for me, because of me," trying to get her words out fast and be careful of them at the same time. "We got into a fight. Not a lovers' quarrel kind of fight, an actual, like, argument."

Nick shook his head. "I wouldn't be too quick to trust her on this one, buddy. I saw heat, anger, intensity. You know, passion."

"Shut up," Charlie and Jude said to Nick at the same time.

Nick laughed.

Then to Jude, Charlie said, "Stan's the one who told me that sometimes you and Cybill used to spend the night in your dad's room at the club. I got mad at you, took it out on him. Said things I shouldn't have. I only feel bad because I caused him to lose his job, give up his job, whatever. It's not what he"—using her thumb rather than her eyes to indicate Nick so she didn't have to look at his smirking face—"is implying."

Jude stared at her hard for several seconds, then nodded. "Okay," he said amiably, taking a pull on his beer, his mood changing abruptly, going back to the way it was before. "I believe you."

"Great," she said, and let out the breath she'd been holding. Then she hit him in the chest. "And you should believe me. I'm telling the truth."

He caught her hand, opened it up so he could kiss the palm. "You're right," he said, smiling. "I'm sorry."

And without another word, Charlie and Jude wrapped their arms around each other's waists, strolled over to the pool table. Charlie almost turned around, aimed a victorious grin at Nick, but then reconsidered. She'd make her point better by ignoring him.

Alice, who'd run out to the street to grab her cell phone from the glove compartment, check to see if Tommy had called or texted—he hadn't—reentered the bar just in time to catch the final reel of the Charlie-Jude-Nick scene. She walked up to Nick, followed his eyes following Jude and Charlie to the pool table. Charlie held Jude's beer as Jude lined up a shot.

"Shouldn't you be off somewhere twirling your mustache or something?" Alice said.

Nick turned to her, seemingly unsurprised to see her standing there. "My mustache," he repeated, puzzled. Then a smile spread slowly across his face, and he said, "Oh, I get it. You mean doing something stereotypically villainous. No, I prefer tying pretty girls to train tracks."

"Sure, I can see how that would be more fun."

"And I'm all about the fun."

Alice looked at his shirt, so glaringly white it was as if it had never been worn before; at his shoes shined to such a high buff they caught the light, threw it back; at his trousers, the crease down the front sharp enough to slice bread. "Yeah," she said, "I immediately sensed that about you."

Someone dropped a quarter in the jukebox and an old Bruce Springsteen song began blasting from the trashed-looking machine. Alice and Nick watched as Charlie climbed on top of the pool table, started dancing with pelvic-gyrating abandon, her short skirt twitching around her hips, her long dark hair swinging back and forth. In no time at all, she'd gathered quite a sizable and enthusiastic audience, male and female, Jude at the front of it, loving every second of the performance, cheering, reaching up to tuck dollar bills in her underwear, give her sips from his bottle of beer.

"You going to go up there with your sister?" Nick said after a while. "Shake your ass too?"

"That's her thing. I wouldn't want to intrude. Besides, she has the more shakeable ass."

"That's debatable."

Normally Alice would have gotten flustered by a comment like that, so pointedly sexual. She understood, though, that he wasn't flirting with her, was just trying to make her uncomfortable, and the knowledge helped her keep her cool. Holding his gaze, she said, "Not if you've got eyes."

A relaxed shrug. "We'll just have to agree to disagree," he said. And then, "Where's Tommy at?"

"Not here."

"So I see. Let me guess, he's having his period. No, wait a second, I know. He decided to stay home and write in his diary."

Tommy didn't write in a diary. He wrote in a journal. Not that Alice was going to make this distinction for Nick, not that he *needed* it made for him. She could tell by the look in his eye that was just trying to bait her into an argument. Well, she wasn't going to engage. That would frustrate him. Drive him up the nearest wall, hopefully.

He laughed, as if he knew exactly what she was thinking. "You don't mind if I take that as a *yes* then, do you?" he said.

Instead of answering his question, Alice asked one of her own: "Any reason you want to mess with the lives of me and my boyfriend, Charlie and hers?"

He tilted back his Budweiser, took a long drink, then handed her the empty bottle. Leaning in close, his lips within an inch of her jawbone so that his words felt like a feather in her ear, "Plenty of reasons but none that I care to share at this point in time."

And without a goodbye or a look or anything, he was gone, walking straight out of the bar and into the night.

CHAPTER SIX

*T*he following morning, Alice was at the club, waiting for Charlie to finish her first-ever private lesson. (How quickly things changed! It was only a few weeks ago that Charlie made her initial appearance—*unwilling* appearance, not at all happy about being dragged—at the club, snapping her thong at Richard in the parking lot, showing off her tattoo. Now it was all, "tennis anyone?" whites, and personal coaches.) Alice couldn't take another day in the house, socked away in her room, avoiding liquids so she wouldn't need to use the bathroom, run the risk of bumping into her mom or Richard in the hall. She was hoping she could talk Charlie into a fruit smoothie or a walk on the beach before her afternoon clinic started, that Charlie wouldn't already have plans with Jude or Cybill.

The lesson was scheduled to last another thirty minutes, and Alice had forgotten to bring a book. She was trying to kill time but it wasn't dying easy. Normally she'd stare at the photograph on the wall of Camilla and Tommy holding the mixed-doubles trophy,

falling into a trance of obsessive wondering, dreaming with her eyes
open: What was Camilla thinking as the shutter clicked? What was
Tommy? Of how in love they were and how in love they'd stay for
the rest of their lives? Or had Camilla started to grow bored with
Tommy and his clean, wholesome affections by this time? Had she
already started looking for newer, dirtier, sicker thrills? Begun culti-
vating an appetite for danger and mayhem?

But Alice was doing her best to break herself of this morbid
habit. Camilla was just a girl, she reminded herself. A dead one at
that. Alice was making her more special than she was, romanticizing
her by demonizing her. And, anyway, she was finally proving to be
Camilla's equal in battle. After all, she hadn't let Camilla destroy her
relationship with Charlie, had she? She'd managed to subvert that
disaster, if only barely. And Tommy had told her he'd never been
happier with a girl than he'd been with Alice. The truth was, were
she to have met Camilla, she probably would have found her surprisingly ordinary, dull even. Camilla only had power if Alice gave it to
her, which Alice wasn't going to do. Not anymore.

Defiantly, deliberately, Alice turned her back to the picture.

She'd just picked up one of the brochures lying on the coffee
table, was reading about the differences between mat Pilates class
and Cardiolates class, when Lucy, one of the club's tennis pros, sitting behind the desk, eating a veggie wrap and tapping every now
and then on the keyboard of the computer in front of her, said,
"How familiar are you with video-editing software?"

Alice looked around, not sure she was being addressed even
though she was the only other person in the room. Frankly, Lucy
made her a little nervous. Lucy was older and pretty and went to an

excellent college, and though she was working at the club this summer, she wasn't really, was more slumming since both her parents
were members and she obviously didn't need the money.

"Me?" Alice finally said.

"Alice, right? You know anything about this stuff?"

"Next to nothing."

"That's still more than me. Will you come over here and take a
look?"

Alice returned the brochure to the pile and walked over to Lucy.
On the screen of the computer was footage, amateur, obviously—
you could tell from the shaky camera work, the low-quality sound—
taken at some outdoor summer party at the club. Members were
milling around in dressy clothes, holding champagne flutes, laughing and talking, some kind of high-class string music playing in the
background. Then Alice squinted, saw the red, white, and blue
streamers decorating the tennis courts and branches of trees, the
American-flag cake on the table, the Uncle Sam hats on several of
the men's heads. Not some outdoor summer party, she realized, an
outdoor Fourth of July party specifically. All of a sudden the people being filmed stopped what they were doing and turned, tilting
their faces expectantly toward the early evening sky. The fireworks
must've been about to begin.

"The club's Fourth party," Lucy explained unnecessarily. "Clay
asked me to trim down this mess of footage—and there are hours
and hours of it—to a snappy two minutes."

Clay was Clay Swaine, the club's tennis director and Lucy's boss.

"Why?" Alice asked.

"He wants to show it at this year's party. How dumb can you

get, right? I mean, why people from this year's party would want to look at people from last year's party, especially since they're the same people, basically, is beyond me. And Clay's given me no time. The party's in two days. Who does he think I am? Sofia Coppola?"

Alice made sympathetic sounds with the back of her throat, was about to return to the couch and the Pilates brochure when something caught her eye: Camilla, the one face in the crowd turned forward, not upward. Camilla, in a white dress that was a special kind of white, the white of chocolate. Of heat. Of lies.

Camilla, five days before she died.

Alice's lungs worked the air but couldn't find any to inhale; it was like there was no oxygen in it. She leaned into the computer, so close she nearly bumped her forehead against the screen. Looking at Camilla, the living, breathing Camilla, the Camilla who could move around freely, no longer stuck inside a dinky little picture frame, all that talk about her not being so special, about her reputation being inflated or overblown or undeserved, went flying out the window.

They were right, Alice said to herself. *Camilla* was *dangerous. A cool blonde with hot impulses and dark edges.* She could credit now the many stories she'd heard about her half sister. They were true, all of them, she could feel it. True and then some. She gasped.

Lucy gave Alice a questioning glance. Before she could follow it up with a questioning question, though, a woman stepped in from outside. She was wearing one of those little sun-visor caps they sold in the club shop and so much jewelry she clanged when she lifted her arm to close the door behind her. "Lucy," the woman said, "there's something wrong with the net on court three."

Lucy put down her wrap. "Wrong?"

"Well, it was a little high so we tried to adjust the height, and the strap broke. Will you come see if you can't do something with it? We only have the court for an hour, and we were hoping to at least get a set in."

Lucy bugged her eyes, a glare of irritation meant only for Alice. Then, turning, said sweetly, "Sure, Mrs. Tilly, be right there. Alice, answer the phone for me, will you?"

Alice stifled a yawn, gave a sleepy nod. Then, as soon as Lucy disappeared through the door, she jumped into the chair, brought her eyeballs back to the screen. Camilla seemed to have caught the camera's attention at the same instant she caught Alice's because all at once it zoomed in on her, ignoring totally the pyrotechnic display going on up above. (Alice could hear the booms in the distance, could see the exploding colors reflected on the upturned faces of the club members.) Camilla was saying something to the guy she was standing with—Tommy! His hair longer, his cheeks fuller, but unquestionably Tommy!—her lips making wheedling shapes, then annoyed shapes, then disgusted shapes. Like she wanted to get away from him but he wouldn't let her go. Like he was being tiresome, a big, fat drag. Finally she twisted free, began sashaying across the grass on long-stemmed legs.

Tommy's expression as he watched her moving away from him made Alice's stomach drop down to her shoes. It was a look of pure anguish. And Alice knew everything he'd said about being indifferent to Camilla by the time she died, about being exhausted by her wildness, her dramatics, her torment, her crappy treatment of him was a lie. He was in love with her, was sick with it. A blind person watching the video could see that. And this was *after* he'd ended the relationship. Three days after if Alice was doing her math right. Well, he might have broken up with Camilla but he hadn't broken her hold over him. He wanted to run after her, fall to his knees before her, wrap his arms around her legs and beg her to take him back. Alice was certain this was what he was feeling, thinking. It was right there in his eyes. It was pumping in her blood.

Alice tore her gaze away from Tommy to follow Camilla, now crossing the lawn. Camilla reached Jude and Cybill, ran her fingers lightly over Jude's bare forearm without looking as she passed, causing his head to snap around, Cybill's right along with it. At last she came to her father and a second man, one with his back to the camera, and stopped. Richard's joy at seeing his daughter was almost palpable, his dark, closed-off face open for once and full of light. She hugged him, kissed him many times, laughed at something he said, making no sound that Alice could hear but taking bites out of the air with her wide mouth, her gleaming teeth.

She was happy, though, in a way that Alice couldn't quite believe. There was something exaggerated about this happiness, exaggerated about her expression of it as well, a too-muchness, like she was performing for somebody. For Richard? Was this part of the act that Tommy had told Alice about, the one Camilla put on for her father to satisfy his perfectionist streak, pretending to be a clean teen during the day, a model daughter, so he'd let her alone to be bad at night? Or was it Tommy she was performing for? Torturing him, letting him see what a good time she was having away from him, the object of every eye, male and female, every fantasy, rubbing his face in her desirability and power, knowing he was tracking her every move, couldn't help himself?

As if Alice's thoughts were directing the camera, it suddenly moved off Camilla's face to sneak a peek at Tommy's. It was everything Alice had feared it would be: a study in desperation and dread, sick-making jealousy. It was Jude he was jealous of, wasn't it? Or was he so far gone on Camilla he even begrudged the affection she showed her dad? When the camera returned to Camilla, she was leaving Richard and the other man. Dr. van Stratten, Alice saw, as he rotated his shoulders at the last moment to give the camera a clean shot of his profile.

Camilla began heading toward the clubhouse. She walked in front of the camera, streaking right past it. Then, all at once, she paused, swiveled, hand on jutted hip so that she was directly facing Alice, giving a long, measured look, unblinking, deeply cool, deeply sexual with those eyes that seemed half full of promises, half full of threats. Alice's heart almost stopped, *did* stop for a second, and then Camilla smiled at her, soft lips parting. Not at her, Alice realized suddenly. At the cameraperson. In that instant, Alice would have given anything—the tip of a finger, a lesser toe, a day off the end of her life—to know who was on the other side of the lens.

And then something fell out of the cameraperson's pocket or off the collar of the cameraperson's shirt. A pair of sunglasses, it looked like. The camera dipped and jostled, took several close-ups of the grass as a blurry hand shot out to retrieve them. And there, staring back at her in not one but two reflective lenses was the sharp-featured face of Nick Chillingworth.

Alice heard the sound of a door sliding shut and looked up. It was Lucy, returning from the courts. She was shaking her head in disgust.

"Did you fix the net?" Alice said, leaning back in the chair, struggling to sound casual.

"Yeah, but those women will probably break it again. They're convinced it's too high even though I broke out the tape measure and everything. Three feet, six inches. Regulation height."

"You should just take it down for them altogether."

"It still wouldn't help them get the ball in the court. They're hopeless. You have any luck figuring out the software?"

"Too high tech for me."

Lucy sighed as she leaned over Alice's shoulder, hit *command Q*. With regret Alice watched the footage disappear from the screen. She began mentally kicking herself for not thinking to email it to her Google account.

"Thanks for looking," Lucy said, picking up her abandoned veggie wrap, taking a bite. "At least now I can tell Clay I tried."

Alice smiled and stood so Lucy could have her seat back. As Alice walked over to the couch, she glanced at the clock mounted on the far wall. Ten more minutes until Charlie's lesson let out. She was picking up the Pilates brochure when her phone rang. She looked down, expecting to see the name she'd been longing to see since yesterday but was now suddenly dreading flashing across her screen. It wasn't Tommy's name she saw, though.

It was Patrick's.

Patrick, who she'd been ducking for weeks. Patrick, whose every voicemail she erased without listening to. Patrick, whose every email she deleted without reading.

She grabbed for the cell before it had a chance to ring a second time, so fast she almost knocked it to the floor. "Hi," she said, her voice breathy with eagerness.

"Alice?"

"Yeah, obviously. It's my phone." Nothing but silence. "Patrick? Are you still there?"

"I'm still here. I just momentarily lost the power of speech. You've been ignoring my calls for so long, I'd forgotten what your voice sounded like."

"Ha ha, very funny," she said, but she was really laughing.

"You sort of caught me with my pants down."

"Wouldn't be the first time."

"I don't have anything prepared to say to you personally. I was all set to leave a message on your machine."

"So pretend I'm my machine. Here, I'll make it easy for you. Hi, it's Alice. I'm not around to take your call right now, but if you leave me a message I'll call you back. Beep."

A beat passed. Then another. And then Patrick said, "Nope. I can't do it. I have stage fright."

"Give me the gist at least."

"Well, first I was going to say something angry and macho about your outgoing message being a big lie since I've left you dozens of messages and you haven't called me back once. Then I was going to say something beg-y and little-girl-y like, please, please, please, call me back whenever you get the chance, please, oh please."

She laughed again.

"So, how've you been? Busy, obviously."

She sighed. "Yeah. Though busy doing what I couldn't tell you. I'm not working. And I'm not painting. Just having this whole new life takes up a lot of energy, I guess."

"Yeah, about that new life."

"What about it?"

"Well, I was thinking of maybe seeing it for myself."

"And how are you going to do that?"

"By accepting the gracious invitation to visit you're about to extend me."

"What's the matter? The big bad city not exciting enough for you these days?"

"Not without you and Charlie in it. Nothing's fun here without you two. Even the fun things, like parties, aren't fun."

"But I'm never fun at parties."

"That's true," Patrick said affectionately. "You never are. So are you going to invite me or not? And remember, I wouldn't have to come up to Serenity Point if you'd come down to Cambridge every once in a while like you promised."

Alice hesitated. The truth was, at that moment, she'd have loved to see Patrick. Just hearing his voice was making her miss him, miss her old life. But she knew the desire was stemming from the fact that she'd hit a rough patch with Tommy, was feeling insecure. Besides, if she said yes, Patrick might take it as a sign that she was interested in picking up where they left off. And she wasn't. And not just because of Tommy. There was a reason she and Patrick had been a couple for more than two years—well, on and off for two years, but mostly on—and yet she remained a virgin. It just wasn't there between them. Not for her, at least.

Patrick continued: "It's not like I think we're going to be sharing a bedroom or anything, Alice. It's pretty clear you're not looking for a boyfriend right now. Not looking to me, at least. It's just, I get some time off from work in mid-August." Patrick's dad and uncle owned a small construction company in Somerville. And ever since he was twelve, Patrick had spent his summers mixing cement, hanging drywall, erecting scaffolds. "I need something to look forward to, you know what I mean?"

The wistful note in his voice was making Alice sad. And he seemed to understand that she had no interest in being romantic, and mid-August was still so far off. If his presence was going to create a problem between her and Tommy, she'd have plenty of time to come up with an excuse. "Sure, you can visit," she said.

"Yeah?"

"Yeah, definitely. Charlie will freak out when I tell her."

"Oh, wow, Alice, that's so great. It'll be like old times."

"We're too young to have old times."

"Okay, like older times."

They talked until Charlie came in from the courts. As they said their goodbyes, Patrick told Alice he'd be glad to see her again. She told him she'd be glad too.

And she meant it.

CHAPTER SEVEN

*C*harlie decided to skip her clinic that afternoon. She mooched a ride into town off Richard as soon as she and Alice finished their smoothies and organic egg-salad sandwiches. She had two errands she wanted to run. Her first was to stop by the local dermatologist's office, talk to him about the possibility of laser tattoo removal.

God, what had she been thinking when she let that skuzzy guy in that skuzzy shop in skuzzy Charleston permanently ink an angel's wing on her lower back? The tattoo wasn't cool or edgy or ironic. It was dumb. A tramp stamp. A stamp that branded you a tramp. And it would keep her from ever really fitting into Serenity Point. As long as it marked her skin, she could never shake her vulgar, low-rent origins: the wine coolers and beer funnels, the trashy-flashy clothes, the loser guys she used to run around with. (Neither Alice nor Maggie were "of" the neighborhood they way she was. They always managed to hold themselves apart.) Plus, she was getting seriously sick of having a tan line in the shape of a Band-Aid.

Her second errand was to pick up something for Stan, a little apology present. She was thinking maybe a book. He was a reader and she wasn't, making a book the last thing in the word she should try to buy him. But reading was the only thing Charlie knew for sure that Stan liked to do. And it was how they'd struck up a friendship in the first place, commiserating over *Tess of the d'Urbervilles*, the assigned summer reading for Wolcott. Though their complaints were of a different order—she bitched she had to read a book at all; he bitched that he'd had to read that book in particular, not one of Hardy's better efforts in his opinion—she was flattered he thought her worth complaining to at all. She was so used to viewing Alice as the brains and bookworm of the family, it was a surprise, and a pleasant one at that, to find a boy who wanted to discuss literary matters with her. And she wanted him to keep on wanting to.

Dr. Larchmont's secretary told her he'd be able to squeeze her in for a quick consultation at two thirty. That was still forty-five minutes off, so Charlie decided to swing by the Serenity Point Book Nook. She entered the store like the books it sold were pornographic ones— head down, face concealed behind a pair of dark glasses. An older woman wearing a cardigan despite the heat of the day, an actual tissue tucked up the sleeve, approached her.

"Can I help you find something?" the woman said, in a tone of voice that made Charlie think she wanted to add, "The way to the local mall, perhaps?"

Avoiding eye contact, Charlie shook her head, walked quickly to the back of the store, like she knew what she was doing. As she roamed up and down the unfamiliar aisles, feeling self-conscious and out of place, wondering how long she'd have to stick around to prove that she hadn't entered by mistake, a bright blue spine caught her eye. Standing on tiptoe, she pulled the slim volume from the shelf. *The Great Gatsby.* She'd been assigned the book in English class last year and had actually enjoyed it. Made it all the way through to the end. She'd even written the paper herself instead of reworking one of Alice's old ones, her usual MO. (Topic: What is the significance of Nick Carraway's description of Daisy Buchanan as "high in a white palace the king's daughter, the golden girl"?)

If she'd read *Gatsby*, Stan must've too. But so what? He wouldn't think she was dumb for giving it to him. And it even sort of pertained to his situation: it was about a poor boy who climbed the ladder of success to dizzying heights, made the move from rags to riches. Sure, he died at the end. But before he got his, he got the girl. For a little while, anyway.

Charlie walked up to the register and handed over the book, looking the older woman straight in the eye this time.

"Oh, Fitzgerald," the woman said, glancing down at the cover. "One of my favorites."

Charlie could see now that the woman had a kind face and that the *Can I help you find something?* question had likely been a genuine one. "Mine too," Charlie said, extra warmly to make up for her earlier rudeness, taking off her sunglasses.

"Is the book for you or someone else?"

"Someone else." A pause. "Actually, you wouldn't happen to have another copy would you? I'd like to buy it for myself, too."

"We have an extra in the back, I believe. Shall I get it for you?"

"That," Charlie said, leaning forward, reaching for one of the butterscotch candies in the silver dish by the stack of bookmarks, "would be great."

As Charlie walked out of the shop, sucking the candy drop, rolling it against the back of her teeth, she realized she didn't have a clue as to where to send the book. She knew Stan lived in the greater New Haven area, but nothing beyond that basic fact. She didn't even know his last name. At least she knew where he worked, though receiving a copy of *The Great Gatsby* at Red Sky might be grounds for dismissal. Or a beating. Well, Stan seemed like he could take care of himself.

Charlie pulled her iPhone out of her bag so she could look up the bar's address. She was a block from the post office when she passed the Crown Hobby Shop. She glanced in the window, less out of curiosity than vanity. The glass was the tinted kind that tossed your reflection back at you, and she wanted to use it as a makeshift mirror. (She was trying out a new hairstyle, half up, tousled in the back, a few strands loose in front, and was eager to see how it looked from different angles.) She took a step closer, leaned forward. And from inside her own image, she saw Tommy van Stratten talking to a salesman. She rapped her knuckles on the window excitedly, waved.

Tommy spun around. When he saw her standing there, he quickly returned the wave, raising his hand and dropping it in under a second. Then abruptly he rotated, giving her his back, began talking to the salesman again. Jesus. Rude much? Did he dislike her or was he buying something embarrassing, something he'd rather she not see—a model train or one of those boat doohickey things that you stuffed inside a bottle? Charlie didn't know what Alice saw in him other than the obvious: good-looking, smart, athletic. Frankly, he was kind of an oddball. Maybe his girlfriend taking her car for a late-night swim in the bay had messed up his brain somehow, made him screwy.

Charlie was guessing that Alice was over her crush, in any case. She hadn't mentioned him in a while and lately when he was around she acted as if she couldn't have cared less, barely noticed him. It would be nice, though, if Alice did find a guy. She spent so much time alone, more every day it seemed like. Charlie worried about her. Alice had always preferred her own company, but in Cambridge she'd had Patrick for those rare moments when she craved actual human contact. Tricky—Charlie's nickname for Patrick—was good for Alice, got her out of her head. Too bad he didn't live closer.

Charlie glanced down at the screen of her iPhone. A quarter past two. She didn't want to risk missing Dr. Larchmont, have him fill her fifteen-minute slot with yet another local matron looking to be shot up with youth serum. (What was that Botox stuff made of, anyway? The blood of young virgins?) So she decided to go back to his office. Then she'd hit the post office. Then she'd walk home. It was a long trek, would take more than half an hour. If Tommy had been a little friendlier, she would've asked him for a ride. God, why did he have to be such an asocial weirdo?

Oh well. At least she'd be getting in plenty of cardio today.

CHAPTER EIGHT

"Girls, we have an announcement to make," Richard said, pushing back his chair from the table, standing up.

Alice had been tuned out for most of dinner, thinking about the footage from the previous year's Fourth of July party. Seeing it had crystallized things for her. She understood now what she had to do: find out what really happened the night Camilla drove her car off Greeves Bridge. Trying to ignore Camilla, to act as if she were dead and buried and therefore in the past, not worth dwelling on, was the exact wrong tactic. If Camilla's final moments remained shrouded in secrecy and rumor and hearsay, if the reasons for her suicide stayed obscure and shadowy, Tommy would never get over it or her. Mystery was so much more potent than clarity, a dream-like/ghost-like presence so much more seductive than any real girl could ever hope to be.

The only way to diffuse Camilla's power was to solve the mystery of her death, and, in so doing, solve the mystery of her. The tricky bit was, Alice was going to have to pull off this feat without letting Tommy know what she was up to. It would be too upsetting for him, too painful. Her first move, she decided, would be to track down Nick. She'd already planned out what she'd say to him when she did, the manner in which she'd approach him, make him squirm with her questions, ooze sweat and fear: *Were you sleeping with Camilla?* (That one was a gimme. Obviously he was. The smoldering look Camilla had shot him through the camera lens told the whole sleazy story.) *How long had the relationship been going on? Who knew about it? Did something happen between you two the night she died—a fight? Were you the reason she was distraught enough to kill herself? If not, what was?*

Hearing those words come out of Richard's mouth, though—*Girls, we have an announcement to make*—caused Alice to snap to, pull her mind back to the present. Did he get Maggie pregnant? Again? She felt her stomach collapse in on itself, the moisture evaporate from her mouth.

And then he said, "We've been thinking of taking a slightly belated honeymoon trip."

"Where are the lovebirds flying off to?" Charlie said, around a mouthful of Luz's homemade raspberry tart.

"The house in Palm Beach."

The house in Palm Beach. How easily the phrase tripped off Richard's tongue, Alice thought sourly. Well, it ought to. He'd had enough practice saying it and phrases like it. Not only did he have a house in Palm Beach and Serenity Point, he also had a house in Aspen, though he referred to that one as "the lodge." Not to mention the co-op on Park Avenue.

Richard continued: "We leave tomorrow evening. It seemed like a good time to sneak off since it's the start of the holiday weekend, which means not much work will be getting done. And free days are going to be so hard to come by once the Art Institute project begins."

"We figured we'd better get it while the getting's good," Maggie said, smiling at Charlie.

Before any of that smile could spill over onto Alice, though, she jerked her head back to Richard, as if something had suddenly and unexpectedly claimed her attention. Alice understood why her mother didn't care to meet her eye because she didn't care to meet her mother's eye for the same reason: Charlie, and the failure to tell Charlie the truth about Richard. Whenever Alice looked at her mother these days, all she saw was her own cowardice looking back at her. It must have been worse for Maggie. On top of feeling like a yellow belly, Maggie had her guilt to contend with. After all, she'd done Alice—done both her daughters—a massive wrong. Alice was glad she knew the score now with regard to her family, was no longer living in a fakey-fake Candy Land rose-colored dream world. Still, her estrangement from Maggie hurt. Maggie wanting to avoid her hurt. Getting stripped of her illusions hurt. And Alice was jealous of Charlie, resented her for being able to bask in Maggie's presence in her old innocence, clueless and the happier for it.

"So you won't be back until Tuesday?" Charlie said, scarcely bothering to conceal her delight.

"Actually, Pie Face," Maggie said, with a laugh, using one of her oldest nicknames for Charlie, "not until Wednesday."

Charlie stood and threw her arms around Maggie, covered Maggie's face in kisses.

Still laughing, Maggie said, "Your mouth's all sticky. Why can't you ever eat dessert without getting it all over yourself? Now you're getting it all over me too." She patted Charlie's back. "Now, sit down and finish your tart like a good girl."

Obediently, Charlie returned to her chair. Picking up her fork, "Wednesday. I can't believe it."

"Wednesday night at that," Richard added.

Wow, Alice thought, he was cutting it close. Wednesday was the eighth. Camilla's memorial was going to be held the next day. But maybe cutting it close was the only way he could cut it at all. Like if he thought about the memorial too much, he'd be overwhelmed by grief, have to call it off. After seeing him interact with Camilla at last year's Fourth of July party, the expression of pure joy on his face, Alice couldn't help but feel more sympathetic toward him and the loss he'd suffered. Whatever his faults were as a father, not loving his daughter enough clearly wasn't among them.

Alice glanced over at Charlie, knew from the expression on her face that she was calculating all the unsupervised time she'd be able to spend with Jude, no parents, no curfew, no limits—heaven. The truth was, Alice was looking forward to the unsupervised time just as much. Not to mention the unsupervised use of Richard's car. Nick had already managed to sneak up on her several times. Now she could return the favor. (Hard to tail a guy when you had no wheels.) After all, she knew where he worked, if not where he lived.

Richard continued: "Now I assume it goes without saying, but I'm going to say it, anyway. There will be no boys and no parties while we're gone."

"Not even the Fourth of July party at the club?" Charlie said.

"The party at the club's fine. No parties at the house, I meant. And your mom and I will be checking in. And when we call the house or your cell phones, we expect you to pick up. If you don't, she and I will be too tense to enjoy ourselves. And if you can't relax on a vacation, what's the point of taking one? Do you give me your word that I can trust you? Charlie?"

Charlie squealed her assent.

"Alice?"

"Sure, you can trust me," Alice said. *About as far as you can throw me*, she added. But only in her mind.

CHAPTER NINE

*T*he following evening, Alice and Charlie were in the kitchen making grilled cheese sandwiches and sweet potato fries, a favorite meal of theirs back in Cambridge. A car had picked up Richard and Maggie after lunch to ferry them to the airport, and Charlie had convinced—Alice couldn't imagine how she'd convinced, but she had—Fernanda and Luz that Richard intended for them to take a paid vacation over the holiday weekend even if he hadn't said so. The two had cleared out an hour ago.

For the first time ever, the girls were all alone in the house.

They decided to spend the night together. The plan was to eat their reasonably nutritious dinner, then gorge themselves on *Buffy the Vampire Slayer*, a show they'd gotten addicted to before moving to Serenity Point but had since abandoned, and Ben & Jerry's Half Baked frozen yogurt. Afterward—and this was not part of the plan, at least not part of Charlie's—Alice would open up to Charlie about Richard, about her paternity. She knew now that she'd have to be the one to do it, to tell Charlie the truth, that Maggie would always find an excuse to put it off.

Alice was in charge of the sandwiches, Charlie of the fries. But Charlie refused to set a timer, preferred a more improvisational style of cooking—"less Nervous Nellie," was how she put it—which meant she sat on the counter, thumbed through an issue of *US Weekly*, speculating on the reasons behind a pop star's recent weight gain, the marital status of a movie star couple, while Alice looked in the oven every two minutes to make sure the fries didn't burn.

Alice had just flipped the first grilled cheese sandwich out of the pan and onto a plate when the doorbell rang. She turned to Charlie.

Charlie lowered her magazine. "Don't look at me," she said. "It's not Jude. Tonight's his biweekly dinner with his mom and dad. You know, one of the two days a month they remember they actually have a son. They drove up from Boston this afternoon."

"Maybe it's Cybill," Alice suggested.

"She's not the drop-by type. She'd call or text first." Charlie pulled her iPhone out of her pocket, glanced down at the screen. "Nope, she hasn't done either."

And no way was it Tommy, Alice thought. If he ever came by the house to see her, he'd throw pebbles against her window or try to shimmy up the drainpipe. He'd never just walk up to the front door and ring the bell. "So, who could it be?"

Charlie shrugged, slid off the counter. "Only one way to find out."

Alice was frightened. Maybe it was because death had been on her mind so much lately, but she saw menace everywhere, especially in the great big empty mansion, the former home of a no-longer-living mother and daughter, on, it was occurring to her now, a particularly isolated stretch of beach. Who would hear her and Charlie if they screamed? The pounding of the surf would drown out their cries.

Alice killed the flame under the pan, reached for the knife she'd used to slice the bread. Then she followed her sister into the entrance hall, her heart jumping every step of the way.

The bell rang a second time. Charlie reached for the knob, but hesitated before turning it. "What if it's a murderer?" she whispered.

Alice lifted the knife, made a stabbing motion in the air. "I'll murder him first."

Charlie laughed. "Maybe he'll be a cute murderer."

"Alice, Charlie," a muffled male voice said, "open up. I have to pee."

The girls stared at each other for a long second, recognition flashing in their eyes at the same moment. Patrick.

"I won't leave the seat up, I promise," he said. "Come on, let me in. Please."

Charlie unfroze first, stepping forward, flinging open the door.

And there he was, all six feet four gawky inches of him, grinning his crooked grin, running a hand through his reddish brown hair, cowlicky and all over the place. "Surprise."

"Tricky!" Charlie screamed, and jumped into his arms.

"Oof, watch the bladder," he said as he spun her around. Looking over her shoulder at Alice, "I know we were talking about me coming in August but my dad gave me the weekend off and . . ."

"And you figured if you asked, I might say no."

"Right. So I decided to just skip that part."

"It's so good to see you," Charlie said to Patrick. Then, turning to Alice, "Isn't it so good to see him?"

It was and it wasn't. She'd wanted Patrick to visit, wanted Patrick to visit badly. But not out of the blue, not with no preparation. She hadn't even had a chance to talk to Tommy yet, find out where they stood.

Fortunately, Charlie didn't wait for an answer. Turning back to Patrick, she said, "You just missed Mom. She and Richard left a couple hours ago. She's going to be so sad she missed you."

"She'll get over it." Patrick dropped his duffel bag to the floor, began craning his neck, looking around. "Nice digs."

"I know, right? Can you believe we live here?"

"I pretty much can't. I thought it was a hotel when I was walking up to it. Or, like, where Queen Elizabeth stays when she comes to America. I was sure I got the address wrong."

"How did you get here? Someone drive you?"

"Bus."

Charlie hit him on the chest. "You should've called. We would have picked you up at the station."

"It was a long ride. I needed to stretch my legs."

"You hungry?"

Patrick laughed. "Do you even need to ask?"

"Perfect because we're just about to eat dinner."

"Let me guess, grilled cheese sandwiches and those orange french fries?"

"And that frozen yogurt with the cookie dough and brownies mixed in for dessert."

"Oh, I love that stuff. But you're not allowed to cheat and pick out all the cookie dough bits."

Charlie retracted her chin. "What are you talking about? Of course I'm allowed to cheat. You're the one who's not allowed to cheat."

"Gee, Charlie, I've missed you."

"I bet. Now, you've got to tell me how you've been doing and how everybody else back home's been doing. And don't be a boy about it. Give me actual details."

"Anything you want to know, I'll tell you. Show me the way to the bathroom first, though. I wasn't kidding about needing it."

"God, you always had the smallest bladder. Tiny tank. Come on," Charlie said, grabbing his hand, tugging on it, "there's one next to the kitchen."

"Tiny nothing. I drank two Cokes and an entire Big Gulp and then the guy next to me had a mini keg in his backpack with this straw thing sticking out of it and . . ."

Their voices faded as they moved deeper into the hall. With a sigh, Alice picked up Patrick's duffel bag, hefted it over her shoulder. It was heavy. Looked like he was planning on staying awhile. Maybe Tommy's aversion to coming to the house wasn't such a bad thing after all.

Closing the door with her foot, Alice followed Charlie and Patrick into the kitchen. The fries were burning. She could smell them. Damn it. She'd remembered to turn off the stove but had forgotten to turn off the oven. She dropped the bag, started to run.

CHAPTER TEN

*A*lice, Charlie, and Patrick walked from the house to the club the next evening for the Fourth of July party. Actually, the configuration was Alice and Charlie on either end, Patrick in the middle, holding hands with both girls.

Alice and Charlie had spent the morning and afternoon showing Patrick around Serenity Point. It had been fun, like the old times Alice claimed they were too young to have actually had. But Alice was starting to get antsy. An entire day down for the count and she hadn't had a single free moment to investigate Nick's whereabouts. Her hope was that he'd be at the party tonight, up to his usual tricks: lurking, skulking, ducking out of the shadows long enough to make a few cryptic yet barbed comments, then retreating back into darkness.

As soon as they reached the garden area behind the clubhouse, the site of the party this year, just as it was last, Charlie spotted Jude and Cybill and broke off.

"Guess Charlie already found herself a love interest," Patrick said as Charlie and Jude fell into each other's arms, began eating each other's faces.

"That sister of mine does not believe in wasting time." Alice watched Cybill take the champagne glass out of Jude's hand so he didn't spill it. Cybill looked at the couple, mouths suctioned together, socketed at the groin, then looked away. She downed the contents of Jude's glass in a single swallow.

"It's good you're more of the cautious type then," Patrick said. "You balance each other out."

He was looking at Alice as he said this in a manner that was meant to be casual but was really deliberate. She knew that he was asking, in his subtle, low-key way, if there was a new love interest in her life as well. She couldn't think what to tell him, how to give him the message to cool it without explaining why she wanted him to cool it. At a loss, she finally just shrugged, said, "Are you thirsty? Because I am."

"How about I get us a couple drinks? I just got this new fake ID from Marcus's older brother. I've been dying to try it out."

"You'll have to try it someplace else. No need for it here. Just go right up to the bar. Nobody'll hassle you."

"Really?"

"Rich people, it turns out, are surprisingly relaxed about under-age drinking."

Patrick raised a fist. "Way to go rich people. Okay, be right back."

When he was out of sight, Alice did a quick scan of the crowd, trying to pick out not just Nick's face but Tommy's as well. Still no word from her secret boyfriend. So secret he was becoming a secret even to her, she thought, a sudden depression filling her.

Secret to the point of nonexistent. Not a call or text or email. (And she couldn't, wouldn't, reach out to him, though it was taking all her willpower not to. Doing so would have meant conceding something, precisely what she couldn't say—dignity? self-respect? the semblance of equality?—that she wasn't prepared to concede.) She looked hard, but it was night and the space was only patchily lit, candles in the shape of liberty torches on the tables and string lights wound around the trees and shrubs, and the partygoers, half of whom had their backs to her, were scattered and moving around. She didn't see Nick or Tommy.

When Patrick returned a minute later, he was carrying three glasses of champagne. Tilting her chin at one of the glasses, Alice said, "It'll go flat by the time Charlie comes up for air."

"Oh, this isn't for her. I got one for you, two for me. And believe me, it won't have time to go flat."

Alice laughed. "Smart."

An announcement was made that the fireworks were about to start. Alice and Patrick positioned themselves a few yards away from the more popular congregating spots on a little rise of land. As the sky filled with bursts of color that turned into bursts of different color that turned into bursts of still different color, Alice resumed her scan of the crowd, realizing it was easier to inspect the faces when they were all clustered more or less together, illuminated and pointed in the same direction. Easier but, alas, no more successful. Still no sign of either Nick or Tommy.

"Hey," Patrick said, nudging her with his elbow, "you're missing the whole show. It's not as good as the one they put on at the Esplanade, but still pretty good."

Alice nodded and turned her head to the sky. The finale had just begun, incandescent eruptions of red, white, and blue.

At one point, Patrick slipped his arm around her shoulders. He'd held her hand earlier, of course, hers and Charlie's. This was different, though. Less friendly, more romantic. Alice hesitated, unsure of whether or not she should push him away, whether she'd be making a big deal out of nothing or acting in good faith, like a responsible and emotionally honest person. And as she vacillated back and forth between the two points of view she stood there, tense and stiff in the semicircle of his arm. The decision was a complicated one because she loved Patrick. Not like she loved Tommy, which was in an obsessive, almost desperate way that made her feel helpless and out of control and a little crazy. Tommy was still so strange to her, his past and his moods mysterious and unfamiliar. She was never sure where she stood with him.

Patrick, on the other hand, she knew inside and out. She trusted him, her confidence in him total, and she was positive that his feelings for her were his feelings for her, weren't mixed up with his feelings for a certain dead girl. And the love she felt for him was straightforward and manageable. Having him beside her was nice. Having his arm around her was nice, too. He smelled the way he always did, she noticed—this was the first time she'd let herself get close enough to him to find out—of sawdust and beer and Old Spice deodorant, a smell she was so fond of she used to steal his T-shirts, wear them to bed without washing them, return them to him when the scent was gone.

And it was as she relaxed into the crook of his arm, giving into her feelings of affection, that she saw Tommy. *Felt* Tommy. He was a hundred feet away, standing with his dad and mom by the giant American flag. His eyes were boring into her so hard they were practically denting the side of her face.

Alice immediately shrugged out from under the weight of Patrick's arm.

He turned toward her, surprised. "What's wrong?"

"I can't do this."

"Do what?" he said, but he hesitated a second before saying it, so she knew he knew what she was talking about. "We're not doing anything."

"Yeah, Patrick, we are. We're acting like things are the way they used to be and they're not."

"But they can be."

"No, they can't."

"Why not?"

"Because I don't want them to be."

She could see the hurt in his eyes before he dropped them. A beat passed. Then he said, "I think you're overreacting here. I was just—"

"You were just what?"

"Al, I—"

She cut him off. Knowing that she was being harsh but needing for him to get the message, for there to be no ambiguity, no confusion, she said, "Stop. Don't play dumb. I know what you were doing. And so do you. And I'm telling you, it's not going to happen."

He stared at her. A muscle in his jaw twitched and the tendons in his neck bunched up and knotted as he swallowed hard several times, his Adam's apple bobbing up and down. He was obviously trying to combat an emotion he didn't want her to see. She looked away. Finally he said, "Whatever you say, Alice," in a quiet voice, and walked off in the direction of the clubhouse.

She turned back to Tommy, but he'd vanished.

Champagne ran through Charlie faster, she swore, than any other liquid. Ten minutes after the fireworks show was over, she separated from Jude and Cybill, ran into the clubhouse. After a quick pee and hand wash, a slightly lengthier primp in the mirror, she exited the bathroom. She was about to return to the party when she spotted Patrick. He was all alone sitting on the couch behind the bar, empty champagne glasses scattered on the coffee table in front of him.

Charlie walked over to him.

He smiled when he saw her, but his smile was sad. "Hey, Chuck Chuck Bo Buck."

"What did my sister do?" she said, putting a hand on his shoulder.

"Nothing she didn't have a perfect right to. Told me she didn't want anything to do with me."

"She didn't mean it."

Patrick let out a humorless laugh. "Oh, she definitely meant it."

"What did she say?"

"That there was no way in hell, basically."

Charlie was surprised to hear that Alice had shut Patrick down so definitively. The two of them had been together for years, since the start of high school practically, and he was so sweet and fun and great. He'd gotten sexier, too. Was finally growing into that gangly frame of his. He was still skinny but not quite so much of a beanpole anymore, all the construction work starting to pay off, building up his arms and back and shoulders. And he had those bright blue eyes that always seemed to be laughing. She'd noticed other girls noticing him—Sasha for one—taking in his cuteness. Plus, Alice was as single as they come. Practically friendless in Serenity Point, too. If Charlie were Alice, sheer loneliness would've driven her into Patrick's arms.

But Charlie wasn't Alice.

"She meant it for now," Charlie said, sitting down beside him. "Not for all time. You don't know what it's been like for us these past couple weeks, these past couple months. All the change has been jarring. She's not herself."

"You don't seem too jarred."

"I roll with the punches better than Alice. It's been crazy, though. It's a whole new life we've been dropped into—new setting, new customs, new people. It's a lot to adjust to. I know Alice cares about you, Tricky. You have to be patient with her."

"I don't think it's a matter of patience. I think she's with someone else."

"No way."

"Are you sure?"

"She would have told me," Charlie said, though as she said it, she wondered, *Wouldn't she?* "Just hang in there. Alice will come around. It's not like you haven't broken up and gotten back together a million times before, right?"

Patrick sighed. "I guess."

"Well, this time is no different." Charlie stood. "Come with me. I want to introduce you to some people."

"No thanks, Charlie. If it's okay with you, I'm just going to sit here and wallow for a while."

She seized his arm, pulled him to his feet. "It's not okay with me. You're going to have fun tonight whether you want to or not. Now, come on."

Patrick grabbed a fresh glass of champagne off the bar top as Charlie dragged him out of the clubhouse and back to the party.

An hour after the party ended, Alice was sitting on the beach on the spot she'd often found Tommy sitting in, a stone's throw from his house, Greeves Bridge in the distance. She'd texted him almost as soon as she'd told Patrick they weren't ever going to happen (the look of surprised hurt on Patrick's sweet face when she'd rejected him, just flat out letting him have it—she couldn't bear to think of it, even if the rejection was for his own good, her being cruel to be kind), asking to meet up. No text back. And no Tommy, obviously. Still she didn't want to leave, head back home, though the night was cold and the sand was wet and she was tired. To leave would have been to admit defeat, that she'd blown it, and that the relationship was damaged beyond repair, over.

And then, the soft swishing sound of footsteps in the sand. *Tommy!* Alice wheeled around.

But it wasn't Tommy. It was Cybill, hands stuffed deep in the pockets of a jacket too big to have possibly been hers, strappy sandals dangling from her fist. Alice turned quickly back to the ocean, knowing that the disappointment would be all over her face, unmaskable.

"Can I join you?" Cybill said, "or do you want to be alone? If you want to be alone, just tell me. You won't be hurting my feelings, I promise."

Alice had never liked Cybill, instinctively distrusted her. She struck Alice as smart and restless and discontented, possibly devious, certainly with an agenda she wasn't divulging. But when Cybill, after a beat, said, "Okay, I get it. Enjoy the night," and started to turn, Alice realized she was desperate for Cybill's company, for *any* company.

"Don't go." Alice blurted the words out. Then followed them up with a mumbled, "I mean, not if you don't want to."

Cybill turned back around. With a shrug, she folded her long legs, dropped gracefully down to the patch of sand beside Alice. And for a while the two girls just sat there, looking at the silvery light the moon cast on the water, listening to the pounding of the surf. Cybill was the first to speak: "So how long have you and Tommy been together?"

Alice felt her jaw fall. "What makes you think . . . I mean, why did you . . . How did you . . ." she said, her mouth going all loose-lipped and sputtery.

"Don't worry. You haven't been obvious. The opposite. I only figured it out tonight and that was by luck. I happened to see Tommy's face when he was looking at you and that guy you know from home. Then I saw the way you looked back at him, put two and two together."

For a moment Alice considered mounting a denial, but then the moment passed. What would be the point? "A couple weeks," she said.

"He didn't seem overjoyed to see—is it Patrick?"

"No, *overjoyed* wouldn't be the word I'd use to describe Tommy's reaction to Patrick." Alice paused, knowing she should be careful here, not disclose too much. But unable to help herself—opening up at last just felt so good—she said in a rush, "I don't understand why he's so mad at me, though. Patrick just showed up on my doorstep. What was I supposed to do? Send him to a motel? And now I can't get Tommy to talk to me so I can explain. Or"—releasing a tense, unhappy snort—"you know, grovel."

Cybill reached into her jacket pocket, pulled out a silver flask. Jude's. The jacket must've been Jude's as well. She unscrewed the cap with fingers tipped in nail polish a shade of red so dark it looked black in the moonlight, took a swig. "Whose idea was it to keep the relationship under wraps?" she said, screwing the cap back on.

Alice held out her hand. Cybill raised an eyebrow in surprise but said nothing as she passed the flask. Alice tilted it into her mouth. The liquid inside was strong. She wanted to cough but wouldn't let herself. Eyes watering, she said, "Whose do you think?"

"I'm guessing his."

"Good guess," Alice said sourly.

"Well, it's not like I don't understand where he's coming from. I'm sure it feels weird dating another Flood girl." Off the look Alice gave her: "Let me rephrase that. Dating another girl living in the Flood house. Still, Tommy's probably not super-psyched at the idea of making small talk with your stepdad while he waits for you to put on your makeup. For him it must be the worst kind of déjà vu. Not that it's any picnic for you either, being the secret."

"Or being the first girl after Camilla."

"She's a tough act to follow. There's no doubt."

Alice couldn't tell from Cybill's tone whether she was being sarcastic or not. Finally deciding that she wasn't, Alice nodded in agreement. Then Alice picked up a fragment of shell, used it to scratch her initials into the sand. "It's like I can't imagine things ever being normal between me and Tommy."

"Once he gets to Harvard and the two of you are out of Serenity Point and in, like, a new context, it'll feel a lot less strange. If you can make it that long."

"That's a big *if* at this point," Alice said, wiping out her initials with a swat of her hand, throwing the shell fragment into the ocean. "I think he's pretty much over it, over me."

There was a second silence, longer than the first.

Cybill broke it by asking, "Does your sister know?"

"I haven't told anyone. I hate keeping secrets from Charlie, but I gave Tommy my word." Alice laughed. "I'm going to have to tell her soon, though. Otherwise Tommy will break up with me and I'll have nothing *to* tell."

"He's not going to break up with you."

"I'm still going to have to tell her. If I don't, she'll figure it out on her own and be pissed."

This time Cybill was the one who laughed. "I wouldn't worry about that."

"Why not? You did."

"Yeah, but I'm not Charlie."

Offended, Alice said, "What's that supposed to mean?"

"Charlie's pretty wrapped up in herself, Alice. Not in a bad way. It's only natural. She's got the person she wants wanting her. And when you've got what you want, you don't spend a lot of your time observing other people, trying to ferret out their motives, figure out what makes them tick."

Alice thought about this last remark, what it implied about Cybill's circumstances and state of mind, Cybill's inner life. She thought, too, about Cybill's earlier observation that her relationship with Tommy represented for him "the worst kind of déjà vu," Camilla redux. Well, Cybill's relationship with Charlie represented the same thing for Cybill: a close friend of hers who fell for her cousin and sometimes more than cousin—cousin with benefits?—got involved with him, and left her suddenly on the outside, unnecessary and unwanted, a third wheel.

The girls were quiet for half a minute or so. And then Alice said, "How are you doing with her and Jude as a couple? It can't be easy."

"No, it's not. But I'm happy for them." Cybill flashed Alice a wry smile. "Most of the time, at least."

"And the rest of the time?"

"A lot of deep-breathing exercises."

Alice sighed. "Jealousy's a bitch."

"Luckily, so am I," Cybill said, and grinned. And as she did, Alice had this feeling that she'd had once before—last week at the Luau Clambake at the club, when Jude got so drunk or high or both that he passed out on the porch, and she and Cybill had watched from the window—that Cybill wasn't bullshitting, trying to come off as hard and cool and above it all, and it seemed to Alice that there was still something likable about Cybill, some shadow of the girl who had been Camilla's best friend.

"I'm sorry," Alice said. She felt like she should say something more, but nothing came to mind.

Cybill shrugged. "It's okay. I've had practice dealing with it. I was jealous when he was with Camilla. Now I'm jealous that he's with Charlie. I'm sort of resigned to the fact that what I want is not okay for me to get."

No, it wasn't okay, Alice supposed. Jude was Cybill's relative. Not a close relative, not a sister, but a relative nonetheless.

"Hey," Cybill said, "pass me that flask, will you?"

Alice did as she was asked. And she and Cybill continued to pass the flask until it was empty.

As Alice and Cybill were parting, Charlie and Jude were coming together. They'd slipped out of the party before it ended, took a walk on the beach. A long one. Or maybe not. Maybe it had just felt long.

They ended up at Jude's, as Charlie knew they would. She hadn't been to his house since the night of strip tennis, when she'd invited him to play by throwing a ball through his window.

"Want to come in for the tour?" he asked.

She nodded.

He reached into his pocket for his keys. It seemed to her that the house was swaying a little, slanting first one way and then the other, and when she looked up, she saw that the stars were swaying, too, swirling brightly overhead. Her knees were shaky from all the champagne she'd drunk and she was shivering, either because it was chilly along the water and she'd forgotten to bring a jacket, couldn't borrow Jude's because he'd lost his at some earlier point in the night, or because she was nervous of being alone—really alone—with him.

She leaned against the wall, watched him as he inserted the key into the lock. His hands, she noticed, were beautifully shaped, the fingers long and tapered. She remembered how they felt against her skin, the texture of the whorls. She closed her eyes and remembered some more.

The sound of a lock being turned. Charlie opened her eyes and they entered.

The house was a blur to her, a jumble of rooms and halls and staircases with Jude's voice laid on top, a string of words running together. She could hear herself saying things back to him, making appropriate responses, her mouth acting independently of her brain. And then, all at once, the scene burst into clarity, became hyper-vivid, the sights as well as the sounds. Jude, she saw, had stopped walking, was standing in front of a closed door. He was speaking.

"And this," he said, "is my bedroom."

Charlie swallowed. The sound it made seemed unnaturally loud to her.

"Do you want to see it?"

She opened her mouth to respond, but nothing came out. Embarrassed, she tried again. Same result.

Gently, he took her hand in his. "Hey, the room's not going anywhere. I can show it to you some other time if you'd like. No rush."

She looked at him, then looked away. Suddenly she caught her reflection in a mirror hanging on the wall opposite. Her face appeared flushed, a little wild. She turned back to him. "No, I want to see it now."

He looked like he was going to say something back, but then didn't. Instead he held open the door. She stepped past him, walked inside the bedroom.

• • •

Afterward, they were lying on the bed, pillows kicked to the floor, comforter tangled at their feet. Charlie was on her side, Jude curled around her. The Band-Aid had peeled off her lower back at some point, got lost in the sheets, and he was running his hand along the bare tattoo, tracing the lines of the angel's wing with his index finger.

"I'm getting it taken off," she said. "I had a consultation with the doctor the other day. I made an appointment for removal next week. I just have to get my mom to cough up the money, which she will, gladly, when I tell her what it's for."

"Getting it taken off? Why?"

"Because I hate it. It's embarrassing."

"It's not embarrassing."

"Yeah it is." Feeling self-conscious and thus hostile, Charlie reached down for the comforter. She pulled it to her shoulders, sat up. "What do you care anyway?"

"I care because it's part of who you are. I care because—" He broke off.

"Because . . ." she prompted.

"Because I'm in love with you."

She covered her surprise with a laugh. "Your timing's off, lover boy. You're supposed to use that line before you get the girl in bed. You don't need it after."

"It's not a line, Charlie. I'm in love with you."

She turned so she could look in his face, gauge his sincerity. Not daring to believe what she saw, she attempted another laugh. "You're drunk."

"I had one glass of champagne."

"Yeah, plus whatever was in your flask. Not to mention whatever was in your medicine cabinet and bong."

"No pills, no pot, scout's honor. And I gave my flask to Cybill before the party started."

Mystified, Charlie said, "Why did you do that?"

"Because I had a feeling tonight would be our first time and I wanted to make sure I remembered it. All of it. No numbness, no blackouts or blank spots."

Charlie lowered her eyes. When she lifted them again, she whispered, "I feel bad now."

"Why? Because you're not in love with me? It's okay if you're not. I just wanted to tell you how I felt, not guilt you into saying you feel the same."

"Because I had the same feeling about tonight as you did and it made me nervous so I did drink. Sort of a lot."

He smiled, brushed a strand of hair out of her eyes. "That's okay. You're not the one with the substance abuse problem. You're allowed."

There was a long silence. And then Charlie said, "And I am, by the way."

"You are what?" A beat, then, "In love with me?"

She nodded.

"Really?" he said, and when she heard the eagerness in his voice, she realized that he'd been downplaying his hopes of reciprocation so she wouldn't feel pressured. "Are you sure? You're not just saying it because I did?"

Instead of answering, she leaned forward and kissed him, crushing her mouth against his, letting the comforter fall to her waist and rolling back with him onto the bed. Like Mrs. Fleischer used to say in the creative-writing class she took freshman year because she thought it meant she'd have to do less reading than in a normal English class: show, don't tell.

CHAPTER ELEVEN

*D*espite crawling into bed at well past three and sleeping fitfully, Alice was up and out the door before eight. The early bird act was partly to avoid a run-in with Patrick, but mostly to ensure that she didn't let another day slip by without making any progress on the Nick Chillingworth front. At the lighthouse, he'd mentioned to Tommy that he was interning for the summer with a Dr. Rose. Alice had done a www.yellowpages.com search, found a single Rose with an MD before his name in Serenity Point: Rose, Stephen.

Dr. Rose's office was located half a mile away from Richard's house. Alice knew it was unlikely that a doctor would be receiving patients at this hour. Still, Nick struck her as the conscientious type. He might arrive for work early to prepare, so Alice would have to arrive even earlier if she wanted to stage a confrontation. She readied herself for the stakeout by filling a thermos up to the brim with coffee. Then she headed out the door, taking care to make as little noise as possible.

Dr. Rose's office was clearly in his house, which was like something out of a Norman Rockwell painting: two-story and yellow and cute as a bug, with cream-colored shutters and a white picket fence, a small garden out front and a well-tended lawn. Alice parked across the street and dropped way down in her seat so that from the outside her car would appear empty. (Luckily for her, in Serenity Point every other car seemed to be a Mercedes SUV, so it was doubtful that Nick would be able to make her from it.) She then unscrewed the top of her thermos, hauled *The Magus*—required summer reading for her honors English class at Wolcott—onto her lap. The copy had originally belonged to Camilla, and when Alice had first pulled it off the shelf last week, she'd found in it a letter from Camilla addressed to her, one of the more surreal experiences of her life. The letter, never sent obviously, was written seven days before Camilla's mother, Martha, had died, a full year before Alice knew there was such a person as Richard, had been such people as Camilla and Martha. Camilla had wanted to tell Alice they were sisters. The letter was still tucked in the pages. Alice used it as a bookmark.

Alice began to read. Not only did she find *The Magus* absorbing in and of itself, but occasionally she'd find passages that Camilla had underlined. These Alice studied with extra attention, trying to understand what about them had caught Camilla's eye, whether it was the phrasing or the thought behind the phrasing that had appealed to her. Every fifteen minutes or so, Alice would look up to see if there was any activity in the house. There never was.

It was as the clock in the dash changed from 11:59 to 12:00 that it occurred to Alice that it was a Sunday, and on a holiday weekend no less, and that Dr. Rose probably wasn't working. Since he was a concierge doctor, same as Tommy's dad, he'd be on call, of course, have to make house visits if summoned. But the likelihood of patients coming by to see him for a scheduled appointment was virtually nil, which meant he'd be giving his intern the day off. Very probably giving his intern tomorrow off, too.

Damn it, Alice thought. At the rate she was going, Richard and Maggie would return from Florida on Wednesday and she'd have succeeded in acquiring not one new piece of relevant information. All she'd have succeeded in doing was alienating the affections of the various boys she was involved with. She was frustrated, no question. Underneath the frustration, though, she recognized the stirrings of a second emotion . . . could it be disappointment? Disappointment over what, she asked herself, almost laughingly. Not locking horns with Nick? And then, with surprise, she realized that yes, that was exactly the source of letdown. But why? She thought about it and the only explanation she could come up with was that she'd been bracing for conflict, gearing up for a knock-down-drag-out, and now she wasn't going to get one; her adrenaline had no outlet.

Alice had just turned the key in the ignition when her cell rang. The number was an unfamiliar one, but the area code told her that the call was coming from somewhere in Serenity Point. Tommy from a hard line? She answered, "Hello?"

"Alice?" a female voice said.

"Yes? Who's this?"

"Sasha."

After a confused beat, "Sasha, hi. I didn't know you had my number."

"I didn't. I got it from your sister."

It was a second before Alice realized Sasha meant Charlie, not Camilla. "Oh."

"You don't mind, do you?"

"Of course not," Alice said, and she didn't. When she'd first met Sasha and Bianca, she'd dismissed them as Cybill's ladies-in-waiting-slash-whipping-girls. Cybill used and abused them, treated them like dirt—lower than dirt—and they loved it, couldn't get enough. And if imitation was the sincerest form of flattery, these girls were the Taylor Swifts of kiss-ups: they dressed like Cybill, wore their hair like Cybill, affected Cybill's preferences and attitudes and viewpoints. But, in contrast to Bianca, Sasha exhibited signs of an actual personality under the clone trappings. Nerve, too. The one time Alice and Sasha had had a private conversation, Sasha had taken a couple shots at Cybill. (Behind-the-back trash talk was a low-level form of rebellion to be sure. Still, it was something; showed she had some spirit to her.) She might be a toady, but at least she knew it. "What's up?"

"Two things, actually," Sasha said. "First, Cybill is having a sleepover at her house tomorrow night and you and Charlie are coming."

Alice laughed. "So, this is a command, not an invitation?"

"Basically, yes. Cybill already talked to Charlie and Charlie agreed."

"And the second thing?"

"I need a cute new pair of pajamas and I was thinking you might also."

"You want to go shopping with me?" Alice said, surprised, a little flattered even that Sasha was interested in hanging out.

"Yes, but this is an invitation, not a command."

"I accept. When?"

"Can you do it soon? That way we can get lunch too."

"Sure," Alice said, delighted to have an excuse not to go home yet. She glanced at the dashboard clock. "How's twelve fifteen? That's in ten minutes."

"Perfect. Let's meet at Je Ne Sais Quoi."

Je Ne Sais Quoi was a boutique clothing shop across the street from the library. It looked a little down-at-heel from the outside, but Alice suspected that the shabbiness was a put-on, an affectation, a bit of faux bohemianism, and that the items inside it would be as breathtakingly expensive as the items inside Neiman Marcus or Lord & Taylor. Alice told Sasha she'd see her in a few minutes and hung up. Her phone had beeped midway through the call. She'd figured it was a voicemail, her mom or Richard checking up on her. But it wasn't. It was a text message from Tommy.

Meet me @ litehouse. 4 p.m. Bring clothes u don't mind getting dirty.

Alice considered her response for several minutes. Should she reply with something funny? (Clothes she wouldn't mind getting dirty? She could make a joke, ask if he was planning on having her wrestle a pig or change a tire.) Or should she reply with something pretend mad? After all, he'd ignored her invitation to get together last night, ignored *her* for days. She could feign ignorance as to his identity—*Who is this?*—like it had been so long since she'd heard from him she'd forgotten who he was, lost his phone number. Finally, though, she settled on short and to the point.

C u there.

Alice dropped her phone in her bag. Then she started the Mercedes and drove into town.

Sasha must have already been in town when she called Alice because
she was standing in front of Je Ne Sais Quoi as Alice drove up. She
was dressed down, for her, in jeans and a spaghetti-strap tank top, her
Cybill-like blond tresses pulled back into a bun, her feet in flipflops,
the nails painted a Cybill-like dried-blood red. A giant frozen coffee
drink was in her hand. She wasn't exactly a pretty girl—her nose was
a little bulbous at the tip, her legs a little heavy in the thigh—but she
was a cute one, bouncy and energetic with round, pink cheeks and a
nice smile, which she was beaming at Alice right now.

Before Alice had a chance to say hello, she said, as if they were
already in mid-conversation, "I'm thinking I want to get a pair of
satin pajamas. You know, like old-time movie-star style."

Alice nodded.

"I saw someone wearing them in a music video this morning."

"Whose video?"

"I can't remember. But the singer looked really good. She also
had on a push-up bra."

"Over the pajamas?" Alice asked, confused.

"No, under. But with the top few buttons undone so you could
see it."

Alice considered. "That sounds like a little much for an all-girls
sleepover."

"You think?"

"Kind of, yeah."

"Okay, I'll lose the push-up bra. But the satin pajamas are okay, right?"

Alice opened the door and both girls walked through it. The store was empty except for a lone salesgirl, extremely pale with a long nose—the better to look down on customers with—and an erect posture. Alice immediately felt self-conscious, slovenly in her YMCA Day Camp T-shirt that wasn't vintage-old, just old-old and her crooked ponytail. The salesgirl had just given Alice and Sasha the once-over, was in the middle of a disdainful *Can I help you?* when Sasha cut her off with a wave of her fingers. "If we need help, we'll ask," she said. "And do you mind getting rid of this for me?" She passed the salesgirl her iced coffee, down to slush, the plastic cup sweating in the summer heat. (Looked like the time she'd spent trailing in Cybill's wake hadn't been wasted after all.) Then, as the salesgirl retreated meekly to her station behind the counter to dispose of the beverage, Sasha grabbed Alice by the hand. "The selection here's not much," she said loudly, "but maybe we'll luck out and find something non-shitty."

Alice, somewhere between embarrassed and impressed, allowed herself to be led to the back of the store.

The girls were browsing when Alice said, "I don't think they sell nightwear in this place. Definitely not satin nightwear."

"That's okay," Sasha said breezily. "I already ordered a pair of satin pajamas from Victoria's Secret online, leopard print. I just wanted to see if I could find something I liked better."

"Oh."

"So, did you have fun at the party last night?"

"Actually, no."

"How come?"

Alice gave her a rundown on the situation with Patrick.

When Alice was finished, Sasha nodded sagely. "Ex trouble. That's grim. He should've known better than to show up at your door with no warning. He seemed like a fun guy, though. I liked his accent."

Alice was so used to Patrick's voice, she no longer noticed he had one.

Sasha continued: "He sounds like one of those characters that Ben Affleck is always playing. You know, those sexy, thuggy, working-class guys, tough but good-hearted."

"That's Patrick," Alice agreed. "Well, except for the thuggy part. He's great. I just—"

"You've moved on."

Alice sighed. "Yeah, pretty much. How about you? How was your night?"

"My night was all right actually because Cybill, shockingly, gave me the time of day." More shockingly, Alice thought, was the way Sasha managed to deliver this line with all the pathos and self-pity wrung out of it. As she did with the next line: "Only when she was out of other options, after Jude and Charlie disappeared." Again, she sounded perfectly upbeat and cheerful.

"Not totally out of other options," Alice pointed out. "She could've hung out with Bianca, right?"

"That's true. I did beat out Bianca, the girl with a personality that's like beer gone flat. Yay me." Sasha held up a green sleeveless shirt with a cinched waist to her chest. "Can I get away with this color?"

Alice regarded her doubtfully. "Green's tough for blondes to pull off. Believe me, I know."

"I didn't think so," Sasha said sadly, returning the blouse to the rack.

"The cut of the shirt's nice, though. Are they carrying it in any other color?"

"Just black."

"There you go. Black looks good on everyone, especially blondes."

"I can't. Black's Cybill's color. She'd kill me."

Alice didn't know what to say in response to this, so she said nothing. Changed tracks. "Speaking of Cybill, I spent a little time with her last night too."

"Really? I didn't see you two together at the party."

"It was after the party, on the beach. We ended up talking for a while. It was surprisingly nice."

"You didn't get all confessional, I hope."

Alice looked at Sasha. "Confessional?"

"Yeah, you didn't tell her anything important, anything you wouldn't want the entire world to know."

Trying to subdue the panic rising in her voice, Alice said, "Wait, Sasha, are you saying Cybill's a gossip? Because she doesn't strike me as one."

"She's not."

"Then why do I have to be careful about what I tell her?"

"You just do. She finds ways to use your secrets against you."

"Like blackmail?"

Sasha considered for a while. Finally she said, "Sort of. Not blackmail like she wants to get money out of you. Blackmail like she wants to get control over you, a way to manipulate you, like, emotionally."

Hearing this made Alice feel slightly better. Because if Cybill had something on her, she had something on Cybill. Alice couldn't imagine Cybill would want it to get out that she was seething with jealousy over the romance between her cousin and her new best friend. Besides, Alice frankly didn't think Cybill would treat her the way Cybill treated Sasha. Alice had never kowtowed to Cybill or acted like she was anything less than Cybill's equal. And Cybill seemed to respect those who pushed back. Tucking her lips into a smile, Alice said, "Luckily, I'm so boring I have no secrets worth telling."

"Then you're safe. Come on, let's get out of here."

"Where to now? I've never been inside Nobby's but I've seen lingerie-type stuff in the window."

"How about a little lunch before we hit the next store? My blood sugar's getting dangerously low." Sasha looked at Alice with poor-me eyes. Her build, though, was too solid, her coloring too ruddy-healthy, to successfully pull off the baby-doll waif act.

Still, Alice laughed, said it sounded like a plan to her.

The salesgirl held open the door for them as they left the store. Wished them a good day, too. She even sounded like she meant it.

After a long lunch, another round or two of shopping, Alice left Sasha to meet Tommy. As she drove across town, she thought about his text message: the arrogance of it, the bossiness of its tone, taking for granted that she'd overlook his neglect of her, drop everything when he crooked his finger. And the worst part was, she was doing just that. It was quickly turning into one of those the-more-she-thought-about-it-the-angrier-she-got situations. And by the time she reached the lighthouse at four fifteen, she'd worked herself up into quite a state.

Tommy was sitting on the curb out front, writing in his journal. While she parked, he slipped the journal into his pocket, stood, brushing sand from the seat of his pants.

"What's with the cryptic text messages?" she said as she got out of the car, deliberately not apologizing for being late, doing her best to ignore how cute he looked in his rumpled khakis and gray sweatshirt.

He smiled. "Cryptic? I was going for mysterious."

"Then you missed the mark," she said, not returning his smile.

"Well, thanks for agreeing to meet."

"I had a choice? I didn't realize. The way your text was phrased, it sounded like an order."

His face fell. "You're mad at me."

"I am, yeah."

"Why?"

"Exactly."

"What?"

He seemed so confused and dejected, her anger vanished, just like that, and she was left feeling confused and dejected too. "Tommy, I'm mad at you because you were mad at me and I don't know why. I don't know what I did to get you that way. At the party last night, you looked at me like I was something you wanted to scrape off the bottom of your shoe. And when I went to talk to you about it, you disappeared and then didn't return my text. And that was on top of our bad goodbye a couple days before." She didn't add, *And you lied to me about not being in love with your ex-girlfriend*, but didn't think she needed to, her case already being plenty strong.

He rubbed his neck with the back of his hand, grinned. "It wasn't *that* bad a goodbye."

Alice made a scoffing sound.

He dropped his hand. Dropped the grin, too. "Okay, I'm sorry. I know I'm moody, temperamental, whatever. But how was I supposed to react? That guy you were with, the one with the red hair, he had his hands all over you."

Alice didn't bother correcting this gross exaggeration of her and Patrick's level of physical intimacy at the party. "Patrick's a friend from home. Just a friend. You have nothing to worry about. And I would have told you that if you'd asked, not run off." Softening her tone: "Look, I know you had a bad experience with Camilla as far as cheating goes, but I don't do that sort of thing. It's not how I operate."

"I know it's not. I'm sorry," he said again. And then after a few seconds of silence, "Hey, will you come with me? There's something I want you to see." He held out his hand.

She wavered for a moment between the impulse to prolong the scene, milk it a bit more, and an interest in seeing what he had to show her. Finally curiosity won out and she nodded, accepted his hand and let him lead her around to the back of the lighthouse where they'd had their picnic days before. Set up on the bluff overlooking the ocean was an easel, a canvas propped against the base, and beside it a wooden stool and a small table with tubes of paint on it and brushes and a palette and bottles of varnish and gels and a stack of paper pads.

"Ta da," Tommy said, reaching inside his sweatshirt, pulling out a bright red artist's smock, looping it over her head. "This was in case you didn't listen, wear clothes you could get dirty."

Too stunned to speak, Alice walked slowly up to the table, touched one of the varnish bottles, one of the gels.

"Do you like it?" Tommy said anxiously. "Did I buy the right kind of paints? I got them at the hobby shop in town. The sales guy said Golden was the best brand. Was he bullshitting me?"

Alice shook her head.

"Are you sure? Because we can go back, switch to whatever you want. I kept the receipt."

"No, honestly, Golden is the best. It's so good I've never bought it for myself. And you got me the heavy body acrylic colors, which is exactly what I would have chosen."

He walked over to her cautiously. "And I picked out three kinds of brushes for you—a bristle brush, which the guy said was for scrubbing color, a synthetic bristle brush, which is for when you need more softness, and then a stable hair brush, which is for . . . I forget what it's for, but it's for something. I don't know what I'm talking about, obviously. I'm just repeating what he told me. Anyway, I'm glad you like your present."

She turned to him, her eyes shining. "Like it? Tommy, I love it. It's the most thoughtful gift anyone's ever given me. Like, ever. In my life."

He shrugged, obviously embarrassed, kicked at a pebble in the grass. "Well, I felt bad that you didn't have the supplies you needed to paint, that they'd gotten lost in the move. I mean, you love to paint, right? So you should be able to. And you said this was a spot you'd especially like to capture so . . ."

"I can't believe you found such high-grade materials at the local hobby shop."

"It's a good little store. Oh, and I saw your sister there. Actually, more your sister saw me."

"Charlie?" Alice said, surprised. "What was she doing in a hobby shop? It must've been an accident. She probably thought that the toys they sold were sex ones."

"She wasn't in it. She spotted me through the window. I was afraid if she got a look at what I was buying, she'd figure out who I was buying it for, so I totally ignored her." He started to laugh. "She probably thinks I'm the rudest person on the planet."

"Usually she's the one bucking for that title."

"Still, I owe her an apology."

Alice stepped closer to Tommy. "And I owe you one. I'm sorry for getting on you about your text message. I thought you were being incredibly controlling when really you were being incredibly sweet."

"We're okay then?"

"Yeah, we're okay. Tommy, we were always okay as far as I was concerned. I was reacting to the energy that was coming off of you. I didn't think you thought we were okay."

Sighing, he said, "I'm working on not doing the shutting-down thing, all right? I really am trying."

"Just know, if something's bothering you, you can tell me."

He nodded at her words, but his face, she noticed, had clouded again, his eyes narrowing so she couldn't see what was in them.

She reached for his hand, not wanting to lose her sense of connection with him, for the bond between them to break when it had only just been reestablished. "Even if you can't tell me what it is specifically—and I do realize that there are limits to how open you can be right now—you can tell me what it is generally. Or you can tell me that you can't tell me. Just tell me something."

This time when she paused, he didn't even nod. And he'd turned his face toward the ground, making it impossible for her to read his expression.

He was retreating back into himself or the past or wherever it was he went to get away from her. Would she ever, she wondered, have his whole attention, have all of him, the way Camilla did? Would he always keep her at a distance? She blinked to cover the feeling of panic welling up inside her. Forced herself to continue: "All I'm asking is that you please don't cut me out. It makes me go kind of nuts when you do that. And—"

Tommy swore under his breath and then, suddenly, he was kissing her. Kissing her and kissing her, kissing her until she couldn't tell where her lips ended and his began, kissing her until her head was bent back to the point of pain, kissing her until she tasted blood in her mouth. He'd never been like this with her before. He was usually gentle, tender, careful even. Not now, though. It was almost as if he were a different person. Less romantic, more passionate. Less passionate, more brutal. She could feel the hard muscles of his arms pressing against her waist and shoulders, the sharp buckle of his belt cutting into her abdomen. His fingers were digging so deep into her flesh she knew they'd leave bruises. She didn't care, she didn't care.

When he pulled away from her, his eyes seemed enormous and

almost black with pupil. Looking into them made Alice dizzy. It was like she was seeing him for the first time, and he her. Like there had been a veil—no, not a veil, a shadow, Camilla's—between them, and now the shadow was gone, chased away. "Come over tonight," he said.

"What about your parents?"

"They're leaving to go to the city in an hour. They have an appointment with their divorce lawyer in the morning. They'll be gone all night. Say yes."

"But we have a guest. Patrick's only staying for a few days and I was away from the house all morning and afternoon and I—"

Tommy's mouth was back on hers. Any resistance that was coming up in her, any doubt or misgiving, he halted it, stole it, swallowed it, whatevered it. It was gone. "Say you will." It was a little frightening, the ferocity of his voice and manner. But it was exciting too. "Say it."

"Yes," she breathed. She tilted her head back so he would kiss her some more, but he didn't. Disappointed, she opened her eyes.

He was grinning at her. "Excellent," he said, and straightened.

She felt weak without his arms around her and swayed for a moment, closing her eyes. When she opened them, she saw that he was walking away from her, down the bluff to the water. "Wait," she called out, still a little breathless. "Where are you going?"

"Home. I've got a few things to take care of before you come over."

"But I can give you a ride."

"No thanks. Come by anytime after seven." He waved without turning around, hands in his pocket, his cool, aloof self again.

She'd think she made up the savage stranger of a minute before if it weren't for the mashed, swollen feeling in her lips, the red indent in the shape of a belt buckle just below her belly button.

Alice watched Tommy until he walked around a bend, disappearing from view. She watched even longer, hoping he'd come back. He didn't, though. Then, not knowing what else to do, she packed up her new art supplies, got in the car, and drove home.

CHAPTER TWELVE

*C*harlie had slept over at Jude's the night before but they did almost no sleeping. And when she returned to Richard's at dawn, she was exhausted, just totally worn out. She sent a text message to Maggie saying that she had a headache, was planning on resting most of the day, so Maggie wouldn't spin into a panic, start concocting lurid fantasies about five-car pileups, freak drowning accidents, serial killers on the loose, when she failed to answer her phone. Then she closed her eyes, didn't open them until the sun had nearly set.

Charlie stayed under the covers, staring up at the ceiling, reliving the previous night with Jude—a dream that came true, better than a dream—as the last of the daylight drained from the room. Soon, she was in the dark. She relived the night some more. Then, realizing that the stabbing pains in her stomach were likely hunger pangs, she shambled downstairs to the kitchen.

Patrick was already there, his head stuck inside the open mouth of the refrigerator. He looked as if he'd been in that position for a while.

"Careful, you're going to get frostbite," Charlie said, pushing him out of the way so she could reach the orange juice.

He grinned at her as he eased his long body onto one of the stools at the counter. "You just rolling out of your crypt?"

She pinched the cardboard spout with her thumb and index finger, was about to drink straight from the carton but stopped herself. "I know, right? Vampire hours." Then, frowning, looking into the fridge, she said, "If I make cinnamon-raisin toast, will you eat some?"

"Sure. But shouldn't you be getting ready?"

She removed a glass from the cabinet, poured juice into it. She took a long drink from the glass, then poured more juice into it. Wiping her mouth, she said, "For what?"

"You're going to that jammie party with Alice tonight, aren't you? Better watch out. I'm seriously considering organizing a panty raid."

Charlie had to open three drawers before she found the one that contained the bread. It was weird having servants. Her own house and she didn't know where anything was. "The sleepover at Cybill's isn't until tomorrow night," she said, pulling out a loaf of honey oat, the closest she could find to cinnamon raisin. "Alice told you about that?"

"If by told me you mean sent me a ten-word text message, then yes."

Charlie caught the look of pain in Patrick's eyes and felt a wince of guilt for being so happy in love when he was so miserable in it. "Eek, so she's avoiding you."

"I haven't seen her at all today. She was in the house at one point, maybe half an hour ago, but she was sneaky about it. Came in and out, quiet as a mouse."

Charlie located the toaster behind the blender—deluxe, four slots, made of chrome, defrost setting for frozen bread—and plugged it in. "Then what makes you so sure she was here?"

"The car was in the driveway and then it wasn't. I guess tonight is the night she's hanging out with Sasha. Obviously I didn't read the ten words carefully enough."

Sasha? Wow, Charlie thought, Alice must really not want to deal with Patrick if she was willing to while away an entire evening with that Cybill reject. Charlie leaned over, ruffled his hair. "I'm sorry, Tricky. Well, I'm around tonight, and I have no problem being sloppy seconds. What are your plans for the evening?"

"I brought a couple of George Romero DVDs with me. I was thinking about maybe scaring myself shitless, breaking into your stepdad's liquor cabinet."

Charlie fed four pieces of bread to the toaster, pressed down the lever. Brushing the crumbs off her hands, she said, "The only thing I like better than being scared shitless is being scared shitless while shit-faced, so you're going to have to let me do it with you."

Patrick's face brightened. "It's a date."

"Boy, am I glad I don't have to go to Cybill's tonight. What a drag."

"A sleepover doesn't sound like a drag to me. Girls stripping down to their undies, getting in pillow fights, comparing breast sizes."

Charlie opened the refrigerator door again, took out the tub of Smart Balance, a knife from the drawer. "You forgot practicing kissing."

He laughed. "Right, so the exact opposite of a drag in my book. How about you send me in your place?"

"Believe me, I would if I could."

Patrick, serious all of a sudden, said, "I don't get it. If you don't want to go, don't go."

"I've got to. Things are touchy between me and Cybill right now. If I bailed last minute, that would be it for the friendship. It's going to be a whole lot of no fun, though."

"I'm sorry I can't help."

An idea coming to her, Charlie looked up suddenly.

"Uh-oh," Patrick said.

"What?"

"I've seen that look before. You're about to ask me for a favor."

"Oh, relax. It's nothing. Barely a favor. Not even a favor, in fact. A question."

"Okay. What is it?"

"Do you have anything on you?"

"What, like pot, you mean?"

She nodded.

"Sorry. I came empty-handed in the drug department. You know Alice doesn't like that stuff."

"Do you think you can get some?" Charlie brought her palms together, made prayer hands. "Please, Patrick, please, please, please. I can't make it through a night of exclusively female company totally straight. It'll end in bloodshed, I'm telling you. I'll kill myself or the girl in the sleeping bag next to me. You don't want a dead body on your conscience, do you?"

"Ah, Charlie, in case you haven't noticed, I'm a stranger in these here parts. I wouldn't know where to call or who to ask."

"Couldn't you find out?"

"How?"

"You have five brothers, three sisters and, like, infinity-number cousins spread all over the Northeast, some of them kind of low-life-y. One of them must know somebody who knows somebody who can get his hands on an itty-bitty bag of weed in the New Haven area."

"Why don't you ask your boyfriend? He looked to me like the type who'd have his dealer on speed dial."

Hearing the words *Jude* and *dealer* in the same sentence made her mood do a dip, but she tried not to let it show. "Yeah, I'm sure he does. Probably shares the dealer with Cybill. Which is the problem."

"How so?"

"I don't want her to know I had to get baked to make it through a night with her. I told you, things are touchy between us."

Patrick looked at her for a long time, then sighed. "All right. I'll put my feelers out. No promises, though."

"But you'll try?"

"Yes, I'll try."

Charlie, grinning ear to ear, "That's all I ask."

The lever on the toaster popped. She pushed it down again. She liked her toast just this side of burned to a crisp.

CHAPTER THIRTEEN

lice closed the door to Richard's Mercedes, shouldered her overnight bag, and walked up the path—crushed seashell, just like at the club—that led to the van Strattens' front door. As excited as she was to see Tommy, she felt bad about ditching Patrick. Felt bad, too, for lying to him about spending the night at Sasha's. Which wasn't to say that telling him the truth about spending the night at Tommy's would have felt good. Still, she'd always been honest with him in the past and had, so far, avoided outright lies. Her behavior, she thought with a sigh, was really getting shameful, just out-and-out scummy. Not that she could do anything about it now.

Shrugging off her guilt, a move she was rapidly becoming world class at, she raised her hand to ring the bell.

It seemed like forever before he opened the door, but then he did. He was wearing the same clothes from this afternoon: khakis and a sweatshirt, both wrinkled, the sweatshirt coffee-stained. His hair was mussed. His feet were bare. He looked beautiful.

"Hi," he said.

"Hi." Alice felt self-conscious suddenly—overly done up—because she'd changed into a sundress, borrowed a little of Charlie's lip gloss.

She felt less self-conscious, though, when Tommy looked her up and down, said, "Wow."

She laughed.

He swung the door open wider. "Come on in."

She followed him from the front hall into the living room.

"Want me to take your jacket?"

She'd forgotten she was wearing one. Denim, so thin it was like a shirt. "Oh," she said, "yeah. Sure."

"I'm just going to hang this up. Be right back."

Tommy disappeared down a hall, a different one. Alice used the time alone to take in her surroundings. At first the room struck her as exactly the kind you'd expect to find in a tasteful but low-key beach house: relaxed and sun-faded, with a sand-tracked-in-from-the-ocean, easy, lived-in type feel. Cozy, in other words. As her gaze continued to wander, though, she noticed that there was something off about the room's casualness. Like it was precisely casual, maniacally casual, *weirdly* casual, meticulously staged and styled by an invisible designer: the peeling paint on the pinewood cupboard somehow contrived-seeming, as if each chip had been administered by hand to achieve that perfect ye-olden-days effect; the slipcover on the couch not merely white, virgin white, unsullied by the touch of a human being; the throw rugs and pillows, the wicker tables and chairs, arranged just so. Alice wanted to put her bag down but was afraid of disrupting the balance and harmony of the room.

Tommy solved her problem by lifting the bag out of her hands.

"Come with me," he said. "I'll show you where you can put your stuff."

Alice took off her shoes, slipped them under her arm and followed him upstairs.

"And this," he said, opening a door, grinning at her over his shoulder, "is where the magic happens. And by magic I mean sleeping. Also, occasionally, homework-doing."

Alice breathed a sigh of relief when she saw his room. It was messy. Not gross messy. Regular boy messy. The bed was half made, cover pulled up hastily over rumpled sheets, a sodden towel draped on the post; there was a pile of dirty clothes in one corner; scattered across the desk were heaps of papers, index cards, one of those hand-strengthener devices, a Harvard University pewter stein cup that appeared old and was crammed full of pens, some of them uncapped and dried-out looking. His laptop was there, too. And so was his journal.

Alice's eye went immediately to his bookcase, which was overflowing, books jammed in every which way. She bent down to get a better look: lots of Hemingway and Salinger and Steinbeck, a few Kerouacs, Hunter S. Thompsons, Philip K. Dicks. Ayn Rand was the lone female.

"How do you feel about Thai food?" Tommy said.

"Um, positive, generally."

"Good. Because I got some delivered. I was thinking maybe we could eat it, then watch a movie or something. I Netflixed a bunch of stuff. I'm kind of going through an eighties high school phase. I got *Pretty in Pink* and *Fast Times at Ridgemont High*. Oh, and also *Dazed and Confused*, which is technically nineties high school, though it's set in seventies high school, so it averages out to eighties high school. And if you don't like any of those options, there's always TV."

"*Dazed and Confused* is one of my favorites."

"Then we're in luck."

Alice nodded that they were, then said, "Where do you want to eat?" The idea of leaving the warm, cluttered cocoon of Tommy's bedroom, venturing back out into the cold, sterile house proper was unappealing to her, so she was hoping he'd say, *How about here?*

Instead he laughed. Said, "Call me old-fashioned, but I'm going to say, the kitchen."

He grabbed her by the hand and they headed downstairs. The layout of the kitchen was as ominously pristine as it was in the living room: vintage-style appliances, white cabinetry, scrubbed wood floor, not a dish towel or napkin ring out of place, the fruit in the bowl so unblemished and perfect-looking Alice first took it for wax. Like robots eat their meals here, not people, she thought as she glanced around. She was afraid to sit on any of the furniture, touch any of the objects, not wishing to begrime them with fingerprints or oils from her skin, and when Tommy asked her if she wanted to carry the plates outside to the beach, she jumped on the suggestion.

Alice did little more than pick at the pad thai and cashew chicken that Tommy had ordered, though both dishes were delicious. She didn't talk much either. She was too busy thinking about what she'd avoided thinking about ever since she'd accepted Tommy's invitation to come over: the thing that was going to happen at the end of the night. The thing that everything else was leading up to. Sex. And she *wanted* for sex to happen, for her first time to be with him, the prospect making her eager, a warmth spreading in her stomach and up her chest. In addition to being eager, though, she was afraid. She was about to enter unfamiliar territory and enter it alone. Tommy was no virgin. Not by a long shot. Of course, she'd always known that. But the way he spoke of his relationship with Camilla he'd made it sound like he was the romantic one, the easily hurt one, the one who was as interested in emotional intimacy as physical. The kisses at the lighthouse, however, told a different story—added a new chapter to the old story, at least—implied aggression, technique, experience. And he seemed so casual now, so confident and easy, sitting there in the sand, legs crossed loosely at the ankle, talking in a drawling voice about his training regimen, John Hughes versus Amy Heckerling, which house he'd been assigned to live in at Harvard, aware that in a few minutes they'd be upstairs in his room, on his bed. A man of the world. Somebody she didn't know. She admired his coolness and was put off by it at the same time.

"All done?" he said, after they'd sat in silence for half a minute. "Ready to watch the movie?"

Alice nodded. It was only when they both reached for the paper bag to dump the leftovers in, their hands brushing, and he looked up at her, startled, that she saw her anxiety mirrored in his face. The sight both surprised and relieved her. It meant that the laidback talk, the relaxed attitude was an act, one he was likely putting on for her benefit, to make her feel at ease, as if he was in control of the situation. The truth of the matter was, he was as scared as she.

He pulled her to him and they kissed. When the kiss was over, they smiled at each other, both calmer. Leaving the mess of dishes for later, they walked, hand in hand, up the stairs and into his bedroom.

• • •

Alice and Tommy were on his bed, *Dazed and Confused* playing in the background. Their clothes weren't off. Not exactly. But they were half off or pushed to the side, treated like minor annoyances. And the two of them weren't lying down. Not quite. Nor, though, were they sitting up. Tommy had twisted his body over hers so that his knees were on either side of her thighs. Their faces were fused at the mouth. His hand was on the back of her neck, his fingers tangled in the hair at the nape. And then he let his other hand fall so that it was resting on her bare hip. The warmth from his palm rolled through her, heating up her chest and stomach and gut. She moaned into his mouth. He bit down hard on her lower lip.

Suddenly she broke away from him. "I'm going to use the bathroom, okay?" she said, picking up her bag off the floor, removing her travel-sized toothbrush and toothpaste from it, discreetly palming the items. It was weird, she knew. They'd already been kissing, full on making out for half an hour at least. So why should she feel compelled to clean her mouth now? But she did feel compelled. Maybe because she could tell how close they were to sex and she needed to prepare—anoint herself or something. In any case, she wasn't about to lose her virginity with less than perfectly fresh breath.

Tommy looked at her, confused. His breath was coming in short, broken-off pants and his T-shirt was hiked up, revealing an abdomen that was like cobblestones covered in skin, impossibly smooth and a rich, even brown from the sun. "The what? The bathroom? Yeah, sure, of course. Second door on the left. Want me to show you?"

"No need. I'll be right back."

He tugged on the leg of his pants. "Okay, I'll, ah, get stuff ready on this end."

Condom, she thought. He was going to find a condom. That's what he meant by getting ready. Feeling a precarious excitement mixed with a disorienting fear, she nodded without looking at him, twisted the knob.

She proceeded quickly down the dimly lit hall, her footsteps echoing remotely. As she walked, the sweat cooled on her skin and the heat left her face. Her pulse resumed its normal, steady beat. She felt as if she'd gotten up from the table in the middle of an unbelievably delicious dessert, gone to check her email or something—like she was prolonging a pleasure, breaking it up so it would last longer.

She'd just reached the bathroom when she noticed a door at the far end of the hall, slightly ajar, a slice of knife-like light falling from it, cutting into the darkness. She paused, standing stock-still at the threshold, holding that position for an interminable length of time. Tommy, she knew, was waiting for her, and she was eager to get back to him, but her eyes kept turning to that cracked door; she couldn't drag them away. She wanted to know what was behind it, the desire irrational yet powerful. And then, a shadow moved across the bottom, so fast she'd have missed it if she blinked. Frightened now but her curiosity stronger than ever—irresistible even—she crept past the bathroom, palms wet, knees weak, continued on her course, the hall seeming to elongate as she went, stretching on endlessly. At last she arrived at the door. Pressing gently on its flat wooden surface, it fell all the way open under her hand, barely needing to be touched. Her throat was so dry she couldn't swallow. After a stealthy glance over her shoulder, she stepped inside.

The room she entered was empty, emphatically so, and silent. (So what had caused the shadow? she wondered. Was the light playing tricks on her? Was her *brain* playing tricks on her?) Also, it was clearly Dr. van Stratten's office. On the wall were his diplomas from Harvard University and Harvard Medical School, both framed, next to a certificate from the Alpha Omega Alpha Honor Society, also framed, and a plaque from the Serenity Point Nursing Home naming him their Man of the Year two years ago. No surprise, the room was as neat as a pin, the desk utterly devoid of clutter, the only objects on it an ink blotter, a pen jar, a crystal paperweight in the shape of a golf ball, and a few photographs. Behind the desk was an old-fashioned filing cabinet. Filing cabinets contained information. On impulse, Alice moved toward it, and, as she did, a floorboard creaked loud as thunder under her foot. She paused, her heart going like crazy. Waited to see if Tommy had heard—and it seemed impossible that he hadn't; the house was so quiet, she so noisy—if he was about to come looking for her.

Five seconds passed. Ten. Twenty. Nothing. She made herself breathe in and out, and then, when her heartbeat was no longer the only sound in her ears, covered the rest of the distance to the filing cabinet. Not allowing her brain to think about what she was doing, she placed her toothbrush and toothpaste on the desk to free up her hands, slid out the top drawer of the cabinet and pulled from it the first file: Abbot, E. With shaking fingers, she opened it. Empty. She reached deeper inside, pulled another file: Briggs, M. the name ringing a faint bell. A member of the club? A client of Richard's? This file, too, was empty. A third: Campbell, O. Empty.

Alice, feeling queerly disappointed, though she didn't know what she'd been hoping to find, returned the files to their proper places, quietly closed the drawer. She was just turning, preparing to leave when she noticed the photographs on the desk. There was a trio of them. One was of Mrs. van Stratten with her pretty face and anxious eyes, no less anxious when she was smiling. One was a family portrait, the entire van Stratten clan in front of a golf cart at the club, stiff bodies, stiff grins, stiffly embracing each other. The third, though, and by far the largest, was of Tommy and Camilla. It wasn't much of a picture: Tommy looking at Camilla looking at the camera, she her usual beautiful, poised self, but he in three-quarters profile, his features blurred as if he'd been caught in the act of turning his head.

It was enough, though.

The wrongness of what she was about to do struck Alice with the force of a thousand tons of bricks crashing down on her. This thing with Tommy, it was psychologically incestuous. It was skin-crawlingly morbid. It was totally and utterly wrong, and not hot-wrong, *wrong*-wrong. What's more, she was implicating him in her weirdness without giving him the full story. It was unfair to both of them.

Besides, how could she ever hope to measure up to Camilla sexually? Camilla, who had, in addition to sex experience, sex instinct. Camilla, who ruined boys, left them forever altered. And not just sensitive, on-the-straight-and-narrow boys like Tommy, but hard-bitten, been-around-the-block ones like Jude, too. Alice flashed back to her conversation with Cybill at the Luau Clambake. Cybill, near tears, had sworn that Jude's relationship with Camilla had changed him from a sweet-natured, fun-loving pothead to a lady killer with a sadistic streak and a serious drug problem. Alice was setting herself up for the biggest fall of all time.

She tiptoed out of the office, closing the door behind her, but then remembering to leave it open a crack. She returned to Tommy's room. He was lying on the bed, bare-chested. He'd turned off the movie and lit a couple of scented candles, bathing the room in a soft, golden glow and perfuming the air, making it smell like a mixture of lavender and vanilla. Music was coming from the computer on his desk, rising up and drifting out gently into the atmosphere, creating a romantic mood.

Alice killed it. Her entry into the room was like a needle being dragged across a record.

Faking distraction and hurry, she grabbed her bag off the floor, hooked it over her shoulder. "I can't stay," she said, hunting around for her shoes, finding them, sticking them under her arm.

Tommy sat up. "What? Why?"

Not looking at him, not daring to, knowing the sight of him shirtless would be more than she could take, would just undo her resolve completely. "I got a call. I have to go home."

He gazed at her in bewilderment. "A call from where? Your cell's in your bag. I heard it buzz while you were in the bathroom."

"I can't stay," she repeated.

"Alice, what's wrong? Did I do something to upset you?"

"I'll call you tomorrow," she said, reaching over to him blindly, squeezing either the leg of his khakis or a bit of bunched-up comforter, before hurrying out the door.

She heard him call her name as she took the stairs two, three at a time, but she didn't stop, not even to put on her shoes, the crushed seashells on the walkway cutting up the soles of her feet as she ran to her car.

CHAPTER FOURTEEN

*B*right and early the next morning, Alice was staked out across the street from the pretty, white-picket-fence house that doubled as Dr. Rose's office. It was the final day of the holiday weekend, but it was also a Monday, so there was a chance he'd be working. More to the point, there was a chance Nick would be working. She'd barely slept but she'd drunk cup after cup of coffee and was agitated besides, so was wired to the point where she could hardly blink.

Tommy had called several times last night. Sent a bunch of text messages, too. So far she hadn't responded. How could she? What could she possibly say? She couldn't justify her behavior, or explain it. Not without being totally and completely honest, which she had absolutely no intention of being. She knew that she'd have to speak to him at some point, but she needed more time to figure out the best way to handle the conversation, the most advantageous strategy to adopt. Until then, she was in full avoidance mode.

Alice picked up *The Magus*, began reading. Almost immediately she fell back into the plot. Stayed fallen until something streaked past her window. Startled, she looked up: a guy on a bike. The guy was in a dark suit and tie and wingtips. His bike was the old-fashioned kind, wide handlebars and a leather saddle and a basket in front. He looked out of place on it in his formal clothes, like the subject of a surrealist painting, a Magritte maybe. He braked just before hitting Dr. Rose's driveway, dismounting and removing his helmet in a single motion. Nick. He lowered his kickstand, reached into the basket for his briefcase, pulling out a lock. As he was spinning the combination, Alice jumped out of the car, ran over to him. He moved so quickly and decisively she was afraid he'd disappear inside the house, be unavailable for the entire day, if she didn't move just as quickly and decisively.

"Nick!" she called out. "Nick!"

He looked over his shoulder. "Oh, hey, Alice," he said casually, like he wasn't surprised in the least to see her at this hour, in this context.

"Can I talk to you?"

"Right now?"

"Well, yeah."

He handed her his briefcase, dropped down and began winding the thread-y part of the lock through the back wheel of his bike and then around the trunk of a thin birch tree. "Now's not so good. How about later? Like after six?"

"*Six?*"

"Yeah, like at the end of the workday. Remember, I'm not on summer vacay. I have a j-o-b job."

"This won't take long."

He straightened. "It really can't wait till tonight?"

She hesitated, unsure of how much of her desperation she should reveal. Finally she said, "Maybe it can, but I can't."

Sighing, he folded his arms across his chest, looked at her expectantly. Now that she had his attention, though, she couldn't speak, the words rushing to get out of her mouth, so many of them, so fast, clogging in her throat, creating a block. After five or ten seconds of silence, he took his briefcase out of her hands and said, not unkindly, "Let's do this another time, okay? I really can't be late or—"

And then, all at once the block cleared, and she blurted out: "You were having sex with Camilla."

Alice didn't think the narrow, crafty face could do wide-eyed. But she was wrong. Nick was staring at her, eyes like saucers. Finally he said quietly, "Are you asking me or telling me?"

So much for a skilled game of cat and mouse. Embarrassed by bluntness, her lack of finesse, she said, "Asking, I guess. I saw this footage of the Fourth of July party last year. You took it. I got the sense that you two were . . . involved."

"It seemed that way to you? Why?" He sounded genuinely curious, not mad or defensive, certainly not guilty.

Alice shrugged, dropped her eyes to her shoes. "I don't know. The way she was looking at you."

He laughed. "With hot eyes, you mean."

"Yeah. Those."

"Ah, but you forget. It wasn't just my gaze that was on her."

Looking up, Alice said, "What do you mean? Who else's?"

"The camera was gazing at her, too, and that's who the hot eyes were for. No, Camilla and I were just friends. She spent a lot of time at the van Stratten house last summer. So did I. We got to know each other."

"Did you love her?"

"Not in the way you mean. I wasn't in love with her."

Alice was aware of a feeling coming over her, a tightening in her abdomen, a constricting of her throat. It took her a second, though, to identify the feeling: relief. But why, she wondered, relief? Why should it make any difference to her if Nick had fallen for Camilla? It's not as though she liked him herself. Jesus, no. Maybe it was just nice to hear that there was a guy out there immune to her half sister's charms. "Why not?" she said. It was an odd question and one she had no right to ask, which she realized as soon as it was past her lips.

Nick didn't seem weirded out or put off, though. More thoughtful. "She had this intensity to her, but at the same time this neediness, this damaged quality. I suppose the mixture scared me."

"It's hard to imagine a guy like you scared by anything."

He smiled, lifted his shoulders, let them drop. "And yet I was. Like I said, though, I did care for her. She tried to convince me to sell her prescription drugs or, even better, to give them to her for free. I shot her down, of course, but she took it well. That's how we first got to talking. We talked a lot after that. She told me what was going on with her. Some of it, anyway, the man-eater parts. She was a funny kid. Open in certain ways, very closed off in others. Mostly, actually, I felt sorry for her."

"Sorry?" Alice repeated, stunned by the word, almost offended.

Nick nodded. He wasn't looking at her, though, was looking at some point between them, looking into the past. "I could feel her sadness, this sadness she was bent on hiding, and hiding two times over, first with the good-girl pose, then with the wild-girl pose right underneath it. But neither was the truth. She was in over her head and didn't seem to know it." Nick's voice trailed off. Alice sensed, though, that he was pausing rather than stopping, that there was something difficult he wanted to say but needed to gather himself first.

She waited. Her patience was rewarded.

"I found her once in the van Strattens' garage. She was lying on a dirty quilt that covered a bunch of boxes of junk in a dark corner, hugging herself. She wasn't crying or making any sound at all, was just sort of curled up and shaking."

"Did you ask her what was wrong?"

"I should've, but I didn't. I didn't want to intrude. I just crept out the way I came. Her back was to me, so I don't think she knew I was there. She must've had a fight with Tommy. Or with Jude. Or with a love interest she hadn't gotten around to telling me about. Or maybe she was crying for some other reason entirely, a reason that had nothing to do with her romantic life. I'll never know because, like I said, I didn't ask."

Alice had never heard Camilla spoken of in these terms—as a person to be pitied—and she could scarcely wrap her brain around the idea. So accustomed was she to thinking of Camilla as all-powerful, a teenage femme fatale, a devourer of males, as someone basically who got other people into hot water, not as someone who got into hot water herself, that the switch was jarring. More than jarring, upsetting. Like, without realizing it, she'd become attached to this version of Camilla. And Alice found herself simultaneously longing to lean forward so Nick's words would reach her faster and to stick her fingers in her ears, start screaming at the top of her lungs, so his words would never reach her at all.

He continued: "I don't think I could've stopped what happened later, with the car and the bridge and all that. Even I'm not that much of an egomaniac. But I could've let her know she had someone to talk to. I mean really talk to. Not just banter with, which is all we'd ever done." He stared at the front tire of his bike, kicked it lightly with his toe, then shook his head. "I failed her is what it comes down to, and for that I feel guilty as hell."

For a while the two of them were silent, just letting Nick's admission lie there between them, neither one touching it.

Alice didn't know she'd opened her mouth until words were coming out of it. "I don't think Camilla killed herself." Her first shock on hearing this statement was that she had no idea she believed it until she said it. Her second shock was the lack of regret she felt at saying it in front of Nick, at being candid with him. She trusted him, she realized. She had no reason to other than that he'd trusted her, sharing with her the secret of his guilt, but she did. Her third shock was his lack thereof. "You don't either," she said slowly.

"Nope."

"But I thought you felt guilty for failing her? That's what you just said."

"I *did* feel guilty for failing her. Still do. The guilt's just for a different reason now." Nick was quiet for a moment, staring down at his feet. Then he said, "When the summer was over and I got back to school, there was a letter waiting for me in my mailbox."

"It was from Camilla," Alice said, telling not asking, though she couldn't possibly have known for sure.

"Right. Only the handwriting on the envelope didn't match hers. I'm guessing that her housekeeper found it on her desk after she died, saw my name at the top, knew where I went to school, and stuck it in an envelope. All that was written was my name and the address for Dartmouth College. No dorm or room number or anything. I'm amazed it even reached me."

"What did the letter say?"

"Practically nothing. Just that she needed to talk to me about Dr. van Stratten, but that the conversation had to be in person, not over the phone or email. It was a note really, not a letter. I bet she was planning on slipping it to me the next time we ran into each other."

"I wonder why she wanted to talk to you about Dr. van Stratten."

Nick hiked his shoulders.

"It could've just been something about Tommy."

"It could've," Nick agreed.

"But you don't think so?"

"I don't, no. Otherwise why all the secrecy? Not wanting to leave an email trail or a phone record?"

"So, is that why you returned to Serenity Point?"

"I needed the work but there are other internships out there. I guess I figured if I came back, poked around a little, I could possibly find something out. Not much of a plan, I realize."

There was a long silence, and then Alice said, "I snuck into Dr. van Stratten's office last night."

At last she succeeded in surprising him. Eyebrows raised, he said, "How did you manage to do that?"

"He and Mrs. van Stratten have an appointment with their divorce lawyer today."

"So?"

"So the divorce lawyer's in New York. The appointment's early. They stayed in the city last night."

Nick, getting it at last, smiled, nodded knowingly. "And Tommy didn't let the opportunity go to waste, did he?"

Alice was annoyed with herself for blushing. Forcing herself to hold his gaze, not to stammer or blink, she said, "We were in Tommy's bedroom, then I got up to go to the bathroom. That's where he thought I went anyway."

Nick started to laugh. "Poor Tommy. He was looking forward to T and A, and all you were thinking about was B and E."

Alice didn't like the dismissive way he was referring to her boyfriend, but she bit her tongue. In a flat voice she said, "It wasn't exactly breaking and entering. The office wasn't locked. I just didn't have permission to go inside."

"What were you looking for?"

She thought for a while, then turned up her palms, a beats-me gesture. "I saw a filing cabinet. I wanted to know what was in it. Simple as that." Thinking some more. "Maybe in the back of my mind was the hope that I could find something on Camilla."

"Was she a patient of Dr. van Stratten's?"

"I don't know. But wasn't most of Serenity Point a patient of Dr. van Stratten's?"

"Seemed like all sometimes."

"Anyway, even if she was, it wouldn't matter. The files were empty."

"Why wouldn't they be? Dr. van Stratten got rid of them all last summer."

Alice could think of nothing to say other than, "Shit."

"Actually," Nick said casually, "I was the one who got rid of them."

She looked at him, startled. "Isn't that, like, not legal?"

"Sure, if I'd been getting rid of them for all time. I wasn't. I was helping Dr. van Stratten go paperless. That was my big job as his intern. Turning his paper charts into electronic medical records."

"I figured he would have done that a long time ago."

"Then you obviously haven't spent much time with him. He's an old-school guy. Needed serious convincing before he'd believe that the Internet wasn't some flash in the pan."

Alice considered for a while. "You don't have access to those records, do you?"

"Not anymore. And I bet he destroyed most of them before the malpractice trial anyway. Claimed his server crashed or something."

She nodded, disheartened.

A beat passed, and then Nick said, "Lucky for you, though, I made copies of everything."

"You did? Why?"

Nick gave a one-shouldered shrug. "Dr. van Stratten believed the customer's always right. That didn't sit right with me. It's a dangerous attitude for a medical professional to have. And maybe I'm an old-school guy, too. Maybe I believe that you shouldn't trust everything to computers, that there should be a hard copy as well."

She waited a moment, then said, "Can I see the hard copies?" holding her breath, knowing she was asking a lot.

She was disappointed but not surprised when he responded with, "I don't think I can in good conscience give you access to the majority of the town's medical records." A long pause. "But"—she looked up at him hopefully—"I will check and see if he had anything on Camilla."

Exhaling at last, she said, "I can't tell you how much I'd appreciate that."

Nick adjusted the straps on his briefcase, made sure it was shut. His wrists, she noticed, were delicate but strong. The wrists of a surgeon. Or a painter.

"We'll be in touch," he said, and turned, starting walking.

And before Alice could ask for a phone number or an email address or their next meeting time, he'd vanished through Dr. Rose's front door.

CHAPTER FIFTEEN

*T*hat night Alice was standing outside Cybill's house, sticking mainly to the shadows, but ducking out every few minutes to see if Charlie was coming into view. After the Tommy debacle, the night of almost no sleep, the heavy-duty conversation with Nick, Alice was tapped out physically and emotionally. She hadn't wanted to run the risk of bumping into Patrick, especially since she didn't have to. She still had a packed bag in the backseat of the Mercedes for the sleepover at Tommy's, which meant there was no need for her to go home, pack one for the sleepover at Cybill's. So she didn't and stayed out all day.

She'd arrived at Cybill's on time, eight thirty sharp. She didn't think, though, that she could face the scene without reinforcement of some kind, which was why she was hanging back, waiting for her sister to appear before making the final steps to the front door. At last she spotted Charlie coming up the sidewalk, shuffling along sort of zigzaggy, humming to herself, playing soccer with a pebble.

When Charlie got close, Alice darted out from her hiding place.

"You're late," she said, linking her arm through Charlie's. "I've been waiting for you."

"I didn't realize we had a date." Charlie pointed at the sky. "Hey, something's covering the moon."

Alice looked up, confused. "What are you talking about? You mean, the cloud?"

Charlie giggled at the same instant the sweet, slightly acrid smell of marijuana hit Alice's nose. "You're high," Alice said.

Charlie's nod was emphatic. "I am, yes. Also, I'm here. And I couldn't do the second thing without doing the first." She jutted out her lower lip: sad clown face. "I kind of want to go back home, though."

Alice put a palm on each of Charlie's cheeks, looked straight at her. Her eyes weaved all around Alice's face. "You can't go home," Alice said.

"But I left Patrick all alone. He seemed sad, only he acted like he wasn't, which was even sadder. Isn't that, like, really sad?"

Alice sighed, said, "Yeah, it kind of is. Hey, you didn't happen to save any of that pot for me, did you?"

Charlie made a shocked face. "But, Allie, you just say no to drugs."

"Yeah, well, it's been a long day. Tonight I was thinking about saying no to saying no."

"But you're the good daughter, I'm the bad daughter. We can't both be the bad daughter." A pause. "Or can we?"

Alice laughed. "Come on," she said, and led Charlie up to Cybill's front porch. Alice rang the bell. Seconds later, Cybill opened the door. She was dressed like a sex bomb about to go off: a skirt that was mini even by miniskirt standards, a halter top made of some slinky black material, and shoes that were spiked rather than heeled. Her ponytail was purposely messy in back, the front teased up into a sleek faux hawk that cut through the air when she leaned forward to kiss Alice's and Charlie's cheeks and reminded Alice of the fin on the back of a shark. She looked the prettiest Alice had ever seen her look, though *pretty* was maybe not the most apt word choice—too soft for someone with a gleam in her eye that was just shy of predatory. Scratch that. She looked the best Alice had ever seen her look, period. Also, coincidentally, or possibly not, the most like Jude.

"Whoa, Cybill," said Charlie, retracting her chin, giving her friend an exaggerated up-down look. "Is this a girls' night or a girls-gone-wild night?"

Cybill grinned. "Who says it can't be both?" She reached out and took Charlie by the hand, guided her inside. Over her shoulder, she said to Alice, "It's so great you two are finally here. We can get started now."

Get started on what? Alice wondered but didn't ask as she followed Cybill's legs, lengthened and muscularized by the high heels, the legs of a sexy assassin in a James Bond movie. The usual suspects were in attendance: a couple of girls from the club, including Bianca and Sasha, in leopard-print pajamas, as promised. They were playing Just Dance 2 on Nintendo Wii, attempting to mimic the movements of the neon silhouettes on screen, all to the rhythm of the Pussycat Dolls' "When I Grow Up." Sasha gave Alice a quick two-fingered wave, dropping the Twizzlers stick in her hand as she did.

When she bent down to retrieve it, Alice was surprised to see, standing behind her, doing a more pelvic-thrusty version of the hokey pokey, the girl whose father was Dr. van Stratten's new boss, the one Dr. van Stratten had asked Tommy to be nice to until he received the job offer. Sloane was her name. She was in Serenity Point with her dad for a ten-day vacation, of which no more than a day or two could be remaining. Was headed to Harvard in the fall, same as Tommy. Her pajamas were frog-footed. They had different Disney princesses on them.

Alice was so relieved by the goofy dance moves and little kid sleepwear—so Tommy *wasn't* just trying to placate her when he told her she had nothing to be jealous of—she almost hugged Sloane during Cybill's introduction. She caught herself in time, though, mimicked Charlie's two-fingered hand wave and laconic *what's up?*

Cybill turned to Alice and Charlie. "You two want to get comfy, change into your jammies?"

Alice declined the offer because she had no desire to be in her Amoeba Music T-shirt and polka-dot boxer shorts if Cybill was going to stay in nightclub attire. And Charlie declined, Alice suspected, because she was too high to be bothered. And she probably wanted to do high-person stuff—stare at the twinkly lights that Cybill had strung up around the room's borders, forage for food in the kitchen, bump into things.

Alice leaned against an armchair and watched the girls shaking to Rhianna's "SOS" while Charlie, wrist deep in a box of Honey Bunches of Oats, shouted words of encouragement and advice— she was seriously into *Dancing with the Stars*—from the couch she was collapsed on. Everyone was having a good, uncool time until they noticed Cybill standing on the sidelines, looking on, smirking.

One by one, the girls were stricken by self-consciousness, wandered off the makeshift dance floor. Shame-faced, they drifted toward Cybill.

Cybill waited until they were all gathered around her and a silence had a chance to develop. Then she waited even longer than that, until the silence stretched to uncomfortable. At that point she said, "Everybody done being a spaz for the night?" When no one claimed otherwise, she picked up the remote, killed the TV. Clapping sharply, she said, "Then it's time to play Questions."

As the girls made their ways to the center of the room, began arranging themselves in a loose semicircle, Charlie stuffed a fistful of cereal into her mouth. "I have a question," she said. "What's Questions?"

With a supple twist, Cybill turned and extended her spine to reach behind the couch, pulled out a brown paper bag. From it she extracted a jumbo bottle of Ketel One vodka, a bunch of small plastic shot glasses. She began filling them. "It's like Truth or Dare except without the dare. The way it works is one person's the questioner. She asks an individual in the group any question she wants, provided it can be answered with a yes or no. Once the answerer answers, the answerer becomes the questioner. If the questioner repeats a question, she must drink. If an answerer takes longer than three seconds to answer, she must drink. If someone in the audience laughs, she must drink. Everybody got it? It's a pretty special-ed game, not hard to understand at all."

Again no one spoke. Cybill began passing out the shot glasses.

The questions started out softball. *Do you still sleep with a stuffed animal? Have you ever cheated on your no-carb diet? Is there a piece of Jonas Brothers fan memorabilia socked away in a drawer in your room?* That kind of thing.

And then it was Cybill's turn. She fixed her gaze on Sasha. "Did you ask your dad for a nose job for your fifteenth birthday?"

Sasha, not missing a beat, said, "Yes. Though technically the request was for a deviated septum repair."

Alice was so impressed by Sasha's response she wanted to break into applause but managed to control the impulse.

Every time Cybill was the questioner, she'd take aim, fire at a different girl, never missing, not once. Alice and Charlie, though, she left conspicuously alone. Finally, Cybill had run out of targets. Alice assumed that she or her sister would be next in the crosshairs, braced herself. When it was Cybill's turn again, though, and she let her gaze travel lazily, lingeringly over the traumatized faces of the girls before her, it was Sloane's that she stopped on. Sloane, who Cybill couldn't have known more than a few days at the most and who everyone else was pretty much giving a free pass to since she was an outsider and only in town briefly and seemed quiet and nice enough.

"Yes or no," Cybill said, "did you once take so many laxatives that poison control had to be called?" Sloane's mouth fell open. (How, Alice, wondered did Cybill come to be in possession of this piece of gossip? Sloane lived in Scarsdale. Did Cybill have spies planted in every Richie Rich high school up and down the Northeast corridor?) When Sloane nodded yes rather than saying it because she was obviously trying to keep from crying, Cybill crowed in triumph, "Nonverbal response. You're in violation of the rules. Bottoms up!"

As Sloane choked down the vodka, Charlie looked at Cybill. "Maybe you should take it easy."

"Take it easy?" Cybill repeated.

"Yeah. Cool it on the raging bitch routine for a round or two. You're the bitch supreme. No one's questioning that. Least of all Sloane." Snapping her fingers, "Hey, you know what? You should try switching from the booze to what I've got in my bag. It'll put you in low-gear quick. Only thing is, do you have a lighter? I left mine at home." Charlie said all this in a light voice. Not seriously calling Cybill a bitch, more teasing her. She was too stoned, Alice knew, to be aggressive.

But Cybill chose to take Charlie's words literally, get mad. And in that moment Alice realized that had been Cybill's plan all along, the whole point of the game: Cybill wanted to go after Charlie without going after Charlie directly, provoke Charlie into going after *her*. Once Charlie made the first move, Cybill had carte blanche, could just eviscerate Charlie with impunity. *She brought it on herself,* people would say of Charlie with a shrug.

Alice was scared for her sister.

"Oh, please, Charlie, get over yourself," Cybill said. "So you're sleeping with Jude. Big deal. It's not like it's that exclusive a club."

Charlie stared at Cybill, and Alice could see that she'd been jolted out of her amiable narcotized state. A hard glint was entering her eye. "If it's not that exclusive," she said, "then why'd you get kicked out?"

"Maybe I decided the club's standards were slipping and dropped out."

"Slipping? Why? Because someone like me was let in? Give me a break. You were out long before I was in."

"Actually, I wasn't talking about you. I will confess, though, that you making it past the velvet ropes wasn't exactly an encouraging sign. I was referring to Camilla. You know, your stepsister, the dead one. When she started sleeping with Jude at the same time I was, I decided that was it for me. We were all close, but there's such a thing as too close. Some things you're just not willing to share. But, hey, I'm an only child. Never really learned how to play well with others. Maybe it's different for you, having a sibling and all. And, you know, growing up poor."

All the blood drained from Charlie's face. "You're lying. You're just saying these things because you're jealous."

Cybill made a mock sympathetic face. "You mean, he didn't tell you? I guess it's not true what they say about honesty being the cornerstone of any good relationship."

"He didn't tell me because there's nothing to tell. He didn't do it. He didn't sleep with Camilla."

"Sure, he did," Cybill said, her voice bright, almost cheerful. "Camilla jerked him around same as she did Tommy and all the other guys in this town. In fact, she treated him even worse than she treated Tommy. Not that he seemed to mind. I think the shitty treatment turned him on, to be honest. He was obsessed with her. Absolutely obsessed. I never saw him like that about any girl. It was somewhere between sweet and pathetic the way he mooned after her. You don't believe me, ask your sister."

Charlie whirled around to face Alice.

Alice looked down at the floor.

"Allie, is it true?" Charlie demanded.

Still looking down at the floor, Alice nodded.

"Why didn't you tell me?"

"I tried to," Alice said, talking fast, too fast. "You didn't want to hear it. I started to say something to you that day on the deck and you cut me off. You said I was fixated on the past. Remember?"

Charlie, ice cold, "Then you should've tried harder."

"Ah, family fight, so cute," Cybill said, with a pout.

"Shut up, Cybill," Charlie said, a low, warning note entering her voice.

"That's sure not something you need to tell Alice. She does nothing but shut up around you. Has been keeping lots of secrets lately." Alice shot Cybill a begging look, but Cybill ignored it. "Did you know big sis has a boyfriend she's told nobody about? Well, I guess I shouldn't call myself nobody. Makes it sound like I have a self-esteem problem."

Looking only at Alice, Charlie said, "She's making this up, right, Allie? Tell me she's making this up."

Alice swallowed hard. Forcing herself to meet her sister's eyes, she said, "I've been—" She broke off. Tried again. "Tommy van Stratten and I have been—" Once more, she broke off. Tried a third time. "The two of us, Tommy and I, we've been dating."

"Since when?"

"Not long. A few weeks."

"A few weeks is as long as we've been here!"

"He asked me to keep it quiet."

"And yet you told *Cybill*?" Charlie said, her voice spinning from her, high and out of control.

"No. I mean, yes, but not on purpose. She guessed."

Charlie's lips turned down at the corners in that way they did when she was acting mad but was really hurt. Alice reached out to touch her but she jerked away like she'd been scalded. "Don't come near me," she hissed. Then she grabbed her overnight bag off the floor, ran out the front door.

When Alice made to follow, Cybill stopped her, putting a hand on her shoulder. "Why don't you let her go, give her a chance to cool off? She's upset now, but it'll be better for her in the long run. She needed to know the truth about Jude. She shouldn't be with someone like him."

Alice shook her head in amazement. "So you're telling me you trashed Jude and ratted me out because you were trying to *protect* Charlie?"

"Believe it or not, yeah."

"How about, or not."

"It's not like telling her made me happy, Alice."

And as Alice stared into Cybill's face, she could see that Cybill wasn't happy. Not one bit. Still, Alice knocked Cybill's hand away and continued to move toward the door.

She stepped outside only thirty seconds after Charlie, but Charlie had already vanished. Alice called her name a couple times. All that came back, though, was her own echo, faint, and then smothered by silence.

Charlie ran the entire way to Jude's. Breathing raggedly, she raised the knocker on his front door, brought it down hard several times. Nothing. She walked around to the side of the house, peeked in his bedroom window. At first she didn't see him.

Then she did.

There he was, lying on the floor, shirtless, headphones covering his ears, eyes squeezed shut, playing drums on his stomach. She rapped sharply on the pane. He jumped up, startled, head swiveling around. Spotting her, he grinned, then walked over to the window. She felt the familiar pull of attraction, his perfect features and graceful legs—Cybill's down to the last lithe contour—his lean abdomen and protruding hipbones. But she resisted it.

With a little difficulty, he opened the window, stuck his head out. "Hey, you," he said. "I thought you were at Cybill's?"

"I was. Now I'm here."

He laughed. "Yeah, so I noticed. What happened? She let you out early for good behavior?"

"No. I just left."

"I'm glad. Going two nights in a row without seeing you is rough." Jude looked up and around at the window frame. Rapping his knuckles against the wood, he said, "You really go for this Romeo and Juliet stuff, huh? I guess I do too. Fuck the door, right?"

"Speaking of fucking, I heard about you and my dead stepsister."

The grin died on his face. "Where? Who told you?"

No longer able to hold back the upset, Charlie began to speak louder, almost to yell. "What does it matter who told me? What matters is if it's true or not. Is it?"

A beat. "It is."

Putting a hand to her mouth, "Oh, God."

He started talking fast. "Me and Camilla—that was ages ago, Charlie. Another lifetime, it feels like."

"It wasn't another lifetime ago, it wasn't even a year ago. Were you . . ." Her throat closed up and she had to pause. She tried again: "Were you in love with her?"

His mouth worked silently for several seconds. And then he said, "Yes."

She waited for him to continue, for him to add on to the statement, qualify it in some way, making it less devastating, reduce the intensity of her pain. When he didn't, she said, "So it wasn't just a sex thing, it was, like, a full-blown romance?"

He shrugged in a what-do-you-want-me-to-say kind of way, his blue eyes dark with emotion, almost purple. *So beautiful,* Charlie thought helplessly as she looked at him. She loved him, she loved just putting her eyes on him, even when he was hurting her to the point that she thought she might die.

"Well," said Charlie, "a full-blown romance for you anyway." She said this purely to wound him, to make him feel just a little bit of what she was feeling, and, with pleasure, she saw that she had. He flinched, looked away. She kept talking: "And you didn't think this was information I should've been given before we got involved? Camilla's my sister. I mean, kind of. In a way."

He looked back at her. "Would knowing it have changed how you felt about me?" he asked quietly.

"I don't know. I do know that the fact that you kept it from me changes how I feel about you now. It makes me think I can't trust you."

The skin over his high, sharp cheekbones stretched tighter, went white, and his eyes hardened. "If you feel like that, maybe we shouldn't be together."

"Maybe we shouldn't."

She held his gaze for one second, then two, hoping he'd take back what he said so she could take back what she said. But he didn't, so she didn't. The tears burst from her eyes almost before she'd turned around, and she ran away from his house as fast as she'd run toward it.

Charlie didn't know where to go or what to do, so she took the long way home. For a half second, she wished she had brought a bottle of something with her, but then she realized that getting drunk wasn't what she wanted right then. What she wanted was to talk to somebody. Her sister. Mad as she was at Alice, Alice was the only one who would understand how she was feeling, was the only one she trusted to help her sort out the events of this shit-show of a night.

Charlie entered the house by the back door. She couldn't imagine that Alice had stayed at Cybill's. Her fear, though, was that Alice had gone to Tommy's rather than home. She climbed the staircase, craning her neck as she ascended to get a quicker glimpse of Alice's bedroom door. To her relief she saw that light was shining out the bottom of it. She took a deep breath, raised her closed fist.

Alice heard a knock on her door. Praying that it wasn't Patrick, but Charlie, who she'd been waiting up for even though her lids were so heavy she felt like sandbags were attached to the ends of them, she shut *The Magus* and returned it to her bedside table. "Come in," she said.

Charlie opened the door. Without looking at Alice, she closed it behind her and moved to the end of the bed. For a long time, she just sat there, saying nothing, bunching and unbunching a segment of comforter. She'd been crying. The way the light was falling, Alice could see the tear tracks on her cheeks. Finally, she said, "I'm still angry at you. The thing is, I'm more angry at other people at the moment."

"Okay," Alice said cautiously, sitting up, her back against the headboard.

"But just because I'm speaking to you doesn't mean I'm done being mad at you."

"I understand. Before we get into a conversation, though, I want to say again how sorry I am. But what I told you at Cybill's is true. I would never have used her as a confidante. She figured out what was going on with me and Tommy on her own, asked me about it. That's the only reason I answered. I was so taken off guard."

"Right," Charlie said bitterly, "because Cybill actually pays attention to people who aren't her and isn't, like, completely self-involved."

Alice swatted the air dismissively with her hand. "Please. That girl's a lurker, always watching other people, secretly scrutinizing them, and not for any selfless reasons, believe me, though maybe she's convinced herself differently."

"What do you mean?"

"After you left, she tried to feed me some ridiculous line, claiming that she told you about Jude and Camilla for you own good, that you needed to know the truth about him. She's a troublemaker."

"She's a psychotic bitch."

Alice nodded. "That too."

The two girls were quiet for a while. And then Charlie said, "Why is it that you couldn't tell me about you and Tommy? That's what I don't understand."

Alice sighed. "It wasn't me; it was him. He just feels weird about the situation. You know, because of his history with the Flood family, with Richard, especially."

Charlie let loose with a sigh of her own. "Yeah. I get that." She did that bunching, unbunching thing with the comforter again. "How crazy is it that both of our boyfriends have gotten horizontal with our dead stepsister? Really"—starting to laugh—"could things get any more fucked up around here? I mean, sick puppy city, right?"

"Actually," Alice said, and paused. She recognized that a rare opportunity was being presented to her. The Tommy secret was out of the bag. And Charlie was in an unusually soft and receptive frame of mind, having just had her world turned upside down by the Jude-Camilla reveal. Alice knew she should come clean to Charlie about everything, about who she was to Richard and who Richard was to her, about Camilla reaching out to Alice before she died, even about her belief that Camilla wasn't a suicide and Nick's agreement to help her prove it. All of it. Now was the time. There was a strange, prolonged kind of charged moment as her eyes held Charlie's. But she allowed the moment to pass or, rather, waited too long to act on the moment so that it was taken from her by an outside force: Charlie's iPhone, suddenly buzzing.

"Jude?" Alice said as Charlie reached eagerly into her pocket, fumbled pulling out the phone.

Charlie looked at the screen, the corners of her mouth turning down. "No. Stan. A text. He got the book I sent him. Just wanted to say thanks."

"I like Stan," Alice said. "He seems like a nice guy, smart and together."

Alice hadn't really been thinking about these words as she said them, was thinking about how to maneuver the conversation back to where it had been before the text message came through, so she was surprised to hear the tightness in Charlie's voice when Charlie said, "What's that supposed to mean?"

"What's what supposed to mean?"

"That Stan's nice and smart and together."

Alice held up her palms, like, *whoa, whoa.* "Charlie, I was just trying to give Stan a compliment. You were mad at me for being dismissive of him a couple days ago."

"And now it's Jude you're being dismissive of. Only you're doing it in this sneaky, underhanded way."

"I have no idea what you're talking about."

"Saying Stan's nice and smart and together you're implying that Jude's none of those things."

Alice paused before responding. She didn't want to stoke the fires of Charlie's rage, but she didn't want to lie to Charlie either. "I don't think Jude is any of those things," she said carefully. "I haven't exactly disguised the fact that I find him to be of, like, questionable character. But if you really care about him, I'm willing to take another look, give him another chance."

Charlie jumped up from the bed. "Forget it. I can't talk to you. I thought I could but I can't."

And for the second time that night, Alice watched helplessly as Charlie ran out the door in anger.

Before exiting the house, Charlie grabbed a bottle of liquor from Richard's cabinet, not caring which bottle so long as it was reasonably full, and stuffed it into her overnight bag. Without looking, she reached into the coat closet, pulled something off a hanger. Then she headed down to the beach.

It was a windy night, chilly for July. When she got close to the water, she turned right, walked until she didn't want to walk anymore, at which point she wrapped herself in the jacket—leather bomber, huge, Richard's, obviously—and flopped down on the sand. She opened her bag, pulled out the bottle. Tossing the cap onto a pile of seaweed, she brought it to her mouth, tilted it back. The liquid inside was disgusting, fruity yet medicinal, like cherry Nyquil, only thicker and more syrupy. She could barely get it down her throat. She looked at the label. Hidalgo La Gitana Manzanilla Sherry. Jesus, just her luck. She'd swiped the drink of choice of the over-eighty set. Whatever. If she guzzled enough of it, it would get the job done. Holding her breath so she'd taste it less, she took swallow after swallow. It dribbled down her chin, sweet and sticky.

Charlie could see Jude's house from where she was sitting. She stared at the window she knew was Jude's. Stared until the light went dead behind the shade. And even then she didn't stop staring.

Charlie must've passed out in the sand, because when she woke up she was in the exact same spot. It was still night, still dark, still cold. The only difference was, she was being kissed. The face and body of the person above her was indistinct, nothing but shadowy outline, and yet, somehow, deeply familiar. Jude.

He murmured her name in her ear, his voice low and husky, as he peeled the jacket from her shoulders. His mouth tasted her neck, her throat, her collarbone, then her lips again. His warm palm slid from her hip to up over her ribcage, and she arched her back so it would be easier for him to free the clasp of her bra.

He'd found her, she realized. He'd forgiven her for the horrible things she'd said, the horrible accusations she'd made. He knew how sorry she was, and he was sorry too. She opened her arms to him, began kissing him back, kissing him harder and deeper, more greedily, than he was kissing her, pushing his lips open with her tongue. She dug her fingers into his shoulder blades, pulling him to her, drawing him closer.

It was in that moment, as she pressed the lengths of their bodies together, that she knew: it wasn't Jude's body she was pressing, it was a girl's.

The shock of discovery made her intake of breath sharp, her eyes snap open wide. She reared back. "Jesus, Cybill. What are you doing?"

"Same thing you were doing," Cybill said, wet-mouthed, her eyes huge and blue-black, bits of moonlight reflecting from the pupils. She leaned forward again.

Charlie began scrambling in the sand, struggling to put some space between them. "Yeah, but not with you. I thought you were Jude," she said, and as she said it the realization that Jude hadn't come looking for her, hadn't forgiven her, sank in. So did the disappointment.

"You didn't know?"

Charlie shook her head. "It's dark. He and I had gotten into a fight. And you look so much like him. It's eerie. You kiss like him. You even—" She'd been about to say, *taste like him*, but broke off at the last second.

A nerve throbbed in Cybill's throat, and she turned away.

Charlie studied Cybill's face in profile, waited for her pulse to come down. She'd just assumed that the reason Cybill acted toward her the way that she did was because she was jealous of Charlie for being with Jude. Was it possible, though, that Charlie had gotten it backward? That it was Jude Cybill was jealous of for being with Charlie? Before tonight, the very notion would have been ludicrous. But now she wasn't so sure.

When Cybill turned around again, Charlie expected to see shame or anger on her face, a mixture of the two. Instead, though, Charlie saw a smile. It twitched at the corner of Cybill's lips and then spilled into laughter. "Makes sense," Cybill said, "since I taught him everything he knows."

"I don't understand. Why would you—"

"For fun," Cybill said, her voice teasing. "Why else? What, you didn't like it?"

"No, I . . . It's just . . ."

Cybill rolled her eyes. "Relax, Charlie. It's only a game. Camilla and I used to play it all the time. In this very spot, in fact. It's why I couldn't resist when I saw you lying there."

Charlie looked at Cybill. Cybill appeared so cool and silvery-slender sitting there in the moonlight, her attitude so ultra-relaxed and contemptuous-amused that Charlie immediately felt unsure of herself. She'd misjudged, she realized with embarrassment. Had overreacted, as usual: shrinking backward, virtue aflutter, mouth a prissy little *O*. Why did she always have to behave like such an easily shocked bush-leaguer around Jude and Cybill? she wondered, her fingers unconsciously running over the tattoo on her lower back, wishing she had a Band-Aid to cover it. Couldn't she, for once, just be cool about the situation? Fake sexual sophistication if she couldn't summon the genuine article?

Maybe then, Charlie thought, with a sickening dip of her stomach, she was making such a big deal out of the kiss because to her it *was* a big deal, her totally extreme, out-of-proportion reaction, a defense-mechanism thing. Like, the kiss felt good, too good, had made her go all hot and cold and quivery. Her heart was still racing from it.

"Plus," Cybill said, "I'm tired of Jude getting all the fun. Thought I'd fuck with him. He likes a little bit of that. Developed a taste for it when he was with Camilla."

Charlie gave a weak smile in response. "Sounds like Camilla got you both to develop a taste for it."

This remark elicited a grin from Cybill, which relieved Charlie, made her feel like she was at least semi pulling off the normal act. Afraid, though, that she wouldn't be able to sustain the light, bantering tone for long, she stood. She began gathering together her bag, Richard's jacket, the nearly empty bottle of sherry, even fishing the cap out of the seaweed. "I've got to go to bed or I really will fall asleep on the beach, get washed out to sea," she said, not quite looking at Cybill. Then, flicking her hand in a goodbye wave—she certainly wasn't going to risk touching Cybill, actual physical contact—she turned.

Charlie waited until she was sure Cybill could no longer see her before slipping her bra, unclasped and dangling off her shoulders, through the sleeve of her shirt, stuffing it into her pocket. She walked the rest of the way home with arms folded across her chest.

Chapter Sixteen

Alice woke up early the next morning. It was a testament to her exhaustion that she'd managed to fall asleep at all so upset was she over the situation with Charlie. The first thing she did when she regained consciousness was rush to her sister's room, fling open the door. Alice was relieved to see Charlie on her bed, if not in it, facedown in a dead man's float, still fully dressed except for her shoes, her feet covered in sand. Alice took the chenille blanket from the armchair, laid it over Charlie's body. Closing the door quietly behind her, Alice headed down to the kitchen.

Patrick was already there, coffeepot in hand. His hair was standing straight up, was almost all cowlick. And he was wearing an inside-out T-shirt, a pair of Rindge and Latin sweatpants that he'd outgrown, his ankles and an inch or so of calf sticking out the bottom. He looked at her. "Thought you were avoiding me."

"Not was. Am. I'm just too tired to do it right now."

"You want some?" He held up the coffeepot, shook it. "It's fresh."

"Sure," Alice said. She pulled out a chair and sat down, stared at nothing as he opened and shut cabinet doors, rattled utensils.

"Here you go."

She watched him as he walked over to her from the counter, his stride naturally springy, bouncy, on the balls of his feet, causing him to slosh coffee over the sides of the mugs. She thanked him, lifted her mug by the drippy handle. For a few minutes, they sipped in silence. Patrick made his coffee strong. And Alice didn't doctor her cup as she usually did, adding a lot of milk and sugar. Black seemed to work faster, go directly into her system, percolating in her blood, sparking her synapses.

Patrick put down his mug. Tilting back in his chair, he said, "It's a fucking nuthouse around here. I heard you and Charlie going in and out at all hours last night, slammed doors, thudding footsteps, raised voices—the works."

"I hope we didn't keep you awake." She sighed. "Well, obviously we did. I'm sorry. In fact, I'm sorry for everything. It hasn't been much of a getaway weekend for you, has it?"

"I don't care about any of that. Are you ready to tell me what's really going on?"

Alice looked at him, at his kind eyes, at the worried crease between his brows, and, as she did, something wrenched inside her chest. She took a deep breath, let it out. Then she said, "I've been seeing somebody, a guy. Charlie found out last night. She was upset. Some other stuff happened, too, but that was the main thing."

"I knew it. Who?"

"You want a name?"

Patrick nodded.

"But you don't know him."

"I want it anyway."

"Okay. Tommy."

"He local?"

It was Alice's turn to nod. She could tell that the revelation had hurt Patrick but he was trying not to show it, which only made her feel worse.

"Any reason you were being so hush-hush about the relationship? This Tommy doesn't have a wife stashed somewhere, does he?"

"No wife. He has a girlfriend, though. Or rather, an ex-girlfriend. Richard's daughter, the one who killed herself last summer."

"So?"

Alice wasn't expecting a question after the Camilla reveal. She figured it would explain everything—it did for her—and was taken aback that for Patrick it didn't. "So—so it's weird for him," she said, stammering, "like uncomfortable, to be going out with me now."

"And his solution to not being comfortable is—what?—to lie? Make you lie, too? Pretend that you're not a couple?"

Trying not to sound defensive, Alice said, "It's more complicated than that. Plus, the not-going-public thing was a short-term solution Tommy came up with, not a long-term one."

"Tommy sounds like an asshole."

Alice gave a one-note laugh. "And this is your totally impartial, totally unbiased assessment of Tommy's character? Tommy, who you've never actually met?"

"I thought he was an asshole before you told me he was making you his secret, like he's ashamed of you or something. I thought he was an asshole when you told me his name was Tommy. What kind of grown guy calls himself by a little boy's name? Answer: the asshole kind."

Alice just shrugged, took another sip of her coffee.

Patrick observed her silently for a few seconds, then said, "I see what's going on here. You're going to write off whatever I say because you think I'm jealous and that I don't get it. Well, I am jealous and maybe I don't get it, but that doesn't mean I'm wrong. You're changing, Alice. I don't know if that's because of your new boyfriend or if it's because of your new circumstances or if it's because people just change, that's the nature of life or whatever. But I do know you need to be careful. Your mom gave up everything for a guy—her husband, her causes, her passions. And it looks to me like you're on the same path. Charlie says you haven't picked up a paintbrush since you've been here. And I heard you ditched Angela when Occupy Boston came around." He was looking her directly in the eye as he spoke and there was something in his stare that made her want to cringe. She dropped her gaze instead.

He pushed back his chair, stood up from the table. "Okay, that's enough tough love for now. I'm going to take a shower. I think you should think about what I've said, though."

He leaned over to kiss the top of her head. At the last second, though, he thought better of it, instead giving her shoulder an awkward squeeze before exiting the kitchen. Her gaze still down, all Alice saw of him was his legs in his too-short sweatpants disappearing through the door. She couldn't remember a time when she'd felt so low.

• • •

Alice had just picked up the two mugs, brought them over to the sink, was rinsing them out when she heard a knock on the door behind her. She turned and saw Tommy through the glass. She stared at him, a sick, panicky-dready sensation beginning to fill her chest. She still had no clue what she was going to say to him. If only he'd come a minute later, she'd have been safely upstairs, could've avoided this encounter. In the small mercies category, though, Patrick had cleared out, so at least she was spared having to introduce the two.

She reached for a dishtowel. Was wiping her hands on it as she walked over to the door, opened it. Instead of inviting Tommy into the kitchen, she stepped out onto the deck. They watched each other for half a minute or so. He looked as if he'd been sleeping even less than she had: bones sharp, dark circles under his eyes, patches of blondish-brown stubble on his cheeks. Also, he looked angry, his jaw clenched, mouth a thin white slash.

Finally he said, "Sorry for the early morning drop-in but I didn't really have a choice," giving his lips a sarcastic twist. "You run out on me with no explanation, then you go dark, don't return any of my calls or texts. And you left this." He held up her denim jacket, tossed it over the back of one of the wicker deck chairs.

"I know my behavior's been"—Alice paused—"weird."

"Is there a reason for this weirdness or is it just weirdness for weirdness's sake?"

"I got overwhelmed. I'm sorry."

"Overwhelmed by what?"

"Being alone with you in your bedroom. At night. No parents around. I'm not . . . I mean, I haven't ever . . ."

Tommy's mouth suddenly softened. So did his tone. "You freaked out because you're a virgin?"

True, if not the whole truth. She nodded.

He reached for her, and she let him take her in his arms. "Oh, Alice," he murmured, "why didn't you say something?"

Say *some*thing? She was afraid to say *any*thing. There were so many things she couldn't tell him: her suspicions that Camilla's death wasn't a suicide, that his father was corrupt, that she'd never measure up to his last girlfriend, the one whose sister she just happened to be even if he didn't know it. She leaned against his chest, closed her eyes.

He went on: "Look, this is scary for me too. Obviously, I'm not a virgin. I was with Camilla. But she was my first, my first and my only. What I have with you, though, is different. It's so much better and so much more real. So, inviting you over wasn't some casual thing that I did just because. You believe me, right?"

Again, Alice nodded. And then she said, "We've been outed," just sort of blurting out the words because it was the one uncomfortable truth she didn't have to feel guilty about, was the one uncomfortable truth that she didn't feel was all or even partially her fault.

Immediately he stiffened. "What do you mean?"

"People know about us."

"How? Who did you tell?"

"No one," Alice said, a little insulted. "Cybill figured it out. She decided not to keep her findings to herself."

Tommy walked away from her over to the deck's railing, leaned against it. As soon as he did, though, he pushed himself off it, crossed to the railing on the other side of the deck, his movements impatient, restless. He folded his arms over his chest, looked at her. "I suppose this makes you happy." His voice was harsh, almost spitty.

"Not especially," she said, surprised by his abrupt swing back to anger. She knew he'd be upset by the Cybill reveal, not this upset, though.

"No? I find that hard to believe since you've been so gung ho about the idea of us going public, even though I told you over and over how dangerous it would be. Now someone's spreading the word for you."

Alice felt a little surge of anger in response to his, but it died out almost immediately. She was too tired to be angry, she realized. She was just tapped out. "I didn't say a thing to Cybill. She guessed. And I certainly didn't ask her to tell other people what she knew."

Tommy let out a snort of disbelief.

Not wanting to look at his face, Alice looked down at her hands, saw the dishtowel in them. And that's when she noticed. Embroidered in the lower corner were the initials MBF. She repeated the sequence in her head, *MBF, MBF, MBF.* And then, suddenly, she made the connection: Briggs, M., the name written on top of the file in Dr. van Stratten's office, was Martha Briggs and Martha Briggs was Martha Flood before she married Richard (Alice had seen the name in the wedding announcement she'd dug up in the Serenity Point Public Library the week before). Martha must've used her maiden name with Dr. van Stratten. Or maybe he'd been her doctor since before she and Richard got together and he never bothered to update her name on the file. In any case, she'd been a patient. This was an important detail. Alice didn't know why it was important, only that it was.

"Admit, though, that you wanted this."

Alice, jerked out of her reverie, looked at Tommy, confused. "Wanted what?"

"For other people to know about us."

"Wanting or not wanting has nothing to do with it. It happened. It just *is*."

"We should've been more careful."

"We *were* careful."

"No we weren't. Not careful enough." He reached out and grabbed her wrist. There was a desperate look in his eyes when he said, "How am I supposed to protect you now?"

"Protect me? From what? What are you talking about?"

His grip around her wrist tightened. His breathing was heavy, irregular, and he was staring at her so hard it was like he was trying to look into her rather than at her. "I can't watch over you all the time. It's just not physically possible."

"Tommy, you're hurting me. Let go," she said. But she didn't think he heard her. Or saw her for that matter, for all his staring. His grip grew tighter and tighter, more and more painful. She wanted to cry out but stifled herself because, as scared as she was, she knew—some animal instinct told her—that she shouldn't allow him to see it. Making her voice cold and hard, she said, "I said, let go."

Immediately his grip slackened. So surprised was she that her bluff had worked, she didn't step back right away, just stood there, watching him. He seemed to be coming out of whatever trance he was in. He looked down at her wrist encircled by his hand, then looked up into her eyes and simply shook his head as he lifted his other hand to his mouth. The expression on his face was one of shock and horror. He couldn't believe what he'd done.

And in a second, an instant, faster than she would have imagined possible, the rage and fear she'd been feeling toward him was replaced by pity. The self-disgust—self-revulsion—was all over his face

And then a voice behind her said, "What the hell's going on here?"

Alice turned. It was Patrick, a towel wrapped around his waist, beads of water from the shower still clinging to his pale, freckly skin. She looked at him, a little out of it from her exchange with Tommy, the high emotion of it. Seeing Patrick without a shirt on for the first time this visit, she realized how much bigger he'd gotten. His shoulders, always wide, were now broad, too, his muscles taut and chiseled. He must've been doing some seriously heavy lifting at work. Before this display, Alice would have said Tommy would've taken him in a fight easily. Now she wasn't so sure.

"Patrick," Alice muttered dazedly, "this is Tommy. We were just talking."

Eyes on Tommy, Patrick said, "You talk with your mouth, not your hands, lover boy."

Tommy released Alice's wrist and, raising his hands above his head, took a step backward.

"That's better," Patrick said. "But it would be even better if you took another step, and then another, and then another, until you hit the water. And even then you should keep going. Come on inside, Alice."

As Alice crossed the threshold, Tommy's eyes sought out hers over Patrick's shoulder. The smile on his face was sickly looking. "Just a friend, huh?" he said to her. Turning to Patrick, "Relax, I'm going."

Alice snapped out of whatever semi-stupor she was in. To Tommy she said, "You, don't go anywhere." And then to Patrick, "And you, don't boss me around. You're not a caveman and I'm not some damsel in distress, okay? We really were just having a conversation."

Tommy shook his head. "Forget it, Alice. We'll finish talking later."

Alice started to say something to him but Patrick slammed the door shut. By the time she opened it, Tommy was already at the bottom of the deck steps, walking across the sand. She called his name but he didn't turn around.

In the late afternoon, Alice received a voicemail from Sasha: "Rager on the beach tonight. Not to be missed." Alice contemplated the message as she three-three-sevened it. Normally she wouldn't have even considered going to the party, not after the day she'd had, not after the last couple of days she'd had, not when there were so many people she was trying to duck. But there was one person she wanted to see more than she wanted to avoid seeing everyone else: Nick. She had to talk to him about the monogrammed dishtowel and M. Briggs. He would have had a copy of Martha's file. She needed him to dig it up, share with her its contents.

She pulled a piece of blank paper from the printer, transcribed Sasha's message onto it:

Rager on the beach tonight. Not to be missed.

She thought about signing the note, but then decided not to in case someone other than Nick opened it. He'd know who it was from. She stuffed it in an envelope with his name written on the top. Then she drove across town to Dr. Rose's office and slipped it under the door.

CHAPTER SEVENTEEN

The party was being held, almost literally, in Richard's backyard. All Alice, Charlie, and Patrick had to do was push open the door that led to the deck, walk down the steps, and they were pretty much there.

Alice looked at her sister. Charlie had been in a funny mood all day. Not bad. Just quiet. Pensive. When Alice had knocked on Charlie's door a few hours before, she'd expected to be told to go fuck herself (only in less polite language). But instead she'd been invited inside. Charlie had been lying on her bed, staring up at the ceiling, still under the chenille blanket Alice had tucked around her that morning. She hadn't looked at Alice when Alice entered. Hadn't spoken either. Finally, Alice, sitting on the footstool of the armchair, uncomfortably perched, had asked Charlie if she wanted to go to a party that night.

"We should," Charlie had said, eyes still on the ceiling. "Tricky's heading home tomorrow. We owe him one good night."

Now here they were. Charlie was dressed casually, bare feet with painted toenails, a tight T-shirt that didn't quite meet the tops of her hip-high Levis, exposing an inch or so of tanned and hollow midriff. Exposing, too, her angel's-wing tattoo. Except not. Alice had noticed—noticed with pleasure—that Charlie had stopped wearing her Band-Aid recently. Only there it was again, just above the waist of her jeans. Had she simply been forgetting to apply the usual covering, remembered tonight, Alice wondered, or had something happened that made her feel the need to hide once more? Alice nearly asked the question aloud but then didn't.

Tonight's party looked almost identical to the first party she and Charlie had attended in Serenity Point: on the beach, kids from the club, bonfire. The only difference was that there were kegs—two of them, rolled up onto the sand like a couple of beached whales—instead of Ketel One and sugar-free Red Bull. Alice let her gaze sweep the crowd. She was disappointed to see that Nick wasn't there yet. She was relieved to see, however, that neither was Tommy.

Jude was standing by the bonfire, on the opposite side that the kegs were on. Alice watched him as he said something that made the girl, one she didn't recognize—small, pretty, long blond hair—next to him laugh. His body language was causal, not caring a bit. His eyes, though, were alert, intent. She was almost positive that he'd spotted Charlie but was pretending not to have.

Alice was about to make this observation to Charlie, ask her what was going on, when something hijacked her attention. Out of the corner of her eye, she saw Cybill, separated from everyone else by a dozen or so yards, sitting at the water's edge, nearly out of sight, her back to the party. Wanting to strengthen her bond with her sister, Alice said, "I can't believe she had the nerve to show up," indicating Cybill with her chin.

To Alice's surprise, Charlie responded with a mild, "Oh, Cybill's all right."

"Are you kidding me? After the show she put on last night? She's about as far from all right as you can get. And it looks like Jude's with me. Those two are usually attached at the hip. He must've found out that she did the dirty to him last night."

Charlie's eyes bugged in her head. "The dirty? What dirty?"

Slightly taken aback at Charlie's intensity, Alice said, "Blabbed about his past indiscretions or whatever to you. You know, his relationship with Camilla."

"Oh. That dirty." Charlie's laugh didn't sound like her normal one. "She had her reasons. In fact, it would be great if you'd act like last night never happened, treat her the same as before."

"You do know she screwed me over in kind of a big way, right? Betrayed my confidence and all that?"

"Yeah, I do. But I'd take it as, like, a personal favor if you'd pretend that she didn't."

Alice stared at her sister for a long moment. The last thing she wanted to do after the week they'd had was start a fight. "Okay. Whatever you want."

"Yeah?" Charlie said, like she was surprised Alice was giving in so easily.

"Sure. Why not? She's your friend."

"Thanks. So, will you and Patrick be okay on your own? I'm thinking about wandering."

"Going to kiss and make up?"

Bug eyes again from Charlie. "What?"

"Sorry. I thought maybe you and Jude had gotten into a little fight or something."

"We did, and not so little. But he isn't the one I'm planning on wandering into."

Alice told her sister to have fun. As Charlie moved away from the bonfire, she turned to Patrick. "Feel like a beer?"

He laughed, draped an arm around her shoulder. "Like more than one."

Charlie approached Cybill from behind, careful to move only when Jude had his back to her so she could avoid his gaze, escape detection. She couldn't believe he was flirting with that blond girl. Not that the girl was a real blonde—those streaks were fooling no one, and neither were those extensions—and not that he didn't have the right to pick up whoever he wanted. Technically, they were broken up.

Besides, it wasn't his faithfulness that she had a problem with. It was his truthfulness. Or lack thereof. He'd lied to her—by omission, but still—had made an idiot of her. Why it bothered her so much that he'd been with Camilla before he'd known she even existed she couldn't have said. It did, though. Maybe because she believed he'd been all-the-way honest with her but, it turned out, he'd only been partway honest. Or maybe because she'd fought Cybill for him tooth and nail, and Camilla got him without really trying, discarded him just as casually. Or maybe because if he'd been as in love with Camilla as Cybill said he was—Camilla, so beautiful, so sophisticated—she didn't see how he could possibly be in love with her, too.

In any case, she wasn't ready to talk to him, or for a reconciliation. Not yet. Not when the terms between them were so unequal.

Charlie was ten feet from Cybill, then five, then one. Her nerve almost deserted her at the last second, and she very nearly turned around, retreated to the safety of Alice and Patrick. But after downing first her own beer, then the one she brought for Cybill, she forced herself to collapse in the sand. For a long time, several minutes at least, Cybill didn't acknowledge her, didn't even seem to notice that there was somebody beside her.

And then she turned.

Her expression was blank, and her eyes seemed to have sunk all the way back into her skull. The work of alcohol and/or chemicals, Charlie wondered, or emotion? As with the other night, Cybill wasn't wearing her hair down and loose as she usually did but pulled back. And her skin was clean of makeup. For the first time, Charlie found Cybill's face beautiful, the moonlight softening her features, rounding them off.

Beautiful and more than a little unsettling.

Looking at it, Charlie struggled to hold the image steady in her mind, Cybill's face slipping, Jude's rising, one blending into the other. And yet, they were two separate people, Charlie reminded herself confusedly. It was funny—funny strange, not funny ha-ha—how fascinating Cybill had suddenly become to her. Before she'd viewed Cybill as an obstacle, basically, the thing standing between her and what she wanted: Jude. Now, though, Cybill was a mystery to be puzzled over.

Or maybe Cybill wasn't a mystery at all. Or, rather, the mystery of Cybill had nothing to do with Cybill. Maybe Charlie's out-of-nowhere fascination with Cybill was just another side of her long-running fascination with Jude. The cousins did, after all, look so much alike. And the ways in which they were different—he male, she female, he dark, she light, etc.—weirdly made their alikeness *more* apparent not less. Opposites yet, somehow, the same.

It was Cybill who spoke first. "I'm Cybill," she said.

Charlie blinked back at her, let out an uneasy laugh. "Yeah, I'm aware of that. We have met."

"Just making sure you didn't mix me up with Jude again. Wouldn't want us to have another case of mistaken identity on our hands, for more hijinks to ensue."

There was a mocking note in Cybill's voice, though Charlie couldn't tell if it was Charlie who Cybill was mocking or herself. Thoughts began pinballing around Charlie's skull, whizzing by so fast, she didn't even have time to think them: Was Cybill amused by Charlie's behavior the night before? Annoyed? Bored? All three at once? Or was the casual act just that—an act? Had she meant it when she kissed Charlie? There was a moment when Charlie thought she had meant it. Or, Charlie wondered, was she guilty of projecting her own desires onto Cybill, allowing wishful thinking to cloud her judgment? The truth was, Charlie hadn't been able to shake the memory of that kiss—the heat of Cybill's mouth, the softness of Cybill's skin. She was remembering it even now.

Well, why shouldn't she let Cybill kiss her? After all, Cybill had kissed Jude. And Camilla. Why not her? Why couldn't she have some fun too?

Charlie leaned back on her elbows, tried to arrange her body in a more relaxed position. "I thought hijinks ensuing was your thing," she said, managing to sound almost as casual as Cybill. "Yours and Camilla's."

"What do you mean?"

"Those games you two used to play."

"The games were really Camilla's. She came up with them and then taught them to me."

"Good. Then you can teach them to me," Charlie said, shocked at her own daring, her heart pounding in her throat.

Cybill cocked an eyebrow. "You didn't seem in the mood to learn the other night."

"Moods change."

"Is that so?"

"Yeah, it is," Charlie said defiantly. She lowered her eyes but raised her face. To her disappointment, though, several seconds passed and Cybill didn't kiss her. She glanced up through her lashes. Cybill, she was surprised to see, wasn't even looking at her, was looking out at the ocean. So she did too.

After a while, Charlie noticed a bottle of Ketel One stuck in the sand. She reached across Cybill to get it. And as she did, she could smell the traces of walnut and coconut on the sheen of Cybill's skin, could see the faint, almost invisible hair on Cybill's forearm. She unscrewed the cap, brought the bottle to her lips. After a succession of fiery swallows, she laid her hand on the back of Cybill's wrist. "Come on, Cybill," she said, "I got the sense that playing with me was something you were into."

"Maybe for me it's not playing." Cybill's voice was soft as she said this, as were her eyes. And Charlie had the feeling—so rare—that Cybill wasn't bullshitting her or testing her or trying to manipulate her. That Cybill was just talking, was saying something because she meant it. And Charlie didn't know how to respond.

Seconds ticked by and then a minute. The girls went back to staring out at the ocean, gazes pointed straight ahead. And then Charlie turned to Cybill at the same moment Cybill turned to her. She looked into the face that was Jude's face but not Jude's face, the eyes that were Jude's eyes but not Jude's eyes, and then she leaned across the sand to kiss the mouth that was Jude's mouth but not Jude's mouth.

"Not again," a male voice said.

Instantly, Charlie pulled away, turned around. Standing behind them was Jude. He was smiling but the smile looked pained. Rapidly, he spun on his heel, began heading in the direction of the bonfire.

"Shit," Charlie said, standing, brushing the sand from the backs of her legs. "I better go talk to him."

Cybill nodded without looking at her.

Head down, Charlie started walking. She only made it half a dozen steps before slamming into someone. Jude? No, Stan. He was wearing jeans and his Wolcott sweatshirt, the hood drawn like he didn't want to be recognized. And why would he want to be recognized? Only last week he'd been serving the kids at the party french fries and lobster rolls, hustling them for tips.

He grinned at her, rocked back on his heels. "Just the person I was looking for."

"Me?" Charlie said, sneaking a quick glance over his shoulder. Jude had already disappeared from view, losing himself in the crowd, twice as big as it was before she sat down with Cybill. The sight sparked a feeling of desperation in her. She had to get to him, find him, make him talk to her. But then, all of sudden, she wondered, why? She hadn't been cheating—they were broken up—or doing anything he hadn't done, for that matter. Besides he was all over that blond girl at the bonfire.

"Yeah, you," Stan said. "I wanted to tell you thanks in person. Didn't think a text message really did the job."

Nervous suddenly, though she wasn't sure why, maybe because she suspected that her gift was stupid, presumptuous in some way—where did she get off giving a guy who was a reader a book, she who skimmed CliffsNotes?—she said, "You don't have to read it, you know. Like, don't feel obligated."

He pulled *Gatsby* from his kangaroo pocket, a page somewhere in the middle dog-eared. "Too late. See?"

She took the book from him, gently thumbed it. "Haven't you read it before, though?"

"Well, yeah. But anything this good is worth a second look. I'm noticing a whole bunch of new stuff this time around."

"Me too."

"You too what?"

"I mean, I've been rereading it, too, though I should still be reading *Tess* for the first time, I know. There was so much I missed when I read *Gatsby* in school that I'm seeing now. Like Jordan Baker. She cheats at golf, so Nick should realize even before he gets involved with her that she's not an honest person. I mean, right?"

Stan looked at her for a long beat, then said, "Charlie, you do realize you've started a book club, don't you?"

Charlie, indignant, "What? No I haven't."

"Yeah, you have. You picked a book for the group—i.e., me—and now we're discussing it."

"That's the craziest thing I ever heard."

"It's true. You're reading for pleasure."

There was a pause, and then she said, "Okay. That I'll accept."

"You'll accept reading for pleasure but not book club? How come?"

She picked a strand of windblown hair out of her mouth, shrugged. "Because reading for pleasure sounds dirty, I guess."

He smiled. "Like something you could get into, huh?"

She couldn't help but smile back at him. "Oh yeah. Big time."

They both laughed.

Alice watched Charlie and Stan talking, laughing. She noticed she wasn't the only one. Jude had dropped the cool-verging-on-indifferent act, was staring at Charlie openly now. The expression on his face was one of intense distress, like the sight of her with another guy was causing him pain, like to actually physically suffer. And the long-haired blonde was nowhere to be seen. And then, abruptly, he turned away from Charlie, his gaze colliding with Alice's. Realizing he was being observed, he rearranged his features into their usual mask of prep-school-rebel aloofness, took an oh-so-casual sip from his beer. Charlie had implied that the fight between them was a big one. *Big enough to end in a breakup?* Alice wondered. Looked like.

Alice and Patrick were hanging out near the kegs. Now that he knew she was with Tommy, he seemed more relaxed around her, like the pressure was off, which, in turn, made her more relaxed around him. Alice was sure it helped that Tommy was nowhere to be seen and there was no competition for her attention. Someone had brought out an iPod stereo, now blasting an old-school Madonna song. Sasha was shimmying to it, shaking her ass, mouthing the words to "Into the Groove" at Patrick.

"I think this is her way of saying she likes you," Alice said.

Patrick winced as Sasha flubbed a simple sit-and-roll, jutting her hip out so far she upset her balance, almost fell. "Oh yeah?" he said, taking a sip of beer. "Well, her mating dance needs work."

"Help her with her moves then. She's a nice girl, actually."

He laughed, having fun. "Like I need to get mixed up with another one of those."

"Okay, well, she's not that nice."

"Now you're talking."

"I'll put in a good word if you like."

"Something tells me I'd do better with her if you put in a bad word."

"I can do that, too. Really, though, do you want me to talk to her for you?"

Suddenly looking serious, almost pained, he said, "I'm not quite there yet, Alice. Okay?"

"Okay," she said quickly. "Sorry."

And then Jude was standing next to them. He appeared jittery, looking all around, jingling the change in his pockets. "Hey—it's Patrick, right?"

Patrick nodded.

"Can I speak with you for a second, Patrick?"

"Sure."

"Like, in private?"

Patrick flicked a glance at Alice. Figuring Jude wanted to have a man-to-man talk with Patrick about Charlie, maybe get some tips on how to handle her from a guy who'd known her a long time, Alice said, "Take your time. I'll be here."

As the two boys went off, Alice stepped closer to the fire, extended her palms to it, the night a cool one. She looked, head lifting, as a spark flew up from the flames and that was when she saw Nick, or at least someone she was reasonably sure was Nick. (It was dark, obviously, so visibility wasn't great and he was standing at a distance.) As soon as her eyes were turned his way, he retreated, rising to the top of a dune, then, after throwing a quick glance over his shoulder—an invitation to follow?—disappeared behind it.

Alice drew a fresh cup of beer from the tap, began moving away from the music and the laughter and the noise. But when she crested the dune, she didn't see Nick. Her gaze roamed the softly dark, softly curved landscape. She wondered for a moment if she'd imagined him, conjured up the shadowy figure framed by the weak light of the moon. A trick of the eye. And then there he was, thirty or so yards away, leaning against an abandoned lifeguard's tower. He was dressed in a neat black suit and tie, his briefcase swinging from the end of his hand—work attire, formal. He'd taken off his shoes, though, tucked them under his arm, rolled up the bottom of his pants. His feet were long and pale.

"Thanks for the invitation," he said, accepting the beer she held out to him.

"Of course. I should tell you, though, that my motives for extending it weren't purely social."

"Neither were my motives for accepting it, so we're even," he said, and grinned, exposing those sharp white teeth.

Everything about him, she noticed, was sharp: teeth, eyes, tongue, edges. Even his body was pure angle, lean and sinewy, the bones prominent, like blades beneath the skin. And yet, for all his spikiness, he wasn't ugly. On the contrary, in a gaunt-faced, high-cheekboned, Adrien Brody kind of way, he was handsome. Alice had never given his looks much thought before, considered whether or not he was attractive, but she saw now that he was. Not to her. Definitely not to her. She could see, though, how he would be to somebody.

"How old are you?" she said suddenly.

If he was surprised by the personal question, he didn't show it. "Nineteen."

There were only two years separating them, a year separating him and Tommy. Alice almost couldn't believe it. He seemed so much older. Like he was already a man. "You're a sophomore at Dartmouth?"

"I just finished my sophomore year. I'll be a junior."

"You're young for your year."

"September birthday. Just made the cutoff. And how did you know I went to Dartmouth?"

"You once mentioned coming down from Hanover."

"Did I? I don't remember doing that."

Fearing that she'd given something away, revealed more than she would have wished—that she paid close attention to his words for one, stored them in her memory—she said, "Well, I do. And what else is in Hanover besides Dartmouth?"

He seemed amused by the touchy note that had entered her voice. "Well, there's a great little pizza joint called Everything But

Anchovies in the town center. The buffalo-chicken pizza is out of this world. Maybe not worth the trip, though, if you don't love the idea of blue cheese dressing instead of tomato sauce. So, how about you tell me what I'm doing here, Alice."

Alice did, starting with the monogram she spotted on the dish-towel in the kitchen, moving back to the name on the file she'd seen in Dr. van Stratten's office, then connecting the two events through the wedding announcement of Richard and Martha that she'd un-earthed the week before in the local newspaper, the *Serenity Point Citizen*. As she spoke, she looked down at her wrist, covered in a bracelet of greenish yellow crystal, borrowed from Charlie to hide the bracelet of bluish purple bruise. The sight distracted her, made her pause, remember the heat of Tommy's grip, the pain of it. She shoved the arm behind her back, continued.

When she finished talking, she looked at Nick. His eyes were bright and he spoke fast, saying, "I didn't know Martha Flood was a patient of Dr. van Stratten's. He never said a word about her. I mean, by the time I was working for him, she was already dead. Still, though, Camilla was at the house constantly. You think it would have come up, if only in passing. I'll check out the file he kept on her as soon as I get home. I assume that's what you want me to do?"

Strangely, seeing Nick's excitement somehow dimmed her own. "It is, yeah. But Dr. van Stratten was a lot of people's doctor. You said so yourself. Like, the entire town's, right?"

This bit of fact-checking seemed to bring Nick down to earth slightly. "I was exaggerating when I said that. But not by much. Your point's taken." He thought for a few seconds, then, making a palms-up gesture, said, "Maybe it's nothing, just a coincidence. Still,

Tommy never mentioned to you that his dad was Martha Flood's doctor, did he?"

Alice shook her head.

"That's a little odd, don't you think?"

"I don't know if it's a little odd or totally normal. Like, why would he want to talk about his dead girlfriend's dead mom and her professional relationship to his disgraced dad? To me, those all sound like topics he'd go out of his way to avoid. Besides, I'd rather have discovered that Camilla had been Dr. van Stratten's patient. Martha's death seems pretty unsuspicious. I mean, you can't get much more straightforward than terminal cancer. It's Camilla's that was mysterious." Alice was about to add that she had no desire to jeopardize her relationship with Tommy—already in serious peril—by chasing after facts that didn't matter, establishing links between people that were irrelevant, but at the last moment didn't, kept her thoughts to herself.

"I hear what you're saying," Nick said. "Nevertheless, the subject rates at least a superficial looking into. Wouldn't you agree?"

Alice unhappily conceded that it did.

He put his hand on one of the lifeguard tower's beams, shook it. "You think the wood on this thing is rotting?"

She shrugged, her mind on other things.

"Only one way to find out." He began climbing the short ladder. From the top he called down to her, "Come up. There's lots of room. Quite a view, too." When she was sitting next to him on the crude wooden bench, "So, how's it going with Tommy? Has he figured out you've been snooping around his dad's office?"

Nick was right. The tower did offer quite a view. Sort of God's eye. Alice could see over the top of the dune to the party happening on the other side. It was only a couple thousand feet away, but it seemed much farther than that, everything appearing miniature and harmless and unreal, the bonfire made of orange cellophane, the people hired actors. Like it was a play Alice was watching unfold rather than life.

"I didn't snoop," she finally said. "I poked around a tiny bit." Off the look Nick was giving her: "Okay, I snooped. And no he doesn't."

"I'd be careful. He's a sensitive lad, that Tommy. Observant."

Alice bristled at the description of Tommy. "I've got the situation under control," she said tightly.

"Actually, Tommy's not the one with the temper. It's his father. He's the one you've got to watch out for."

Before she realized she'd done it, Alice had shoved her bruised wrist behind her back again. "Like I said, I've got the situation under control."

He laughed softly. "Whatever you say."

The two lapsed into silence for several minutes, both of them with their thoughts.

And then Nick broke the silence, saying, "Oops. Apparently I spoke too soon."

Alice glanced up. "What?"

"Maybe that temper's hereditary after all."

She turned to follow the line of his finger. It was pointing at the party, but the scene had changed completely since the last time she'd observed it. Tommy and Patrick were standing by the bonfire, on the flat spot where Sasha had been dancing. Angry words were being exchanged, though Alice was too far away to make out exactly what words, could just hear the hard, sharp sounds. The boys began circling each other. People had stepped back to give them space, but also to look on, the crowd perking up, rousing itself, sensing that something nasty, vicious, ugly, and very, very fun to watch was about to go down.

Tommy delivered the first blow, connecting with Patrick's nose. There wasn't much shoulder in it, but it was hard enough to give Patrick a dopey-dazed look, cause him to stagger back a few feet. Patrick shook his head a couple times, like he was shaking off the pain, then came at Tommy, driving his fist into Tommy's temple so hard it sent Tommy dancing, almost into the bonfire. Tommy recovered quickly, though, launched himself at Patrick.

Alice had seen enough. She moved to the ladder. Nick blocked her, then put his hand on her shoulder. "The cavalry's coming. You might want to hang back."

"Cavalry? I don't see any cavalry," she said, conscious, as she spoke, of Nick's hand on her. She could feel the warmth of his palm through the fabric of her shirt.

"Not see, hear."

Alice listened and she could pick up, very faintly, the strains of a police siren. "I don't care," she said. "I'm not going to stand here while they kill each other."

"They're not going to kill each other. Just bash each other's brains in a little bit, get their frustrations out. The cops will break it up before they do any real damage."

"I'm still going down."

"Okay, but I wouldn't if I were you. Not if I were me either."

"Why not?"

"I apply to medical school next year. Contrary to what you might expect, a criminal record doesn't improve your chances." His smile was less mocking than teasing. "And besides," he added, "this isn't just underage drinking anymore. Actual physical violence has occurred. They might haul a few people in. Not that they'll be able to hold them, not for long, not if they're local. They'll have to cut them loose after half an hour. Still, they'll do it just to prove they have some authority. Small-town cops and their fragile egos."

"I'm going anyway."

Alice shook Nick off, clambered down the rungs of the lifeguard ladder and hurried up and over the dune.

Charlie couldn't believe it. One second she was talking to Stan about the only serious book she'd ever actually read all the way through—and she was holding her own, too, she could've sworn!—the next second Tommy and Patrick were beating the shit out of each other in front of an enthusiastic crowd. She'd turned to Stan to say as much when Jude flew from the upper-right corner of her vision, landed on top of Stan. Stan was on his feet practically immediately. It was almost as if he'd been expecting the attack. The two boys just started throwing punches, arms a moving blur. Then the cops were there, everything dissolving into a chaos of noise and lights and rush, the *thump thump thump* of music no one had thought to turn off.

Alice grabbed Charlie's arm. "What's going on?" she said, her breath coming fast, in uneven little bursts.

"I don't know. Everything was normal. Then, all of a sudden, it was an outtake from *Fight Club*."

"Well, something must've happened."

"Yeah. I mean, obviously."

"Who started it?"

Charlie looked at her sister. Why was Alice asking these questions? Where had she been? And with who? Clearly not Tommy or Patrick. And why was she so out of breath? Before Charlie had a chance to give voice to her curiosity, though, one of the cops killed the stereo. Her head snapped around.

The two sets of brawling boys had been pulled apart. Tommy and Patrick had received the worst of it, Tommy's eye already bulging in its socket, Patrick's nose a mushy smudge of blood and snot. Jude and Stan hadn't had as much time to inflict damage on each other, but they were pretty beat-up-looking, too. What had gotten into Jude? Charlie wondered. Forget that. No need to wonder. She knew very well what had gotten into him. Jealousy. He'd taken a swing at Stan because he couldn't take one at Cybill. Poor Stan. She was his bad luck charm. Anytime he was around her his life immediately got shittier. And then, as the cops were reaching for their cuffs, about to start fitting them over the boys' wrists, another thought occurred to her, and as it did, a desperate sort of swelling panic rose up in her chest and throat. She spun around to Alice. "We can't let them take Jude in."

"Charlie, don't worry. He's a rich kid at a beach party with two kegs of beer. They won't do anything to him. They just want to prove they have some authority. They'll cut him loose after half an hour."

"No, they won't."

"What do you mean? Why not?"

"He's carrying."

"I thought he wasn't using anymore," Alice said. And then, as if realizing how stupid this remark was, how useless, said, "How do you know?"

"I don't know. Not for sure. But I think he and Patrick went off together earlier."

"They *did* go off together earlier. I saw them." Recognition dawning: "*That*'s what Jude wanted with Patrick? To buy drugs?"

Charlie cut her eyes away from Alice's. "He was upset."

"About what?"

"Something he saw me do."

"You mean, you talking to Stan?"

Charlie's laugh was short and hard, a single syllable. "Okay, by a couple things he saw me do." Her brain started jumping ahead: if Jude got caught with the drugs and he didn't go to jail, he'd go to rehab, for sure, the one that was so bad he couldn't even tell her about it, the one that his politician father sent him to before so he wouldn't disgrace the family. A second stint would break him. Cybill knew it. That's why she was so ferociously protective of him, endangering her own reputation to safeguard his. And now Charlie knew it, too.

Starting to catch Charlie's panic, Alice said, "So Patrick's also carrying?"

"Just pot."

"Since when? He'd know better than to come with drugs if he wanted to get back together with me."

"He got it after," Charlie said uneasily, looking down at Stan's copy of *Gatsby* in her hands.

"After what?"

Charlie hesitated, wanting to lie but afraid to. "After I asked him to."

Alice's eyes went wide, like she couldn't believe what she was hearing. "Jesus Christ, Charlie. You asked him to *score* for you? He doesn't have zillionaire parents like everybody else here. He can't afford a fancy lawyer if he gets busted. Something like this could completely fuck up his future. How could you be so stupid? So selfish?"

"He wasn't able to get much. I'm sure Jude bought all he had." A beat. "Pretty sure, anyway."

Alice clutched at her hair, her eyes wild. "I don't know what to do. I don't think there's anything we *can* do."

And then someone—Bianca, Charlie saw, when she craned her neck—yelled out, "Hey, you can't arrest Jude and Tommy. It was the other two who started it. We don't even know who they are. They crashed the party."

Murmurs of agreement from the crowd quickly turned into choruses of agreement. The cops began conferring with each other, mumble-mouthing in a tight circle. Then an older cop, heavy in the gut but strong-looking, the one who seemed to be in charge, said, "Serenity Point residency passes, everybody. Let's see them. Come on, come on, we don't have all night."

There were a few bitches and moans, but people complied willingly enough, holding out the passes so the cops could shine their flashlights over them, match names with faces. The only two unable to produce: Patrick and Stan.

Charlie almost couldn't believe her eyes when the cops unlocked the cuffs binding Tommy and Jude. Seeing Jude rub his wrists together, she was nearly faint with relief. No drug bust, not even a drunk-and-disorderly. The good feeling only lasted a second, though. Ended as soon as she caught sight of Stan's face. His summer job, his scholarship to Wolcott, his hopes of a scholarship to Yale—everything would turn to dust, and all because of her. A bad luck charm was right. The cops started leading Stan and Patrick to the parked squad cars, the bubble lights still spinning.

"Hey," Jude called out. "I'm the one you should take in. I hit him"—pointing to Stan—"first."

The heavyset cop said, "Looks like he hit you back, son."

"I'm not your son. Not unless my mom's been clowning me all these years. And he was just defending himself. I don't know what got into me. Oh yes, I do. All that beer I illegally obtained with my fake ID."

Jude was lying to the police now, Charlie knew. Goading them. (When she was talking to Stan she'd heard Bianca, behind her, bragging about buying the kegs, getting them delivered to the house while her parents were at the club playing tennis, hiding them in the garage under her dad's Porsche tarp.) Charlie's panic began to turn to terror.

The heavyset cop stared at Jude, chewing the inside of his cheek, for what seemed to Charlie like forever but in reality was probably only a couple seconds. Then he pulled out a key, undid Stan's cuffs. Jude stuck out his wrists so the cop could slap the cuffs on them. The cop shook his head disgustedly, turned away. Once again, Charlie was hit by a rush of relief so powerful she thought she might pass out from it. Jude was safe. Jude *and* Stan were safe. But what about Patrick?

Charlie swung her gaze over to Tommy, anxious to see if he was going to do for Patrick what Jude had done for Stan. And she wasn't the only one. Many of the faces in the crowd were aimed in his direction. His eyes, though, were trained on the ground, stayed trained as the heavyset cop seized Patrick by the arm, started frog-marching him up the beach.

And then the cops were gone in a burst of blue-and-white light, and it was just kids again. A weak, fluttery feeling in the pit of her stomach kept Charlie from moving. All she could do was watch Alice run up to Jude. "Did you buy him out?" Alice said.

Jude turned from her politely so he could spit out a gob of blood-flecked saliva. When he turned back, he gave her a confused look. "Did I buy who out of what?"

"Patrick. Did you buy him out of whatever drugs he had on him?"

"Of course," Jude said, as if insulted. "I was about to go on a bender. You think I'd half-ass it?"

Alice threw her arms around him. He looked at Charlie over Alice's shoulder, the expression in his eyes unreadable. When Alice released him, he began walking down the beach, toward his house. Alice glanced at the patch of sand where Cybill had been sitting, expecting to see Cybill brushing sand off the backs of her legs so she could go join her cousin. But Cybill was already gone.

The cops had confiscated the kegs, not to mention killed the mood. Soon everybody began following Jude and Cybill's lead, heading home or up to the strip of road at the top of the beach where the cars were parked.

Charlie was tucking her Serenity Point residency pass back in her wallet when a split-lipped Stan approached her. She started to speak. He flashed his palm. "Don't say it," he said. "This one wasn't on you."

It was, of course. But she didn't have the heart or the energy to tell him so.

"And it looks like I was wrong about your boyfriend," he said. "So, I'll see you around, Charlie."

Wordlessly, she held out the copy of *Gatsby* to him. He took it, squeezed her shoulder. As she watched him walk down the beach, heading in the opposite direction Jude and Cybill had headed in, a feeling started to creep over her, a mixture of shame and guilt and regret. Tears burned her eyes. Alice slipped a hand in hers.

"Come on, it's late," Alice said, her voice soft. "Let's go home."

The two girls walked in a silence until Richard's house loomed in front of them. Alice's brain was buzzing with so many thoughts she couldn't think them, never mind direct them or put them in any kind of order, certainly never mind voice them. All she could do was stare dumbly at her feet, watch them traversing the sand, one in front of the other. Charlie seemed similarly preoccupied.

Finally, Charlie spoke: "You didn't want to bring Tommy back with you? Mom and Richard come home tomorrow. Sleepovers won't be so easy after that. No walking straight through the front door and up to your room, that's for sure."

Tommy. The most sensitive of sensitive subjects for Alice right now. And, not coincidentally, the subject she most wanted to avoid. Smiling weakly, she said, "Then I guess I'll just have to make one of those sheet-rope thingies that girls make on TV, toss it out the window so he can climb up," and hoped that would be enough to make Charlie back off.

It wasn't. Charlie persisted: "Are you mad at him, though? Letting Patrick just take the fall like that. I mean, Jesus."

"I'm grateful to Jude. What he did was really brave."

"That's not what I asked."

Alice sighed, kicked at a small mound of sand in front of her. "I know it isn't. I'm just not sure how to answer. I guess I don't feel right judging him, judging the decisions he makes. There are things going on with him, with his family, his dad, really, that I don't know about. My sense, though, is that they're bad. You should've seen the inside of that house, Charlie. It's control freak central. Like beyond creepy."

Charlie nodded, though more in a "I hear what you're saying" way than in specific agreement. And Alice could tell she was far from through with the matter, was about to approach it from a different angle.

Heading her off, Alice said with a grin, "Hey, how come your lipstick's all rubbed off?"

Charlie's hand fluttered unconsciously to her mouth. "It was? I mean, it is?"

"Oh yeah, big time. It's almost as if you were wearing none at all."

"Maybe I forgot to put in on tonight."

"Nice try. It was perfectly applied when we arrived at the bonfire. Then I saw you at the fight and it was mostly gone."

"You must be eating more carrots than I realized to be able to see in the dark like that."

"The question is," Alice continued, ignoring Charlie's snotty, sarcastic tone, "who did you rub it off on? It wasn't Jude and it wasn't Stan." She nudged her sister playfully in the ribs. "So, who was it?"

"Probably the cup of beer I was drinking from. Not all of us are little goody-two-shoes teetotalers. So, are we going to talk about what to do about Patrick, or do you want to keeping wasting time with this dumb gossipy stuff?"

Chastened and a little hurt, Alice said, "God, I was just kidding around. You don't have to snap at me. And besides, what can we do about Patrick? We're not eighteen and we're not related to him. There's no way they'll release him into our custody. The important thing is, none of this will go on his record. Thanks to Jude, there's nothing *to* go on his record. We're probably just going to have to let Mom and Richard handle it tomorrow. Do you know what time they're supposed to get back?"

"The plane's scheduled to land in the early evening, six thirty, I think. So they should be back at eight o'clock-ish."

"That's late. We could call his mom. Mrs. O'Brien is such a worrywart, though. She'll flip out. And how's she going to get down here? Bus? Train? Besides if we involve her, Patrick will never forgive us, basically."

Charlie considered. "Maybe we should just wait until morning to make any decisions. I mean, we know he's safe. He's got no drugs on him. And it's a jail in Serenity Point, so it's unlikely he has to worry about not dropping the soap."

"The soap?" Alice said, confused. "What soap?"

"It's an expression. Like, if you want to avoid prison rape, don't drop the soap in the shower."

"There's an expression for that? Wow."

The two girls were laughing softly as they came up on the steps of Richard's deck, began climbing. It wasn't until they reached the top that they saw him: a man, lanky-limbed and lean-jawed with a worn, handsome face, straw-colored hair spilling over the collar of his battered corduroy jacket. He was leaning against the far railing, long legs crossed at the ankle, a duffel bag and an instrument case at his feet. Charlie's father, Alice's too, or so she thought for almost all her life. Phil.

CHAPTER EIGHTEEN

*A*lice ran, jumped into Phil's arms. Burying her face in his neck, she inhaled his familiar scent: soap and cotton and the smoke from the bars and clubs he played in that seeped into the fabric of his clothes, wouldn't wash out no matter how many times Maggie laundered them.

"Hi, baby," he said, in that laconic way of his. Like it'd been days since they'd last seen each other, not months. Like he'd just come back from the store, not another continent. He brushed her hair back from her forehead, his calloused fingers snagging on the loose strands.

"You're here," she observed pointlessly. "In America, I mean."

He confirmed that he was.

"I was at a party. We both were." Alice turned to Charlie, who was hanging back, arms folded tightly across her chest, eyes pointed down at the wooden slats of the deck.

"How you doing, Charlie horse?" he said softly.

Charlie lifted her eyes. "I'm fine," she said, her face composed, her voice free of emotion. "A little tired, though."

"Yeah, I can understand that. It's late."

"Right. So I'm going to bed."

"Charlie—" Alice started.

Charlie spun around. "No," she said, her cool, dispassionate tone coming apart at the seams, her voice breathy with rage. "He can just leave when he feels like it, so I'm entitled to do the same." Not waiting for a response, she pushed past Alice and into the house, slamming the door behind her.

Phil looked at Alice. He gave a low, sad laugh. "That went well."

"She's just being"—pausing, searching for a neutral word—"difficult. You know she gets the meanest when she's the most upset."

"I do."

"I'll go get her."

Phil rubbed his eyes tiredly with the back of his hand. It occurred to Alice to wonder when the last time was he slept. He had his bags with him and that sunken-cheeked, haggard look he got when he was on the road too long. "I'd appreciate it if you would," he said. "I'd rather let her be, let her come to me in her own time, but I don't have that luxury tonight."

"Why not?"

"I can only stay for a few hours. I've got to catch the 6 a.m. bus back to New York. I'm flying to Prague later in the day. I was supposed to go straight from Tokyo, but I wanted to see you two girls first, so . . ." He trailed off.

Alice finished for him: "So you're taking the roundabout route. From the capital of Japan to the capital of the Czech Republic via the Connecticut shore."

He nodded.

"You got picked up by that pianoless quartet again?"

"I did. Another tour of duty. European tour this time."

"Congratulations," she said, knowing how much he loved playing jazz trumpet, how rare the opportunities for him to do so professionally were, most of his work coming from sitting in with rock bands whose music he hated and had no respect for.

"Thank you, baby."

She looked at him, into his calm eyes, the palest of blues, the color of sun-bleached denim. He knew that she wasn't really his daughter, but he didn't know she knew, and he wasn't treating her any different than he always had, was still calling her baby, smoothing back her hair. Emotion surged in her chest She turned away from him so he wouldn't see it. Then she said, "Stay here. I'll bring her down."

Alice entered the house. As she walked deliberately around to the front, passing the portraits of all her Flood relatives going back generations, the men and women with Richard's face, Camilla's face, *her* face, and mounted the massive staircase, she knew the time had come. She had to tell Charlie the truth. If she couldn't find the courage to do it for herself, she'd do it for Phil.

She knocked on Charlie's door.

"Go away," was the muffled response.

"I can't do that," Alice said, and entered.

It took Alice longer than she thought it would to tell the story. It came out in bits and pieces, mostly because of Charlie who alternated between fits of rage and fits of sorrow, interrupting her every other second to pelt her with questions and tears and recrimina-tions. Finally, though, Alice made it to the end.

Charlie was hugging her pillow, eyes swollen and red-rimmed. "Poor Dad, poor Dad," she said over and over again.

"Yeah," Alice said, suddenly feeling more exhausted than she'd ever felt in her life. "He got a rough deal, no doubt about it."

"He let us think all those bad things about him so we wouldn't think bad things about Mom."

"He did."

"Like she deserved his loyalty after the shit she pulled."

"I know."

Abruptly, Charlie threw down the pillow, stood. "I'm going to go see him." At the door, she hesitated. Turning to Alice she said, "Will you come with me?"

"You two should have some time alone together."

"Why?"

Because you're his daughter and I'm not, Alice said but not out loud. Out loud she said, "I'll be down in a bit."

Charlie nodded, shut the door behind her.

Alice sank back onto the bed.

Alice had closed her eyes, just thinking she was going to rest them for a second. The next thing she knew Charlie was shaking her by the shoulders.

At last Charlie let go. "Great. You're alive. I couldn't tell there for a second."

Disoriented, Alice pushed herself up off the pillow. "What time is it?"

"Almost five thirty."

Five thirty. Alice had been asleep for nearly three hours.

"Dad called a cab to take him to the station. It just got here. It's waiting for him in the driveway. He wanted me to get you, though, so he can see you before he goes."

Alice looked at Charlie's face. It was composed but her eyes had a blurred, pink-tinged look. The edges of her nostrils, too. "Did it go okay? I mean, did you talk?"

"We did. It was good, really good. I'm so glad you told me, Allie. I don't think he was going to. He would have let me go on blaming him instead of mom, protecting her even though she doesn't deserve it. He'd have gone off to Europe thinking I hated him . . . " Charlie squeezed her eyes shut as though to ward off this horrible thought. "Anyway, you have to move. He's got to leave in the next few minutes if he's going to make that train."

"But wait a second. Did—"

"We don't have a second. We can talk later. Come on, we have to go downstairs now, before he gets in the cab."

Dazedly, Alice let Charlie pull her to her feet. The two girls stumbled out of the room and down the staircase. They opened the front door.

Phil was leaning against one of the columns, duffel bag slung over his shoulder, instrument case in his hand. A Toyota Prius the color of a school bus was parked in the driveway. Stenciled on the passenger's side were the words *Serenity Point Yellow Taxi Co.*

Alice just stood there, hovering in the doorway, until Charlie gave her a small push forward.

Alice and Phil, only a few feet apart now, regarded each other.

One of those long, long moments. In the leeched, early-morning light everything seemed pale and sad, including his face. Alice stood there, clutching her elbows, doing her best not to let anything happen inside her. She'd thrown herself in his arms when she first saw him. But then she'd simply been reacting, operating on the level of pure animal instinct. Time had passed, though, enough for rational thought to have come into play, and now she felt self-conscious in his presence, aware of how flimsy her connection to him was, of how little claim she truly had on him, of how exhausted he must be from his scene with Charlie, his real child.

"You know," he finally said.

"I know," she said back.

"Did your mother tell you?"

"Only after I made her."

There was a pause, and then he said, "It doesn't change things for me, you know."

"Actually, I didn't know. How could I? You don't call. You don't write." She tried to keep her voice light and easy as she said all this, but it changed midway through. Became heavy with emotion, a trembly little catch in it.

Phil expelled a deep breath, looked out at the horizon, allowing his gaze to float awhile. And then he turned back to her, his eyes falling softly and evenly on her face. "Because," he said, "I figured everybody, me included, needed time to adjust to the new circumstances. It wasn't because I stopped loving you. I never stopped, will never stop. You're my daughter. Do you understand me?"

Alice felt the loose parts inside herself suddenly coming together, drawing tight. And she was unable to see, tears were so clouding her vision. Unable to speak either, emotion fisting up her chest, jamming in her throat. All she could do was nod. And when Phil stepped forward, covering the distance between them, and wrapped his arms around her and squeezed, she squeezed back, as hard as she could.

Alice felt a second pair of arms, Charlie's, wrapping around her, this pair wrapping from behind. And they stood there like that—Alice, Charlie, and Phil—in a three-person embrace, until the cabbie honked his horn twice, impatiently.

Phil patted the top of Alice's arm, then the top of Charlie's, so they'd release him.

"Okay, babies," he said, his voice thick, "I've got to get going. I left all my numbers with Charlie so you'll both be able to reach me if you need me." Then he said what he always said before he went on the road: "Be good girls. Listen to your mother. I'll see you soon." He hugged them each again once more, then he began striding across the small patch of grass over to the driveway.

Alice and Charlie stood side-by-side, frozen in place, watching Phil as he folded his long form into the body of the cab. They listened as the engine choked to life. Once the car began to move, tires churning on gravel, though, they unfroze. They ran after it, following it all the way to the end of the driveway. They waved until they couldn't see it anymore. Waved even after that, Phil's kisses evaporating on their cheeks.

CHAPTER NINETEEN

After seeing Phil off, Alice and Charlie returned to Charlie's room, Alice's limbs heavy and dumb as she climbed the stairs. She knew Charlie would want to talk, and though she didn't feel up to a long and involved conversation about their deeply screwy family situation, was trying to get herself up to it for Charlie's sake. When she opened the door, though, Charlie headed straight for the bed, collapsed on it. Grateful that the therapy session would have to be postponed, Alice collapsed beside her.

She'd just curled into fetal position when she felt something digging into her side. Reaching under her hip, she pulled out a cell phone, Charlie's. *New voicemail,* the screen said. It was from Maggie. Alice turned to Charlie, but Charlie was already asleep, snoring softly.

Alice hit play: "Hi, Pie Face. It's early and you're probably still sleeping. If you wake up and that headache hasn't gone, I want you to take two Tylenol right away. Don't wait or it'll get worse. As soon as you open your pretty eyes. Richard and I are on our way to the airport. We decided to take a morning flight back instead. The trip was fun but we would have had more fun with you and your sister. Give Alice a kiss for me. See you in a few hours."

Alice wanted to roll her eyes, say something sarcastic, if only to herself about Maggie's faux maternal concern, but she couldn't. The truth was, she didn't think Maggie was being phony with the voice-mail, exhibiting faux maternal anything. And the fact that Maggie wasn't being phony or faux made her feel sad. For Maggie, for Phil, for Charlie, for herself.

Ignoring the female robot voice running through the list of options for message disposal, Alice slipped the phone into her pocket. She curved her body in the S of Charlie's, sank into a deep sleep.

Alice was roused by two noises. The first was her ringing cell phone. The second was the sound of one hard object being slammed repeatedly into another hard object. Experiencing a momentary bout of amnesia, she looked over at Charlie, sleeping peacefully beside her, then at the electric clock propped up by a copy of *The Great Gatsby*—what was Charlie doing with *Gatsby*? Had she used it to kill a bug or something?—on the nightstand. It was a few minutes past eight.

The cell rang again. Groggily, Alice pulled it out of her pocket. Patrick's name was flashing across the screen. The events of the previous evening came rushing back at her. Fumbling for the answer button, she wondered if the police were now letting you make your one phone call on your own cell.

"Patrick, hi," she said, trying to sound alert, like she'd been awake for hours, not pounding her ear on a goose-down pillow while he sweated it out behind bars. "Did they say when they're going to let you out?"

"I am out. I'm here, in fact."

"Here where?"

"Here at the house. Who do you think's been banging on the door for the past fifteen minutes? I bet I've broken every knuckle in my body."

"Hang on, hang on," Alice said, crawling over Charlie. "I'll be down in two seconds."

More like ten. Still, though, fast. She flipped the lock on the door, flung it open. Patrick's arm was raised, hand curled in a fist, like he was getting ready to knock on it again.

She gave him the once-over. He was sporting a few cuts and bruises, a fat lip, coagulated blood in the rim of one nostril. And his clothes were a little worse for the wear, his shirt missing a button and a sleeve and his belt, for some reason, hanging out of his pants pocket instead of looped around his waist. Otherwise, though, he seemed undamaged from his night of brawling and big-housing, his eyes clear, his skin flushed, even fresh-looking.

"How'd you get out?" she said, still speaking to him through the cell. Realizing what she was doing, she closed the phone, tucked it in her pocket. "Prison break?"

"Nothing that dramatic."

"Then how?"

He dropped his eyes from her face to his shoes, the left one untied. He knelt to tie it. "They just let me out."

"They didn't require the presence of a guardian or an adult-type person of any kind?"

"Nope."

"That seems weird."

"I was thinking more lucky but okay." He stood. "Look, Alice, they unlocked the cell door for me, opened it. I wasn't about to question them, ask them if they were following proper protocol or whatever. They told me I was free to go, so I went. Walked straight back here."

"I would've picked you up if you'd called."

"I didn't want to bug you." Patrick's mouth stretched into a grin. "Besides, I don't think you'd have heard if I did."

"Yeah, I was pretty zonked," she admitted.

"Plus, the exercise was good for me. It helped clear my head."

"Helped sober you up, you mean."

"That too. And if you want to give me a ride so bad, give me one now."

Alice looked at him, surprised. "To where?"

"Greyhound station. I'm going to put myself on a bus back to Boston before I get in any more trouble."

She sighed. "Yeah, that's probably a smart idea. Not that I'm not sorry to see you go. But this place might have it in for you. Sometimes it's better to run than to fight."

He touched his bloody nostril with the tip of his finger, winced. "Yeah, I've already tried fighting and that didn't work out so great for me. One night in jail was plenty. Unless you think I can talk that Sasha chick into conjugal visits."

"Doubtful."

He laughed.

"Will you let me take you to breakfast before I drive you to the station?"

"Sure." He patted his flat stomach. "I could go for some bacon and eggs and pancakes right about now."

"How about turkey bacon, egg whites, and gluten-free pancakes? You're in Yuppieville now, remember? Greasy-spoon food is hard to come by."

"I really must be hungry because that still sounds good."

Alice turned, about to head to the staircase. "I'm going to go wake up Charlie," she said.

Patrick put a hand on her arm. "Let her sleep."

"You sure?"

"This isn't goodbye, just goodbye for now. I'll see her again soon. And a little alone time wouldn't be such a bad thing, would it?"

No, it wouldn't. In fact, Alice was just thinking how nice it would be to sit with Patrick in some sunny café, sweating pleasantly in the heat, eat until she couldn't eat anymore, knowing she could spend the rest of the day napping. She checked her pockets for her car keys and cell phone. "All set," she said, stepping outside, reaching to close the door behind her.

"Uh, Alice?"

"Yeah?"

"You might want to put on a pair of shoes."

She looked down at her bare feet. "Oh. Right."

Alice retrieved her shoes, Patrick his bag. And then, after Patrick ripped off the other sleeve of his button-down so he more or less matched, the two piled into the Mercedes and lit out for the town center, passing Luz and Fernanda in Luz's old pickup on the long driveway.

Alice and Patrick spent nearly three hours at the Arcadia Café, lingering over plates with crusts of toast on them, smears of ketchup, sipping cup after cup of coffee, talking. He didn't bring up Tommy or Tommy's less-than-honorable behavior the night before, for which she was beyond grateful. And neither, obviously, did she. Mostly they spoke of the past, of things they'd done, times they'd had, people they'd known. Finally, the emptied-out restaurant began to fill back up with lunch trade. Over Alice's protests, Patrick paid the bill. They then returned to the car and Alice drove them to the Greyhound station.

The next bus back to Boston didn't leave for forty-five minutes, so she sat with him on one of the hard wooden benches beside the vending machines, kept him company. They held hands but didn't really talk and there was a distant, sad feeling between them. When the announcement was finally made that the 1:15 p.m. to South Station was ready to board, they both stood, smiled at each other uncertainly.

She walked with him outside. At the bus's door, he stepped out of line, fixed her with his pale blue eyes for a long moment before gazing off at the parking lot, flat and gray and smelling of diesel. His hair lifted slightly in the breeze. Under his freckles and contusions, his face was pale. At last he turned back to her. "Take care of yourself, Al."

"You too."

"And if something's ever wrong, really wrong, you call me. I'll come running."

She nodded.

He started to say something else, she could see it in his face, but then didn't. Just nodded back.

She watched him mount the steps, hand his ticket to the conductor, then watched him through the dark glass as he found a seat and settled in. As she did earlier, Alice waved until the vehicle had driven out of sight and beyond.

She'd parked directly in the sun, so the car was like a heat box. She drove home without bothering to roll down the windows or turn on the air-conditioning.

CHAPTER TWENTY

*A*lice's plan was to crawl into bed, not crawl out again for ten or twelve hours. Just as she was about to turn into the driveway, though, she noticed a slinky black Town Car at the end of it, a man in a dark suit behind an open trunk, struggling to remove several sets of luggage. Richard and Maggie, back from the airport. Of course. How could she have forgotten the voicemail that Maggie left Charlie? The newlyweds had pooped out on their honeymoon, taken an earlier flight. So much for sleeping through their home-coming.

Before she'd made a conscious decision to do so, Alice ground her foot into the gas pedal, shot past the house. No way was she anywhere near the right state of mind to make it through a run-in with those two. Once she hit the beach, she pulled over to the side of the road, parked. She listened to the radio for a while, a classic rock station. When they started playing AC/DC's "Highway to Hell," a favorite of Patrick's, though, she flipped it off. Decided to take a walk instead.

She'd only gone a couple hundred yards when she reached the lifeguard tower, the site of last night's impromptu meeting with Nick. As she touched one of the support beams, the wood rough and splintery under her palm, she remembered that it was surprisingly spacious inside, cool and dry with a wide-planked bench. Maybe she could stretch out up there, take a nap. It didn't occur to her that someone else might have had the same idea until she climbed to the top.

Not that Tommy was sleeping on the bench. He was sitting on it, though. His journal was spread open across his lap, and he was writing in it intently. So intently that he didn't see her until she saw him. Their eyes met, two of hers, one of his, the right eye puffed up and purply, sealed shut.

He closed his journal, slipped it in his pocket, then scooted over so she'd have enough room. She climbed the rest of the way up the ladder, dropped down beside him. Neither spoke. For a long time they took refuge in the view, gazing out at the ocean, hard and blue and, today, smooth-looking, extending in three directions at once. It was Alice who finally broke the silence. "There's something I have to tell you," she said.

"Okay."

There was another silence as she tried to choose her words. And then, tired of being careful with him, of tiptoeing around secrets, his and now her own, she just let the words come, fall out in whatever order felt natural: "I don't believe Camilla killed herself. I've been looking into her death. That night I stayed over at your house—was supposed to stay over, whatever—I broke into your dad's office, opened up his filing cabinet."

Tommy stared at her for a long beat, then let out a soft laugh of disbelief. "So that's what the toothbrush and toothpaste were doing in there. My dad asked me about them."

"He was Martha Flood's doctor. You never told me."

"No. I didn't."

"Why?"

"Why didn't I tell you?" That soft disbelieving laugh again. "Because I didn't want you to know, obviously."

"Was he Camilla's doctor, too?"

Tommy's eyes suddenly flashed with anger. "Do you really think I'd let my dad get that up close and personal with my girlfriend? See her naked, examine her, pinch her, prod her, all that?"

Her voice tentative, nearly apologetic, Alice said, "I didn't know if it would be up to you. I kind of get the sense that he calls the shots in your house."

"Most of them, but not all. Not all," Tommy repeated, sighing and closing his eyes, the anger dying down as quickly as it flared up.

For several seconds Alice gazed at his still face with the closed lids, perfectly beautiful and serene, even with the plum-colored shiner. She began picturing him resting in the most permanent way possible: in his coffin. And once she started, she couldn't stop. Shaking her head to rid herself of the ghoulish image, she said, "I don't see why you'd keep the Martha thing from me. Who cares if your dad was her doctor?"

Tommy, his eyes still closed, "I thought you might."

"Why, though? So she died under his watch. It's not like cancer doesn't kill a lot of people. It's pretty much an act of God. Unless—" Alice paused.

And as she did, Tommy's eyes blinked and opened wide. Wet and scared, they were on her. But she wasn't looking back at him. Instead she was staring down at the tops of her thighs, working her way through the set of known facts, the slow, steady buildup of revelations paralyzing her.

She flashed back to the club's Luau Clambake earlier in the summer.

It was just after Dr. van Stratten's malpractice trial had ended, was the family's first public appearance since the verdict had been handed down. They were treated like lepers at the party, like what they had was contagious, people afraid even to go near them, never mind talk to them. And then Richard, as casual and relaxed as could be, had strolled up to Dr. van Stratten, slapped him on the back, asked him about his golf game, kissed Mrs. van Stratten on the cheek, shook Tommy's hand. And once Richard did this, other people began approaching them, too, tentatively at first but soon boldly. It was as if the all clear had been given. Richard had single-handedly saved the van Strattens from social ruin that night, and Alice had admired him for the magnanimity of the gesture.

What if, though, the rescue had been performed not out of kindness, as she had thought at the time, but out of obligation, or worse, self-preservation? When Martha was alive, Richard had had a problem: a mistress he was in love with and a wife he wasn't, a wife already knocking on death's door. And Dr. van Stratten had had the solution: the means of giving the wife a gentle nudge through that door. What's more, he had a professional disposition that was of a people-pleasing bent, or rather, according to Nick, a people-with-money-pleasing bent. What if Richard and Dr. van Stratten had come to some sort of mutually beneficial arrangement? Had killed Martha Flood together? Were each other's alibis and each other's covers?

"Unless," Alice continued slowly. "Unless—"

"Oh, Jesus, oh, no," Tommy moaned.

"God was given an assist."

"I don't know for sure. Neither did Camilla."

"But you both suspected?"

"She did. I didn't." Tommy paused. She saw him swallow. Then he said in a lower voice, almost a whisper, as if it hurt his throat to utter the actual words, "At least I didn't until later."

Alice felt dizzy suddenly, like she was swaying, or the tower was. She was right about Richard: he was a wife murderer after all. Saying something just to prove she could, "How could your dad do it?" She tried to laugh, but her tongue wouldn't roll, lay there at the bottom of her mouth. "Technically, I mean, not morally."

"It's so easy, Alice, you can't even believe. In Mrs. Flood's condition, stage IV breast cancer, the cancer already spread to her liver, she was just incredibly vulnerable. If she missed her medication a single day, she'd go downhill so fast your eye wouldn't even see her. And that's pretty much what happened. She was improving, improving, improving, and then she was dead. Almost as soon as they sent her home from the hospital under my dad's care. I'm talking days, not weeks. The type of cancer she had could take a wrong turn at any time, but hers took a really wrong turn at an especially opportune time. Opportune, I mean, for your stepdad and my dad. Not so opportune for Mrs. Flood."

"And Camilla knew about my mom? That she and Richard were involved?"

"Yes. I don't know how she figured out about the affair but she did."

"She wouldn't tell you?"

"I wouldn't listen." Dropping his face in his hands, "God, why wouldn't I listen?"

His shoulders were shaking and he was producing these weird strangled, hiccup-y sounds, like a kind of dry sobbing. To comfort him, Alice considered revealing her true relation to Richard—after all, she was implicated in this crime, too, even if only genetically—but then decided not to. Her plan, she realized, could backfire, could make him feel worse, not better: he failed to save not just his ex-girlfriend but her half sister. And the guilt was clearly already almost killing him. If he took on any more, he might break. "When did you think Camilla was right?" she said.

Tommy looked up, laughed. Made a sound that was laugh-like, anyway. "When it was too late, of course. When she was already dead. I wasn't ready to hear it before, I guess. That's really why we broke up. I mean, the cheating was a problem, but I was getting sort of used to it even though she was throwing it more and more in my face, gossiping about it with Nick, the two of them snickering at me, laughing outright sometimes. But I couldn't let her talk about my dad that way. To me, my dad was a great man. Not a good man maybe. A great man, though. I knew he was kind of an asshole as a person, a tyrant in the house, pushed me and my mom around. But as a doctor he was the opposite of an asshole. He was a healer. He had control over life and death. And he'd built this thriving practice from scratch. Other people, rich people, powerful people, people who ran companies, were at the very tops of their fields, came to him, depended on him to cure them, to make them better. So to listen to Camilla question his professional integrity was not an easy thing for me. Like I said, he's an asshole, but also he's . . . he's . . ."

"He's your dad," Alice finished for him.

"Right, he's my dad."

"What changed for you after she died?"

Tommy looked away from Alice, his eyes positively fleeing hers.

"You think your dad killed her," she said, speaking the words almost before she thought them, as if her mouth was working faster than her brain. And when there was no denial, the dizzy feeling came rushing back at her, bringing with it a sense of claustrophobia as well, like the walls of the lifeguard tower were shrinking, closing in on her.

After a minute or so of shocked silence on both sides, Alice said, "But how would your dad know that she suspected him?"

This time Tommy didn't even look at her.

"Because you told him," she said, again speaking the words before she knew she'd thought them.

"Camilla was dead a few hours later."

The silence that followed this statement was beyond shocked. It was empty, totally white and blank. For a second Alice was breathless with hatred of Tommy, the hot, dark emotion surging through her body, causing swirling black dots to break out behind her eyes. He didn't just fail to save Camilla, he practically helped murder her. But then Alice reminded herself that the only thing he was truly guilty of was trusting the wrong person—his dad, who he was hardwired to trust, like genetically programmed to put his faith in—and the surge passed, her vision cleared.

"What about Richard?" she said.

Tommy stared at her, lips parted slightly as he struggled to understand her meaning. When comprehension at last arrived, he said, his voice rising, "Like, was Mr. Flood involved in hurting Camilla? My God, no. Never. He loved Camilla more than anything. I don't even know for sure if my dad hurt her. Not for sure."

"Seems like a pretty safe assumption to make to me."

A heavy sigh. "To me, too. If he did"—breaking off, trying again—"if my dad did do something to Camilla, no way was Richard a part of it."

Relieved to know that there was a limit to her biological father's evil, Alice was quiet for a moment. Then she said, "Is that why you didn't want anyone to know we were dating? Because it might get back to your dad?"

Tommy managed a guttural, "Yes."

"So, he's the threat?"

No response. She turned to him but couldn't see his face. It was averted, aimed at the floor.

"Tommy, is that right? Is he the one you wanted to protect me from?"

His head stayed down.

"Tommy, look at me. Please. Tommy."

Finally he lifted his face, raised his eyes. They were a horrible sight to behold, one sealed up inside its swollen, livid socket, the other dead-alive, full of torment. "That's the thing," he said miserably. "I can't protect you from him. I can't even protect me from him. That's why I didn't speak up when the police led your friend away in cuffs last night, slunk off like a coward. I'm terrified of him, of what he'll do."

"There's no reason you're going to have to protect me. He won't find out about us."

"He will."

"How? It's not like he's plugged into the teen grapevine. And I promise I won't start hanging out at your house, wearing your varsity letterman jacket, asking your mom to show me baby pictures."

She intended the last line as a joke, but Tommy didn't laugh, didn't even appear to have heard her. "Everything I love, he tries to destroy. I can't let him destroy you, too. Not like he did Camilla."

Tommy's lips were still moving but the words they formed were lost to her. Blood was rushing to her ears, and the sound took up all her hearing. He loved her. That's what he was telling her, that's what he meant. He loved her as she loved him. She felt a peace and sweetness spreading through her.

The blood died down in her ears. She could hear again.

"My dad's stronger than I am," Tommy was saying, "smarter than I am, tougher than I am, more everything than I am. And I—" He stopped, unable to continue, an anguished sound coming from the back of his throat.

She thought he'd turn away from her, not want her to see him in so raw a state. After all, he'd always been guarded around her, closed off even, careful of what he said, determined to protect her and himself. That masculine-code-of-silence thing, absorbing pain, never showing any. Stoic. But the look he was giving her now was one of extreme vulnerability and openness, and it moved her. He was trusting her with his secret and his shame: he'd been the victim of his father. All at once, she felt overwhelmed by emotion, almost as overwhelmed as he was.

"Tommy," she said, managing to keep her voice from cracking but barely, "what happened to Camilla wasn't your fault. You couldn't have known."

He lurched forward suddenly, leaning into her, and moaned, "I hate him."

She put her arms around his shoulders and drew him to her.

His next statement was unclear, emerging muffled and muted because his mouth was buried in her neck. She could make out the words *I'm* and *sorry* and *Camilla,* but couldn't tell if it they formed a complete sentence or if a couple nouns and verbs had gotten lost on the way.

It didn't matter. She stroked his hair, bent to kiss his cheek. At the last second, though, he turned, instead meeting her lips with his own. She opened her mouth in surprise—she'd only meant to comfort him—but that just drew him deeper inside her. She couldn't believe the intensity of his need. She could feel it in his kiss. It was beyond hungry, it was devouring. For a moment she thought of resisting. This was too much, too soon. Emotions were heightened and all overlapping and jumbled up. Not just his but hers as well. She needed a chance to think this through, decide if this was what she really wanted.

And then she thought, *Yes. Yes, it is. Yes, yes, yes.*

She fell back onto the wooden bench. He fell with her.

CHAPTER TWENTY-ONE

*T*he night before the memorial, Alice dreamed of Camilla. They were on a train, the two of them moving quickly from compartment to compartment. The seats were filled with people from the club, their faces and eyes all pointed forward as she and Camilla lurched down the aisles. Though she didn't hear anyone behind them, Alice knew they were being pursued.

They came to the end of another compartment.

Alice stopped. "Can we rest for a second?" she said, bending at the waist, both hands on her knees, sucking air.

Camilla, in the white dress from last year's July Fourth party, turned to her. "Later. Not now. We have to keep going." Her words were urgent but her voice was not, was, in fact, inflectionless, lifeless, matching her face, which was blank and glazed over.

"Why?"

"So we don't get caught."

"By who?" Alice said. And when Camilla didn't respond, "Camilla, who's after us?"

"Not after us. After me."

"Just you?" Alice was ashamed of the question even as she asked it.

"Yes, but if I leave you behind, you could get mistaken for me. Things could happen to you. Bad things."

Craning her neck, looking forward, Alice said, "But we're at the end of the train. No more cars. What do we do?"

"We keep going, like I said."

Camilla opened the door in front of them. There was an on-slaught of streaming air so powerful it felt to Alice like a series of blows to her head and body, one after another. Camilla stepped out onto the tiny platform, the very last bit of train. It was night, the black surrounding them so utter Alice could see nothing in it but Camilla's pale face, Camilla's glowing eyes.

"Go where?" Alice's words were torn apart by the wind almost as soon as they were out of her mouth.

Camilla gestured to the surrounding darkness.

"How?" Alice said.

"We jump."

"If we jump, we die."

"Maybe, maybe not." Camilla glanced over Alice's shoulder. "We're not alone anymore."

Just as Alice was about to turn, find out the identity of their pur-suer, Camilla reached for her hand, pulled her out onto the platform. Now instead of pushing her back, the air suctioned her forward.

"Come on," Camilla said. "There's no more time." She swung her legs over the railing.

Not knowing what else to do, Alice mimicked her. They were

leaning forward, grasping the metal rod with their hands. Alice could feel the vibrations from the train's engine traveling from her feet up her legs to her back, even to her neck.

"Are you afraid?" Camilla said.

As Alice nodded she could scarcely bring her eyes up to Camilla's face. She dreaded the look of contempt she knew she'd find there, contempt or the former blankness. But Camilla's expression was one of kindness and sympathy.

"It's easy to be brave. Just don't think. Do you trust me?"

"I trust you," Alice said, discovering the truth in the words as she spoke them.

"Then do as I do."

And with that command, Camilla released her hold on the rod. Instead of falling into the darkness, though, she waded into it, like it was made of water rather than air. It swallowed up her feet first, then her knees and thighs, circling her waist and breasts. In no time at all, there was nothing visible but the top of her head. Then just a few strands of floating blond hair. Then not even that. She was gone, without a ripple or trace.

Alice tried to undo her grip on the rod so she could follow but was unable to. She was too frightened. Her hands only curled around the rod tighter. She couldn't bear the thought of disappearing into that deep darkness. Even less, though, could she bear the thought of disappointing Camilla. She licked her lips. No thinking, just acting. On the count of three, she told herself, she'd let go. "One . . . two . . ."

And just before her mouth formed *three*, she woke up.

•   •   •

A decision had been made to hold the memorial at the club. Alice was wearing a dress she'd run into town a few hours earlier to buy. She'd realized that morning that she owned no black formal wear. Had been forced to go to Richard for the necessary funds when Maggie proved unavailable, was tied up on the phone with a caterer or a florist or something.

Alice had found Richard in his office, sitting in his leather chair, the back so high it resembled a throne. His face was pointed toward the window, the view of the ocean outside lovely and vast, sparkling blue stretching out all the way to the horizon. She didn't think, though, that he was actually looking at it. Or rather, he was looking at it without actually seeing it. A legal pad was in front of him and a fountain pen, the legal pad unwritten upon, the pen capped.

Hating to ask him for anything but unable to think of an alternative—she'd so looked down on Charlie for accepting that iPhone from him—she'd said, "I don't have a dress," getting right to it.

Richard had gone from staring blankly out the window to staring blankly at her face. Seconds ticked by. Then more seconds. She was about to give up, forget it, just make do with whatever was in her closet, let him go back to zoning out at the Atlantic, when he blinked twice, his eyes slow-focusing on hers. "For the memorial, you mean?"

She'd nodded.

He'd reached for his wallet. "Then you'll have to get one. But you'll need money to do that, won't you, sweetheart?"

It was the first time he'd used a term of endearment with her. And it had made the skin over her entire body go hot and crawly, too tight over her flesh.

"How much, do you think?" he'd said, looking up at her.

"You tell me. I'm not used to shopping at anything but thrift stores."

"I should imagine a couple hundred would cover it. But spend as much as you like. Here," he'd said, handing her a credit card, shiny and black with the familiar—familiar from TV commercials, not from life—logo of the Roman soldier guy in profile at the center of it. "Take my AmEx. I'm low on cash at the moment."

She'd pocketed the card without saying thank you.

"Can I give you a lift?" he'd said.

"I'd rather drive myself."

He'd smiled at her but his eyes were sad. For a second, she'd felt sad, too, then, reminding herself who he was—a liar, a cheater, a killer, a monster—toughened up. "I'm not really in the mood for company. You know how it is." She'd meant to sound hostile and, with pleasure, realized that she did.

He'd nodded. "I do. Okay, well, be careful."

She'd exited the office, leaving him to his blank legal pad and spectacular, if unseen, ocean view, and headed straight up to Je Ne Sais Quoi. Walking through the door, credit card in hand, she'd told the snooty salesgirl what she needed, let the salesgirl clothe and un-clothe her like a doll until something suitable was found. She'd signed the bill without looking at it. Had worn the dress out of the store.

The hours since Maggie and Richard had come back from Palm Beach had been strange ones. Apart from Alice's scene with Richard in his office and a brief encounter here and there, the sisters had managed to avoid the prodigal honeymooners almost entirely. Alice hadn't returned home the previous day until well after nightfall. By the time she was ascending the front staircase to her room—and *ascending* was the word for it, floating up to the second floor as if on a cloud—dizzy-dazed, thrilled, reveling in the loss of her virginity, still smelling Tommy on her skin, Charlie, eyes puffed with sleep, hair a rat's nest, was just emerging from hers. Maggie and Richard were out, presumably at the club for dinner. The two girls had decided to walk into town, get something to eat, then take a cab back after the rest of the house had, hopefully, gone to bed.

Alice and Charlie had lucked out: all went according to plan. The windows in the master bedroom were dark when they'd returned from Blue Basil, the house silent. It had been a surprisingly fun night, both girls feeling loose, a little unsprung. Charlie was in especially high spirits since she'd used her fake ID to purchase several penacaradas, an apparently lethal Thai cocktail, a mixture of rum and coconut milk and God knows what else, and had become part of a conspiracy besides, allowing Alice to talk her into not telling Maggie that she knew the truth about Richard.

"Okay, okay, my lips are sealed," Charlie had said after Alice impressed upon her, several times, the need for complete secrecy, the importance of not letting on to Maggie that she was in any way wise to what was going on. "You don't have to tell me again. Message received. Mum's the word when it comes to Mum."

Alice, relieved that Charlie was complying with her wishes, not giving her the usual fight, had leaned back in her chair. "Great. You get it."

"I get it, yeah. I'd have to be severely retarded in the head not to get it." A pause. "Only, actually, I sort of don't get it. Why all the"—raising her index finger to her face in a shushing gesture except missing her lips, hitting her cheek instead—"hush-hush, cloak-and-dagger business? I mean, what's up with that?"

"I just need a bit more time to, like, work things out," Alice had said. Quickly adding, "Not much more time, though."

Charlie had picked up her glass, roughly the size of a fishbowl and containing a liquid that managed to look both froufrou and sinister at once, then put it down again. She'd waggled a finger at Alice in cheerful reproach. As she did, the tiny paper cocktail parasol she'd stuck behind her ear fell to the tablecloth. "You're being annoyingly vague," she'd said, "but I'm going to let you get away with it."

"I appreciate that."

"Just this once."

"Thank you."

"I'll play dumb with Mom and Richard, pretend like I'm still in the dark."

"I really am grateful," Alice had said. And when she saw that wasn't enough, buttressed it with, "Like, beyond grateful."

Charlie had nodded, finally satisfied. "So long as you know how nice I'm being."

"I really, truly do."

A few minutes later, the girls had walked out of the restaurant. (Well, Alice had walked. Charlie more lurched.) Alice had scooped a handful of mints on the way out the door on the off chance that their mom was still up and in a breath-sniffing mood. She'd left the waitress a very large tip.

●　●　●

The day was dedicated to grieving. Consequently, mandatory family breakfast had not been mandatory that morning. Alice had run downstairs early, grabbed a bottle of extra-strength Tylenol in case Charlie woke up with a hangover, which she never did, and one of the brown paper bags of fruit Luz had picked up at the farmers market earlier. Alice had smuggled the goods up to Charlie's room. While they were sitting on Charlie's bed, cross-legged, peeling back the skins on a pair of bananas, Maggie had knocked.

"Girls," she'd said, poking her head around the door, "the memorial starts at four so we should be dressed and ready to go over to the club no later than three thirty, okay?"

"Is Richard coming with us?" Alice had asked.

"No, he's going to head over earlier."

"Why?"

Maggie had appeared surprised by the question. "Why? So he has time to prepare, I should imagine. He wants to make sure everything's ready, that the club's organized the event according to his specifications. This is something he's obviously very anxious to go smoothly."

Alice had nodded like she understood, but the truth was she didn't. It was a mystery to her how Richard had been maneuvered into staging the memorial in the first place when it was apparent from his encounter with Muffie Buckley that it was pretty much the last thing he wanted to do. And then she thought, *Maybe not such a mystery after all.* Maybe guilt was dictating his behavior. When she and Charlie had moved into his house those many weeks ago, Richard had maintained that Camilla died in a car accident, a sad but by no means unusual case of a young driver losing control of her vehicle with fatal consequences. It wasn't until Alice met

Cybill at the summer solstice party that she learned Camilla's death was widely regarded as a clear-cut instance of suicide, a girl out of her mind with grief over the loss of her mother deciding to end it all. Richard's denial, his refusal to accept the facts—and while these facts were in question at the moment, *he* had no idea they were in question, that they'd ever been in question—signaled to Alice a man on bad terms with his conscience. And now she grasped how he got there: he'd snuffed out the life of Martha, which he believed had, in turn, snuffed out the life of Camilla. A memorial might be his way of trying to atone.

Alice had been too preoccupied with these thoughts to engage with Maggie. And Charlie had been too busy not looking at Maggie to engage with Maggie either, Alice was noticing. If Charlie didn't snap out of it, start acting like her usual good-natured self, Maggie would catch on that something was up. Might have caught on already. She was studying Charlie, a peculiar expression on her face.

Alice had covered by saying, "Of course we'll be ready at three thirty, Mom. Death talk is kind of heavy so early in the morning. You just took us by surprise, that's all. Right, Charlie?"

When Charlie remained stubbornly silent, Alice had shot her a look, and Charlie managed a grudging, "Uh-huh."

Maggie had looked at Alice in mystification and Alice mouthed the words, "Boy trouble."

Maggie had given an understanding nod, ultra-subtle, back, then said, "Honey, do you have anything to wear today? I've been going through your closet in my mind and I'm coming up empty."

"Don't worry. I've got stuff," Alice had said, not realizing at that moment that she didn't.

"Okay, good. And, baby, when you pull back your hair, make sure you don't let it get too flat on top. Poof it a little. It drags your whole face down when you forget to. All you have to do is tease a couple of strands at the front and . . ."

Just how to blame are you? Alice had asked herself as she watched Maggie delivering this extremely familiar piece of grooming advice, looking so innocently and cutely momish standing there in the doorway: hair rolled up into curlers, skin iridescent with cold cream, little cotton balls stuffed between her freshly painted toes. *What do you know? Did Richard tell you how he cleared the path for you, disposed of your predecessor? Did it bother you or were you so overwhelmingly happy to have what you wanted after all those years of being denied that you didn't care?* And the biggest question of all: *Did he tell you about the act when it was a done deal or when it was still in the planning stages?* No, not the biggest question of all. The biggest question of all because it was the question underneath every other question: *How much am I going to have to make myself hate you when I find out the truth?*

For a second, Alice had wished passionately, with her entire heart and soul, that she could just drop it, drop all of it: forget about Camilla and Martha, the secret history of Maggie and Richard's relationship, the Dr. Kevorkian-like antics of Tommy's father. But she couldn't drop it. It was far too late in the game for a memory wipe. She had to see this thing through to the bitter end, no matter how much she didn't want to, no matter how painful it became, no matter how high the cost.

As soon as Maggie shut the door behind her, Charlie had collapsed back on the bed, jammed a pillow over her face, and screamed into it. Alice had understood just how she felt.

CHAPTER TWENTY-TWO

*A*t a quarter to four, Alice followed Maggie and Charlie inside the clubhouse. There was a blown-up picture of Camilla—a school photograph it looked like, a cropped shot of her head and shoulders against a solid blue background, her smile broad and uncomplicated and totally false—placed on easels at various spots around the room. Guests, mostly members but not all, were clad in gloomy-colored clothes, not the usual pastels. And classical music was being pumped into the air at a low volume via overhead speakers. And yet the atmosphere, Alice observed, was oddly party-like: cheese-and-cracker plates were circulating; lavish flower arrangements were decorating every table; dressed-up people were chitchatting with one another; there was even the occasional burst of laughter, though always cut off at the halfway mark, as if the person abruptly remembered that any expression of joy in the present circumstances was in poor taste.

In the back corner, Alice spotted Tommy standing with his father and mother. Standing with his mother at least. There was a small but distinct space separating him from Dr. van Stratten, his shoulders angled away from his father an all-important degree or two. He was speaking in body language, his message subtly delivered yet emphatically clear: a rejection of Dr. van Stratten. Tommy was wearing a dark suit and a matching pair of dark glasses, either to hide his black eye or his red-rimmed ones. Maybe both.

When Tommy saw Alice, he gave her a nod of acknowledgment, very slight. It was enough for her, though. Honestly, it was enough for her just to be in the same room with him, to know he was only a couple feet away, to know what they were to each other, what they'd become yesterday in the lifeguard tower: real boyfriend and girlfriend, in love and sleeping together. She gave him an even slighter nod back, then turned so as to avoid the temptation of focusing on him, risk tipping off his father that something was going on between them.

Nick, she saw, had come to pay his respects, too, also at the back, but in the opposite corner. He was dressed, as usual, in a neat suit and tie, white shirt, wingtips. Though for once his clothes didn't cause him to stick out. His face, however, did, its angularity and sharpness and general lean-and-hungry look making most of the faces around him appear piggy and complacent. He was standing in front of the memorial guest book, a pen in his hand. At the sight of him, Alice's heart leapt, caught on her ribs. All day long she'd been wanting to swing by Dr. Rose's office, wait until he came out for lunch or a breath of fresh air, tell him about her encounter with Tommy (minus the fade-to-black part, of course; her sex life was her business), dissect it with him, hear his thoughts.

There hadn't been enough time for a stakeout, though. Not enough time and, also, as much as she'd wanted to tell him about the encounter, at the same time she hadn't wanted to tell him about it at all. She was afraid to, frankly. Was afraid even to go near him because she sensed that when he looked at her, he'd know what she'd done with Tommy. Would be able to see it in her eyes. It's not like she thought her loss of virginity was a visible thing. It wasn't like the loss of a tooth. But Nick was so smart, so perceptive. He'd be able to tell. She just knew it.

Still. He was here. And there was no way she was going to let him escape today without coughing up his basic contact information. He glanced up suddenly and their eyes met. Now her heart was beating so fast and loud it sounded like a fist pounding on a heavy door. What would he do when he read the truth in her face? What would he say?

But Nick did nothing. Said nothing. He merely winked at her, then returned his attention to the guest book.

So he didn't notice anything different about her after all. Huh. Relieved that her secret was safe from him, but—unexpectedly, weirdly—disappointed, too, she moved her gaze along. The bar was open in the dining room, and, surprise, surprise, Jude and Cybill were striking a pose against it. (Guess they'd mended whatever rift had taken place at the bonfire.) The cousins were the only two in the club in pale clothes, Jude in his seersucker suit and Cybill in a dress that Alice recognized from the Fourth of July video as well as from her dream, the white one that belonged to Camilla. Alice wondered if it had, in fact, belonged to Cybill and Camilla had borrowed it for the occasion, or if Camilla had later given it to Cybill, or if maybe Cybill had just taken it from Camilla's closet after Camilla died—a keepsake. Jude was holding a glass of something clear. Vodka most likely, since Ketel One was such a hit with the Serenity Pointers. Both he and Cybill were watching Charlie from their respective perches. Neither, however, approached Charlie.

No one was approaching any of them, Alice realized, not her or her sister or her mother. Plenty of covert glances, though, were being thrown in their direction. Well, it was to be expected, she supposed. It's not as if people could offer them condolences on the loss of a person they'd never met. As Richard's stepfamily, their status was weird, ambiguous, contradictory: they were intimates and strangers at the same time.

Charlie turned to Maggie. "Where's Richard?" she said. Her tone was casual, but her hostility showed in the way she was holding her body: head thrust aggressively forward, eyes narrowed, hook-like, at the corners, elbows jutting out of her torso at sharp angles so that the top layer of her San Pellegrino was spilling over the rim of her glass.

Fortunately, Maggie seemed too preoccupied to notice. "I was just wondering the same thing."

"So, what's the answer?"

"I can't give you one. He must be around here somewhere."

"Well, I don't see him."

"He left for the club a full hour before we did." Maggie smiled. "I can't imagine he got lost on the way."

Not returning the smile, Charlie said, "But shouldn't he be on hand to, like, talk to his guests or whatever?"

"He'll turn up."

"Yeah, but when? This feels kind of awkward. Like he's using us to do his dirty work or something."

Maggie's patience finally snapped. "Awkward for you, devastating for him. And what dirty work exactly are you doing? I don't think you're in danger of breaking any child labor laws sipping mineral water while your stepfather takes a few minutes to be by himself before delivering a speech memorializing his dead teenage daughter." Then, softening her voice, "I'm sure he's someplace private, mentally preparing. As you can imagine, this isn't easy for him. People will just have to wait until afterward if they want to say something."

"In the meantime," Charlie said, "they can just stare at us, whisper behind their fans."

"Gee, I will be so glad when you and this boy that you're apparently having such trouble with make up because you really are acting like a little pill."

Charlie released a snort of air but otherwise didn't react to the name-calling.

For another ten minutes or so, Alice, Charlie, and Maggie stood in a stiff cluster, not speaking or even really looking at each other. At last the grandfather clock struck four and people began drifting toward the garden area out back. Maggie put down her water glass and followed them. After exchanging a quick glance, Charlie and Alice did the same. It hadn't occurred to Alice until that moment how odd it was that a memorial service was being held at a country club. Or maybe, she thought as she stepped outside, it wasn't odd at all. The club certainly seemed prepared to accommodate: the croquet set had been removed, the little holes left by the wickets filled in, rows of folding chairs had been placed under a striped canopy, and there was a sort of makeshift stage at the front with a lectern on it, behind which, Alice assumed, Richard would be addressing the crowd. People began seating themselves, leaving the front row empty for immediate family, the center spot of which was already claimed.

The sight of Richard's mother and Camilla's grandmother—Alice's grandmother too, Alice realized—made Maggie stop, if just briefly, in her tracks. Mrs. Flood was wearing a chic navy suit and spectator pumps. Her hair, the same as her son's, every bit as heavy and lustrous, only her shade of gray was the silvery gray of smoke rather than the steely gray of a gun, was twisted up into an elegant chignon. Her strong features were poised and her body language stylish, her back perfectly straight in her chair, her legs crossed supplely at the knee, her hands folded gracefully in her lap. She must've been very beautiful when she was young, Alice thought, since she was very beautiful now and she had to be coming up on eighty if not already past it.

Alice broke away from her mom and sister. "Hi, Nana," she said, the name Mrs. Flood had requested she and Charlie address her by when they'd visited her at her house in Darien earlier in the summer. Alice was afraid that Mrs. Flood would take a look at her, start to unravel just like the last time. Mrs. Flood, though, was prepared this time for the shock of the resemblance. She smiled at Alice composedly, tilted her cheek to accept a kiss, then patted the chair next to her. Alice sat down.

It occurred to Alice that she'd never had a grandmother. At least, she'd never had a grandmother that she'd met, both Maggie's and Phil's moms having died before she was born. Mrs. Flood, though, was everything she could have wished for in one. She hoped

Mrs. Flood was similarly pleased. Then again, Mrs. Flood's only other granddaughter was Camilla, so her standards were no doubt extremely high.

Alice noticed that Mrs. Flood was looking at her expectantly. It hit her that she didn't know what to say. After fumbling around in her head for a suitable topic of conversation, she said, "Pretty day," embarrassed to have to resort to weather talk but unable to come up with anything else.

Mrs. Flood agreed that it was.

"Was your drive down okay?"

"Oh yes, easy as could be. Richard very sweetly arranged to have a driver pick me up."

"Is he nice?"

"She. And quite nice. Kerry is her name. Kerry will be taking me home as well."

Mrs. Flood had an accent, Alice noticed. Not a city or regional accent, an accent like people from her hometown had, like Patrick had and like she and Charlie had escaped having because Maggie had freaked out anytime either showed the slightest sign of developing one, but an accent like actresses in black-and-white movies had. Faintly British. Enunciating every word fully, her *t*'s hard and crisp. Avoiding contractions.

Alice was ransacking her brain for yet another benign question when Mrs. Flood reached out and took her hand, squeezed it, as if to tell her that conversation wasn't necessary. Gratefully she squeezed Mrs. Flood's hand back and, heeding the silent advice, went into observer mode. She focused her attention on the line of people continuing to file into the garden. Sasha, who Alice had somehow missed in the clubhouse, was with her parents, as was Bianca. Sasha caught Alice's eye, smiled, and made a face as she followed her mom and dad down a middle row. Lucy, the tennis instructor, was in attendance, as were Fernanda and Luz, a teary-eyed preteen girl holding Luz's hand. Must be Luz's niece, the one Camilla had tutored.

Finally everybody was seated, including her mom and sister, Charlie next to her, Maggie next to Charlie, as far away from Mrs. Flood as politeness allowed. The two women nodded at each other but did not speak. And then Alice heard a hush fall, felt a slight stirring of air and twisted her shoulders to look: Richard striding down the narrow aisle and up to the stage. His face was so white and rigid it was less like his face, more like a mask of his face. When he was parallel with the lectern, he turned, stepped behind it, his movements stiff, as if his joints needed oiling. For a long time, he just stood there staring out at the collection of people assembled before him. A small wind gusted and his hair lifted; the cuffs of his pants snapped against his ankles.

At last he cleared his throat. "My daughter's life was far too short. And she was taken from me far too soon. And not a single day goes by that I don't think about her or wish that it was me under those six feet of dirt instead." He lifted his hand, curled it into a fist, and brought it down so hard that it smashed through the thin plank of wood covering the lectern. There was a collective gasp from the crowd.

Richard gazed down at his hand, now uncurled, absently, as if it didn't belong to him. Blood trickled from it onto the stage floor. With a ghastly sort of composure, he dragged it across his chest, smearing red on his lapels, his tie, his pristine white dress shirt.

Standing there, the breeze mussing his hair, the sun touching his wedding band, making it glitter, he seemed entirely unaware that he'd done anything at all strange. "Not a single day," he repeated quietly.

And with that, he stepped off the stage and strode back down the aisle and into the clubhouse. The door closed behind him. Silence welled.

Ten minutes later, everyone was back in the clubhouse. There'd been a period of confusion after Richard's exit. His speech was so brief in length, so abrupt in delivery, so violent in execution that the mourners didn't know what to do, what was expected of them. Was that all there was? Or was somebody else going to say something? They looked around at one another in dismayed bewilderment.

And then Mrs. Flood had risen from her chair. "Thank you all for coming. Your presence means so much to me and to my son, Richard, and to every member of our family. We would be honored if you would join us for refreshments inside the clubhouse."

Maggie had stood alongside her mother-in-law. "Yes, please join us," she'd said.

The two women had such natural authority that the air of uncertainty immediately dissipated and everyone began to stand, pleased to be directed, told what to do.

It shocked Alice how quickly the atmosphere returned to normal, or at least an approximation thereof. Sure, people seemed a little subdued, were glancing nervously at her mother, her grandmother, at the door, checking to see if Richard would be making a reappearance, what kind of mood he'd be in when he did. Still, they

didn't start fiddling with their car keys, ignoring the plates of sandwiches and salads and desserts the club staff members were placing
on the tables or the bar, once again very much open and serving.

.   Alice let her gaze drift to Nick, at the back of the room, naturally. She was hoping he'd stick around for a bit. Was eager for the
chance to get him on his own, more likely now that the business part
of the memorial service had been taken care of and people were feeling less inclined to be on their best behavior, less inclined to make
sure others were too. And then, suddenly, he was on the move,
reflective sunglasses on, carving his way through the crowd. At first
she thought he was headed for the bar. But as he walked straight on
past it, she realized he was headed for the door. She couldn't let the
opportunity to speak to him slip through her fingers, not without
knowing when the next one would arise. She said, "Excuse me," as
she edged by her grandmother, ignoring the curious looks her mom
and sister shot her, followed him around the side of the clubhouse.

Alice didn't dare call attention to herself by yelling out his name,
so she just tried to catch up with him. His pace, though, was, as
always, brisk. And he stayed well ahead of her until he reached the
row of tennis courts. His bike, she saw, was on the first one, chained
to the net post. He knelt down to fiddle with the combination on
the lock, removing his sunglasses so he could see better.

"Anyone ever tell you you move too fast?" she said, a little out
of breath.

"Only ex-girlfriends."

She laughed.

He turned to her, squinting, gave her a slow up-down. "Maybe
you could move fast too if your dress weren't so tight."

It hadn't occurred to Alice until he said it that her dress—a black sheath that ended well above her knee—was rather formfitting, especially for her. She avoided the temptation to pluck at it, try to stretch it out. Kept her arms at her sides.

He stood. "No, really, Alice, that's quite a mourning costume you got there. And so versatile. Doubles as a cocktail dress."

He was right. It did. Cut high in the leg, low in the breast.

"Can you even breathe in that thing?" he said.

He was enjoying her discomfort. She could tell. Forcing herself to look uninterested, bored even, she said, "Please. Like I'm going to take fashion advice from a guy who dresses like a Mormon missionary."

Now he was the one to laugh. "I was going for junior G-man, but okay. So, what's up?"

She sensed that he was done testing her for the day, that they'd tuned into each other's attitudes and would be okay from here on out. Handing him her phone, she said, "Program your number into this, please."

He took it, began fiddling with the buttons.

"Your email address, too."

"There," he said, handing the phone back to her. "Now I'll be at your beck and call morning, noon, and night. Anything else I can do for you?"

When she started to speak, he held up his palm. "Wait, of course there is. You want to know about Martha Flood's file. Well, I read through it carefully and I found nothing suspicious in it. There's a history of heart disease in her family. She suffered from a few yeast infections in her twenties, the occasional migraine. She was on atenolol to lower her blood pressure and Lexapro to lower her anxiety. Then, naturally, in the last couple years she was on medication to treat her cancer. All the drugs van Stratten prescribed, though, were standard regimen drugs. No funny business with the dosages either. Seems like he was on the up and up." After a pause, "We're looking at the wrong guy." After another pause, "Or we're looking at the right wrong guy, only we have to look a little harder."

"Actually, I less wanted to talk to you than talk at you."

He gave her a curious look. "Okay," he said. "Sure. Shoot."

Alice thought for a while, gathering her words together in her head, understanding that she had his attention now, could afford to take her time, get it right. At last she began to speak, relaying everything she'd learned from her run-in with Tommy yesterday. Not *everything*, obviously, not the stuff that wasn't his business— the personal stuff, the lie-in portion of the run-in, basically—but almost everything. She hoped he wouldn't give Tommy his usual hard time. Not because she was protective of Tommy, though she was, intensely, especially after seeing how much pressure he was under, how close to snapping he was, but because she was protective of herself now, too. She was realizing suddenly that she was in a lot deeper than she'd been only twenty-four hours ago, the decision to have sex with Tommy putting her in a lot deeper.

In a certain sense, what she was doing was a betrayal of Tommy. She knew that. In a more important sense, though, what she was doing was saving Tommy. She believed that Dr. van Stratten was dangerous and a bully and a murderer, and that he had to be stopped. Tommy wasn't in a position emotionally or psychologically to take his father down—you couldn't ask that of any son—but she was. At least with Nick's help she was.

Nick was quiet for a long time after she finished. She could see that his mood had changed. He seemed not just surprised by what she'd told him but disturbed as well. For the first time since she'd known him, he looked young, like his actual age.

Finally, he said, "Wow," shaking his head. "Dr. van Stratten was as bad as we thought he was—worse. A murderer two times over. Jesus, a dying woman and a teenage girl he'd known almost all her life."

"I'm shocked," Alice said.

"Yeah, no kidding. Me too."

"No," she said, "I mean, I'm shocked that you're shocked."

"Why wouldn't I be shocked? It's one thing to think something about someone, another to know it." He looked up at her. "You understand what I'm saying?"

She nodded that she did. Then she said, "Though I feel I have to say it because someone has to say it—we don't have anything like definitive proof that Dr. van Stratten murdered Martha, never mind Camilla. All we have is suspicions."

"And the suspicions of his only son. Which is kind of damning, if you ask me."

"More than kind of." Alice sighed. "Look, I think Dr. van Stratten did it, too. I could see how much it hurt Tommy to admit that that's what he believed. All I'm saying is we're jumping to a conclusion—the likely one, I agree—still, we are jumping. Not that we shouldn't or that we're wrong to. I just wanted to point out that's what we're doing. I just wanted to, like, take note."

"Jumping to a conclusion? More like baby-stepping to a conclusion. And I'm sure it did hurt Tommy. I mean, who wants to think his dad's a bad guy?"

"Nobody."

"Your stepdad, too, also a pretty bad guy. Not lead-villain bad but second-lead-villain bad."

"Richard isn't my stepdad."

Nick looked at her with raised eyebrows. "Just because you wish something's true doesn't mean it is."

"Yeah, I grasp that concept," she said, irritated. "Have been grasping it since I was, like, six. Richard really isn't my stepdad."

"I must be missing some key piece of information here because I'm not following."

Alice took a deep breath, supplied him with the key piece.

When she stopped talking, he gave her a look that was deep and searching, maybe a little pitying too. "This changes things," he said softly.

"I don't see how."

He turned away from her, gazing out toward the ocean, a blue line in the distance, massaging the back of his neck with his hand. Still gazing, "Richard Flood isn't just some random rich guy your mom married in a quickie ceremony a couple weeks ago. He's blood. Your blood. If you pursue this thing to the end, you'll ruin his life. He'll wind up rotting away in prison because of you. Can you handle that?"

"After what he did to my sister, no problem. He killed her, Nick. I don't care if he killed her directly or indirectly. He's responsible. He and Dr. van Stratten."

Nick stood perfectly still with his profile to her. Even the hand that had been rubbing his neck had stopped moving. "Your sister?"

"Camilla. She's also my blood. She died when she wasn't supposed to and somebody has to pay for that. And I want you to help me make that somebody pay, both those somebodies. I can't do it on my own."

Nick turned to her, studying her with absolute calm, and she let him, willing herself not to flinch under the scrutiny of those penetrating eyes, those eyes that missed nothing, gave even less away. "Okay," he finally said. "I'll help you."

Alice silently released the breath she'd been holding. Said, "So, what next?"

"Well, we think we know what happened. What we need now is the definitive proof you were talking about earlier."

"Right," she said, "definitive proof." Then after a beat, "How do we get that?"

"Here's how we're not going to get it, from looking through Dr. van Stratten's whitewashed files. And Tommy's testimony doesn't help much either since it's all hearsay. Camilla must've had proof."

Alice instinctively felt that what Nick was saying was right, but it took her nearly a minute of hard thinking to understand why. "Okay, yes," she said. "Otherwise what reason would Dr. van Stratten have for killing her?"

"Exactly. She started screaming murder about her mom, he could've just dismissed the accusation as the ramblings of a griefcrazed teenager and people would have bought it. Camilla was a wild kid, troubled, and he was a pillar of the community and all that. And it's not like Martha Flood didn't have terminal cancer. And it's not like Richard Flood wouldn't have backed him up one hundred percent."

"So we need to find that proof."

"We do. Because once we've got the proof, we've got Dr. van Stratten. And once we've gotten Dr. van Stratten, we've got Richard."

"How's that?"

"I highly doubt the doc will be taking the fall for the both of them. Think about it."

Alice did, then said, "So, any ideas on how to find the proof?"

"Not off the top of my head, Clarice Starling, no. I'm not Hannibal Lecter. Give me a couple hours to chew on it."

"Of course. Sorry. I didn't mean to be impatient."

Nick exhaled heavily. "Don't apologize. You're eager, which is totally understandable. Dr. van Stratten had a nurse who was with him for a long time, Candace. She was fanatically loyal when I was there, but that was then. Maybe she's not so loyal anymore."

Alice, excited, "Do you know how to get in touch with her?"

"I don't even know her last name," he said. And then, before Alice's disappointment had a chance to sink in, "But I do have the address of Dr. van Stratten's former secretary, Barbara Allard. That's why I was hovering over the guest book, to see if she'd written it down. Thought I'd have better luck pumping her for information at her house than at a memorial. She'll know where Candace is."

"Nick, that's great."

He nodded, then turned away from her again, back to the ocean, his gaze inching along its surface. "So, how's your friend doing?"

"Tommy's my boyfriend, not my friend," she said, making her

voice hard, her eyes, too, assuming Nick was getting ready to have a go at Tommy. She'd thought he was going to lay off Tommy for once but she should've known better, should've known he couldn't resist.

He looked at her. "No, I meant the red-haired kid."

"Patrick?" she said, surprised. "Patrick's good. Great, in fact, since he's back in Cambridge, out of this snake pit."

"Glad to hear it."

Alice stared at Nick, her brain going *click*, *click*, *click*. And then she said, "You're the one who got him out of jail."

Annoyed, "Patrick told you? Wow, I really misjudged him. I thought he could be trusted to keep his mouth shut."

"He did keep his mouth shut. It's just, it's the only explanation that makes any sense. I can't believe I didn't figure it out until now."

"It was nothing," Nick said sullenly, kicking at a loose piece of gravel. "They weren't going to book him or anything. I just got him sprung a few hours early is all. Spared him the indignity of having to call his mom."

"Still, it was a nice thing for you to do for him."

"It was a nice thing for me to do. But it wasn't him I did it for." And with that, Nick swung his leg over his bike and pushed off, steered himself off the tennis court, then up over the ridge of grass to the crushed seashell road.

Alice tracked him until he pedaled all the way down it, disappeared through the tall front gates. Watching him, she felt, for the first time, a twinge of regret over sleeping with Tommy. Had she made a mistake? she wondered. Allowed herself to get swept up in the moment? Was he the right guy for her?

And then she mentally gave herself a snap-out-of-it slap. Of course Tommy was the right guy for her. So smart, so athletic, so handsome, so sensitive. What she was thinking? And who did she wish had taken his place? Nick? Sure, Nick, as established, was good-looking if you liked them bony and intense. Sexy even. But he was also rude and weird and loner-y. And besides, she barely liked him, never mind loved him. Tommy she loved.

She shook off her doubts. And then, with a sigh, she turned, walked back up to the clubhouse.

CHAPTER TWENTY-THREE

*C*harlie sneaked out to pee—she didn't really have to go, just wanted to duck out of sight for a minute—then flushed the toilet, lifted the latch on the door. As she stepped out of the stall, she was shocked to see Jude sitting on the counter, in between two sinks. He looked like his beautiful, raffish self: crisp, white shirt; hair brushed back from his forehead matinee-idol style; long, cool fingers raised and splayed in an abbreviated wave.

"What are you doing here?" she said.

He grinned. "You mean, in the one place you figured there was no danger of bumping into me?"

"Yeah."

"I just wanted to remind you to wash up after going tinkle. Jasmine-scented hand soap?" he said, holding out the pink plastic bottle to her.

She pushed past him, twisted the tap, thrust her hands under the stream of water, not bothering with soap. "You'll get kicked out of the club if someone sees you in here."

"I'll tell them I'm going through a gender identity crisis."

"I'm serious. Some nice little old lady will come in and have a heart attack right next to the paper-towel dispenser."

"Fine," he said, and grabbed her by the dripping wet hand, shoving the bathroom door open with his shoulder.

The coatroom he pulled her into was dark. Empty, too, except for a couple of wire hangers dangling loosely off the metal rod, and smelled of floor polish and mothballs and lavender sachet. Though there was a door and it did close, it was missing its upper half, presumably so people could hand their outer garments to an attendant more easily. But if she and Jude moved deep enough into the shadowy interior, they were, for the most part, concealed from view. A large mirror was mounted on the back wall, and in it was reflected the hallway, the dining room—at least a segment of it—where everyone from the memorial service was now congregated. Charlie glanced in it to see if anybody had noticed Jude dragging her off. Nobody, it appeared, had.

She turned to him. "So, what is this? An ambush?"

"How else am I supposed to get you to talk to me?"

"You could try calling."

"I have tried calling. And texting. And emailing. You haven't picked up or written back."

"You want to talk to someone so bad, why don't you talk to that little blond cheerleader chick? You seemed to like talking to her at the bonfire well enough."

"She's not a cheerleader. She's a flag girl. There's a difference. And she has a name. I just can't remember what it is right now." He smiled at Charlie in a teasing, gentle way. When Charlie didn't smile back, he said, "Come on, you know she meant nothing to me. I was only trying to make you jealous."

Charlie looked away from his face and down at her wet hands. He took them in his, brought them to the breast of his shirt and tenderly dried them.

"Oh, Jude," she said, "you ruined your beautiful shirt."

"It's just water. It'll dry."

For a long time Charlie stared at the soggy prints on his chest, at the small patch of dark hair now visible through the transparent fabric. Then, withdrawing her hands from his, tucking them under her arms, she said, "The lack of response wasn't just me being rude. I didn't listen to your voicemails, or read your emails or texts. I was afraid to, afraid of what you'd have to say to me."

"You mean about Cybill?"

Charlie, keeping her head down, nodded.

"She told me what happened."

Charlie looked up. "She did?"

"Yeah."

"What did she say?" Charlie asked, curious to hear the answer since she wasn't quite sure what happened herself.

"She said that you were both drunk, that she kissed you, took you by surprise. I mean, that is what happened, right?"

There was a two-second pause, *one, two*, between Jude's question and Charlie's response. She knew instinctively that if she lied here, colluded in Cybill's lie—same difference—allowed Cybill to shield her, she'd be crossing some divide she couldn't uncross. She'd be in league with Cybill against Jude. Even if she didn't mean to be or want to be, she would be. And if she had any hopes of her relationship with him being an open and honest one going forward, she needed to be both those things with him now. She took a deep breath, looked him the eye, and then she lied. "Right," she said.

Jude sighed. "I should never have flown off the handle like I did. The thing is, there'd been a bit of overlap between Camilla and me, and Camilla and Cybill so the topic was sort of a sore one."

"There was a Camilla and Cybill?" Charlie said. And then she thought, of course there was. Camilla was super-sexual and great-looking. She would have been heavily recruited by both teams.

"I mean, no, not officially. They were only messing around. It was nothing. Still, when you're into a girl, you don't want to see her with someone else, even another girl. I don't care what the men's magazines say."

Charlie felt a pang of jealousy toward Camilla, unsure if it was on Jude's behalf or Cybill's. To get away from her confusion, distance herself from it, she said, "So, that's why you said, *Not again*."

Jude gave her a queer look. "What?"

"When you saw me and Cybill, you know, together, you said, *Not again*."

"I did? I don't remember. Mostly I remember taking out my rage on your nice waiter friend."

"I've never seen you so mad."

"You've been pretty mad yourself lately."

"I have, yeah."

"You can't stay that way for much longer, though, can you?" His voice took on a pleading edge. "I was involved with another girl, yes, but that was before I even knew there was a you."

"I'm not mad at you, Jude, not now. How could I be after what you did for Stan?"

He grinned. "You liked that?"

"It was the bravest thing I've ever seen anybody do."

His grin broadened.

"Also the stupidest."

His grin disappeared.

She was quiet for a moment. Then she said, "I don't even think I was mad at you at the time. Not really. More hurt. Not that I had any right to be." She shook her head at herself. "No, I had a right. You should have told me. Camilla wasn't just any girl. She was Richard's daughter. And"—the words hard for Charlie to say, but she was determined to say them—"you loved her."

"Yeah. About that."

"About what? You loved her. You told me you did." Charlie was taken aback by her tone, which was almost indignant. Like she *wanted* Jude to say he loved Camilla, though nothing could have been further from the truth.

"I know I told you that. It's just your question took me by surprise and I wanted to answer it honestly."

"And you did answer it honestly. You answered *yes*."

He sighed. "I answered honestly and I didn't answer honestly. I should've said I *thought* I loved her. Our relationship—mine and Camilla's, I mean—was intense, but it wasn't real. She wanted me as a drug buddy and a fuck buddy and that was it. Anytime I tried to talk to her, get close to her, she shut me down. I guess that was what she had Tommy for, an actual boyfriend to do actual boyfriend things with."

There was a little bitterness in his voice as he made this last state-ment, Charlie noticed, but only a little.

He continued: "I never felt like so much of a girl as when I was with her, always wanting to have conversations when she just wanted to have sex." He let out an unhappy laugh. "Camilla messed me up because she was cold to me emotionally. But at the same time there was all this heat coming off her, like, physically. It wasn't real heat. It was just sex heat. I confused the two. Easy enough to do under the circumstances, I suppose. Anyway, I was obsessed with her without being in love with her, if that makes any sense."

"It does," Charlie said.

"That's why I freaked out when I saw that Nick guy watching us play tennis. He knew me during the worst of it, when I was a complete and utter basket case, just totally at the end of my rope, confused and angry and desperate. He reminds me of a time in my life I'd rather forget, basically." Jude released a deep breath, let his gaze wander around the room. Then he said, "In some ways, my relationship with Camilla was the opposite of my relationship with Cybill, which is extremely tight, obviously, but not sexual, not any-more, not ever, not really. But with you"—bringing his gaze back, letting it fall fully on Charlie—"I get everything. Physical closeness and emotional closeness. I've never been as happy with anyone as I am with you."

He leaned into her. She stayed still, did nothing to stop his approach. When he reached for her hand, though, she stepped back.

Clearing her throat, trying to keep emotion from making her voice break, she said, "The problem for me now isn't Camilla."

"What is it?"

"It's the drinking and the drugs. I can't handle knowing that every time we get in a fight, you're going to go off on some bender. It's too much responsibility for me. More than I can take."

"My staying sober is not your responsibility and you shouldn't feel like it's yours. It's mine, entirely mine. And just so you know, I didn't go off on a bender. I thought about it, came close, but I didn't."

Charlie turned down the corners of her lips, gave him a look, like, *How dumb do you think I am?*

"I didn't," he insisted.

"Jude, please. You cleaned Patrick out, bought all the weed he had. I saw you."

"Yeah, but I ended up not using it."

"You threw it out?"

"No, I gave it to Cybill." Off the look she shot him, "What? Just because I can't smoke a joint without making a mess of myself doesn't mean she can't."

"Okay, well, swilling vodka in the middle of the afternoon doesn't exactly make you the poster boy for clean and sober living either. Getting loaded? Not one of the twelve steps I've ever heard of."

"Vodka?" he repeated, puzzled.

She threw up her hands. "Or gin. Whatever clear liquid you were knocking back with Cybill at the bar earlier."

"You know what's also a clear liquid? Water. That's what I was knocking back with Cybill at the bar earlier."

"Oh."

He reached for her hand. This time she let him take it. "I'm telling you, I'm not doing that shit anymore. No drugs and I'm limiting myself to one unit of alcohol a day. I've turned over a new leaf. Which is not to say that it's all going to be smooth sailing from here on out, that there will be no bumps in the road or . . ." He trailed off, bit his lip.

"Or what? What's wrong?"

"Nothing. I was just trying to throw another metaphor into the mix but I couldn't think of one. Anyway, I want you to know that I'm trying, really trying."

"Why would you do all this? Change your whole life?"

"I already told you. Because I love you."

Charlie melted. It was the only way to describe what was happening to her internally: her insides just dissolving into puddles of tenderness. In that moment, hearing those words, nothing else mattered, not what he'd done in the past, not what she'd done in the past—none of it. His face began floating toward hers. And as it did, she looked into the mirror behind his head, found herself staring into the reflected eyes of Cybill, standing at the edge of the dining room in that white dress, as intent and watchful as a ghost.

As damned, too.

Charlie was startled, felt as though her heart had ceased beating altogether, and then she wasn't. Suddenly the backs of her legs tightened and a shudder of excitement ran the length of her entire body. Holding Cybill's gaze with her own, not letting it go, she dreamily mouthed the words, "I love you too," and brought her lips to Jude's.

CHAPTER TWENTY-FOUR

*I*t was past midnight, how far past Alice could only guess. She'd just sent a text message to Nick setting up a time tomorrow to meet and strategize but had failed to check the clock on her phone's screen. She was sitting alone on the beach, a few feet from the bonfire pit, the spot Tommy was so fond of. It was where he often came to write in his journal when he couldn't sleep, gaze out at Greeves Bridge, inflicting on himself the view of Camilla's grave site to feel the pain-pleasure of guilt, shame, remorse—take your pick or mix and match—to torture himself, basically. Alice recalled Nick's words about Camilla being in over her head and not knowing it, about the dry sobbing in the van Strattens' garage when she believed she was alone and unobserved. Thought, too, about the boys who had loved her and cared about her and sensed she was in trouble but could do nothing to save her.

Remarkably, the memorial had ended only a short time ago. Mrs. Flood hadn't stuck around long after the service's completion, disappearing into her chauffeured vehicle and heading back to her house in Darien while Alice was on the tennis courts with Nick. Maggie and Richard weren't far behind, though they were heading to the hospital rather than home. (Maggie had found Richard in a corner of the kitchen, ignored by the staff bustling around him, nursing his hand. It wouldn't stop bleeding. She took him to the emergency room to get it stitched up.) With those three out of the picture, the atmosphere in the clubhouse had completely degenerated. Or elevated, depending on your point of view. People were laughing and talking, telling jokes, eating the food and drinking the alcohol that Richard had paid for, their ties loose, their jackets thrown carelessly on the backs of chairs, the women's high heels kicked off, tossed in a pile.

Alice didn't begrudge the general high spirits, find them disrespectful or distasteful or anything like that; slightly manic merrymaking seemed to her a perfectly reasonable response to having the long, dark shadow of death cast over you, even if only for a few minutes on a lovely summer's day. She couldn't participate in it, though. So she'd sat at the top of the staircase that led to the guest rooms on the second floor, peered through the slats in the banister.

From that vantage point, removed and partially concealed, yet also privileged, Alice had watched the scene unfolding below. She'd spied Tommy wandering the hall, the porch, even ducking his head into the girls' bathroom. She knew he was looking for her, but she didn't care to be found, which was why she leaned back into the shadows. Not that she was avoiding him. Not exactly. It's just that if his dad was as treacherous as he believed, maybe it was best that they only meet when they were certain no one would spot them, definitely not when Dr. van Stratten was in the immediate vicinity. Besides, the

encounter with Nick had unnerved her as far as Tommy was concerned. Made her doubt Tommy, doubt herself. The effect was tem-
porary, she was sure, but she wanted to wait until it wore off before
facing him. After a while he gave up, returned to the dining room.

From her perch Alice had also spied Charlie, emerging from the
coatroom, hair in disarray, straightening her skirt, tugging it down over
her hips, and Jude emerging a discreet thirty seconds later, tie crooked
and shirttails hanging out the back of his pants, bumping shoulders
with Cybill as he entered the dining room and Cybill exited it.

Tomorrow morning Alice would have a talk with her sister. Tell
Charlie to get her act together with Maggie, ease up on the snotty
little bitch routine. Otherwise she'd blow her cover, blow both their
covers. Fortunately, she and Jude appeared to have reconciled, which
meant her mood around the house would be much improved so Alice
wouldn't be put in the position of endlessly making excuses for her.

Also in Alice's crosshairs: Dr. van Stratten. He was a handsome
man, no question, tall with an erect carriage and a lean, disciplined
body. And his face, so like Tommy's, possessed a strength and resolve that Tommy's lacked. But Alice could see his ugliness, too.
Could see it in the cold way he spoke to his nervous wreck of a wife,
could see it in the dismissive attitude he took toward his sensitive,
high-strung son, could see it in the blend of obsequiousness and
contempt with which he treated his former patients, many of whom
were guests of the service, as they offered him condolences as father
of the onetime boyfriend of the deceased. And from twenty feet over
and fifteen feet up, Alice could feel his need to dominate and control
every situation, to bully and oppress every person. He was smooth
and he was menacing. She would've liked to have watched him

interact with Richard, get a sense of their dynamic, of how things stood between them, but of course there was no chance for observation since Richard had ducked out so early.

Still, Alice was glad that Maggie and Richard had gone to the hospital because it meant he would come back to the house all patched up and as good as new. And she wanted him healthy and at full strength when she took him out. Took him and Dr. van Stratten both out, this pair of powerful males that preyed on vulnerable females: Martha, sick with a wasting disease, easy pickings; Camilla forced by her perfectionist father to split herself down the middle, construct two identities, in order to survive; Mrs. van Stratten, that traumatized shell of a woman, a victim who sought out her abuser; and Maggie, a shell of a woman in a different way, surrendering her personality entirely to her new husband.

These two preyed on vulnerable males as well. At least one, anyway. When Alice went up against Dr. van Stratten, she'd also be avenging Tommy, who was being eaten alive, eaten from the inside out, just ravaged and consumed by his guilty feelings for what he'd done to Camilla, giving her scent to his father and thus inadvertently becoming an accessory to her murder.

Well, their predatory days were over. No more feeding on the weak and helpless for them. They were about to find out how the other half lived, to see what it was like to be damaged instead of damaging. They were about to fall victim to a malignant force, a force that wished to hurt them, scare them, exploit them, violate them, make them snivel and suffer and beg for mercy. They were about to get theirs.

In spades.

ACKNOWLEDGMENTS

I'd like to extend my deepest gratitude to my agent, Jennifer Joel, and to the entire team at Razorbill, my editor Jocelyn Davies and my publisher Ben Schrank especially.

Thanks always to my parents, Bill and Margie, and my brother, John.